CLASSIC
REVENGE
A Silver Sleuths Mystery

CLASSIC REVENGE

A Silver Sleuths Mystery

•

Mitzi Kelly

AVALON BOOKS
NEW YORK

Published by Thomas Bouregy & Co., Inc.
160 Madison Avenue, New York, NY 10016

Library of Congress Cataloging-in-Publication Data

Kelly, Mitzi.
    Classic revenge / Mitzi Kelly.
        p. cm. — (The silver sleuths mystery series)
    Includes bibliographical references and index.
    ISBN 978-0-8034-7769-8 (acid-free paper)   1. Older
people—Fiction.   I. Title.
    PS3611.E454C57 2010
    813'.6—dc22

                                                    2010002302

PRINTED IN THE UNITED STATES OF AMERICA
ON ACID-FREE PAPER
BY HADDON CRAFTSMEN, BLOOMSBURG, PENNSYLVANIA

In loving memory of my parents, Lewis and Lucretia Rothman, who gave the gift of humor to all their children and taught us that anything is possible if you have laughter in your heart. I love them and miss them dearly.

Many, many thanks go to all the people who have encouraged me in my writing career, and to those I have crossed paths with who keep life interesting. First, and foremost, my love and gratitude go to my husband, John, and my son, John Lewis, who support me with understanding and patience and who are the *wind beneath my wings*. I want to thank my brothers—Lewis, Pat, and Stan—who keep the laughter coming even after all these years and whose love and support I would not want to live without. I'd like to thank my extended family who I feel proud to be a part of: the Michons, Barbers, Fryars, Rothmans, Sheffields, and all the cousins, nieces, and nephews who descended from these families and married to different names. I realize, as family, they couldn't choose me, but I'm honored they kept me!

A special thanks to my good friend and fellow author, Ronni Hoessli, who has encouraged me to write for years and gave valuable editing tips when I was in a hurry to get to the next scene.

Huge thanks go to Michael and Celeste Wall who introduced me to Sandra Lucchesi, who introduced me to my intrepid agent whom I adore, Susan Cohen at The Gersh Agency. I value these new friendships and appreciate all the advice and support.

I wish to extend a very special thank you to my editor, Chelsea Gilmore. She is one special lady. We hit it off right from the beginning and her enthusiasm for this series is something I will always cherish. I thank her for all the advice and hard work and I'm looking forward to our growing relationship.

To all the others along the way, I thank you for your encouragement and support.

Prologue

Patience and careful planning were the keys to success. It would all be over soon. Gone would be the venomous hatred that had been a constant companion for the last several years. It would simply disappear, vanish into thin air, and then life could get back to normal, a life with dreams and goals before it had been so callously destroyed.

Rubbing gloved hands together made the predawn chill bearable. There was little that could be done, however, for protesting muscles made stiff from crouching behind the cover of landscaped shrubbery and new spring flowers for over an hour. April in Texas was, to state the old axiom, unpredictable. Yesterday the high temperature had reached eighty-four; now it hovered at forty-five degrees. Proper foresight would have demanded a thick sweater.

It was the last mistake that would be made.

The sun finally started to rise, spreading soft, pink

light across the dark, cloudless sky. Slowly, the light became brighter, glistening off dew-dipped blooms while birds began to sing out cheerily to one another. There was no appreciation, though, for the glory of a bright, new day, the promise of the kind of day that just made you happy to be alive. Yes, someone was surely happy to be alive, even for just a few short hours.

Weeks of surveillance had revealed that the movements of the people inside the sprawling two-story stucco house could be monitored simply by observing which lights came on and off. They thought that they were safely tucked away in their home in this upperclass neighborhood. How utterly stupid.

Like so many of their neighbors whose backyards ran up to the many acres of undeveloped land that ran parallel to the highway, they refused to erect a fence, probably an informal announcement that they owned more property than they actually did. What it announced, in fact, was that they did not have a pet they had to keep enclosed. A pet that could have warned of unwelcome intruders coming right off the highway and through the wooded area into the yards of the unsuspecting residents.

That knowledge brought a smile, but it was without humor. Anticipation grew as daylight settled in. Any minute now the bathroom curtains would close.

The soft, sweet scent of lavender filled the bathroom. It was Susan Wiley's favorite bath oil, and today she added a generous amount to the water in the antique claw-foot tub. She then lit the four candles arranged on the vanity. She loved the ritual of preparing and then soaking in a relaxing bath, a time when she was all alone and her mind drifted lazily, reflecting on personal goals, planning a vacation trip, or just enjoying the pure luxury of solitude and quiet.

With her sleeve, she wiped the fog from the ornate oval mirror and glanced critically at herself. Her face belied her true age, a fact she was modestly pleased about given the years of stress and anxiety she and her husband had endured while running their own business. There had been many hard, lean times, more than she cared to remember, but through hard work and perseverance, and most importantly, by working as a team, she and Sam had succeeded. Yes, it had all been worth it.

She was slowing down now—there was no point denying it—but at seventy-two she figured she had earned the right not to have to race through each day hoping to get through a to-do list. Since their retirement three years ago, though, life had definitely gotten easier. With a full-time housekeeper and a full-time social calendar, she and Sam were enjoying the fruits of their labor. Just as it should be.

Susan dropped her robe, walked barefoot across the marble floor, and stepped into the tub, sinking into the hot, fragrant water with a sigh. Today was a special day, one she was looking forward to immensely. With their housekeeper, Claire, at the grocery store and Sam at his weekly golf game, she would pamper herself with a long soak in the tub, give herself a facial, manicure and pedicure, and then get her hair done before meeting Shelley Rivers, her sister-in-law, for lunch. But this evening was what she was most excited about. Tonight, she and Sam would be celebrating their fortieth wedding anniversary. Sam had told her to dress up for dinner. He would be taking her someplace special. It was amazing to her how, after forty years, every moment with Sam was still special, a fact she thanked God for each and every day. He couldn't have blessed her with a better man.

Susan leaned back and closed her eyes, her mind aimlessly conjuring up her wardrobe as she wondered what she would wear that night. Maybe she would buy something new, something in blue perhaps, Sam's favorite color. She heard the bathroom door open before she had made up her mind whether it would be a dress or a pantsuit, but she smiled anyway. Sam must have planned an earlier surprise. It would be just like him to cancel his golf game to spend the day with her. An expression of love and welcome softened her face as she slowly opened her eyes.

At first she couldn't see the shape clearly. The tulip lighting cast shadows onto the velvet-covered wall. Suddenly, her smile vanished and her eyes opened wide in shock. There was a stranger walking toward her. No, not a stranger, her mind registered—this was someone vaguely familiar . . .

Susan sat up straight, the water sloshing over the side of the tub. She tried to release the scream bubbling in the back of her throat as she watched something being plugged into the wall socket. She saw the evil grin and the glittering eyes at the same time that she realized something electrical was going to be tossed into the water. She tried to scramble out of the slippery tub, but there wasn't enough time.

Why? her mind screamed silently, her mouth forming a word that made no sound—but she would never know the answer to her last question.

Chapter One

With a clarity born out of months of self-deception, Trish Anderson knew the moment of truth had arrived. She either faced her personal demons here and now, or she would forever be wondering *what if*. She sat quietly at her kitchen table, hands clasped tightly in her lap, her gaze glued to the opening into her living room where it would all begin.

It was a beautiful clear morning, the sun already warming the air. Birds chirped their singsong messages, lawnmowers roared across yards that desperately needed care after the weeks of rain the month of May always seemed to bring, and dogs barked ferocious warnings to passersby on the sidewalks. Trish usually started Saturday mornings quite late. She would sit at the kitchen table with coffee and a chocolate doughnut . . . or two, still in her pajamas while she struggled with the daily crossword puzzle in the paper. But this wasn't a usual Saturday morning.

The closed windows shut out the noise and the drawn blinds shut out the light. It was so quiet she could actually hear herself breathe. Her eyes darted quickly to the refrigerator but she pulled them away with a sigh. It didn't take a degree in psychology to know why she was hesitating. It was going to take a lot of sacrificing to reach her goal. And there was no point denying it—she wasn't big on sacrifices.

Well, time to bite the bullet, as they said. Taking a deep breath, she stood up and rolled her head from side to side to loosen the tension that was beginning to creep up the back of her neck. She could claim a headache, go back to bed, and postpone the inevitable, but the thought of having to mentally gear up for this moment again had her placing one foot in front of the other as she steadily made her way to the living room.

Trish now stood courageously in front of her tormenter, the cold, black steel contraption, and once more studied the many features of the new exercise equipment. She wasn't stalling. She was downright intimidated. Apparently it did everything from trimming your waist and thighs to performing major organ transplants. But which of the many gadgets attached to the machine did what? Flipping through the accompanying manual last night had been no help; it may as well have been written in Japanese. She preferred the hands-on approach anyway. "Learn as you go" was her motto. Well, now it was time to put her hands on and start learning.

Trish straightened her spine and strengthened her resolve. First, she'd do the thing where you sat down and pushed the pedals with your feet. It was supposed to tone your calves and thighs while adding muscle. It looked safe—and besides, her legs could definitely do with a workout. Pleased, she nodded to herself and hiked her leg up to maneuver onto the bicycle seat. That's when the loud peal of her doorbell shattered the quiet.

Startled, she screamed before she could stop herself, the leg she was balancing on almost buckling beneath her. Taking a calming breath, she glared resentfully at the torture device. "Safe and easy, my butt!" she muttered under her breath as she regained her balance. "You were saved by the bell, you lucky heap of metal, but you haven't beaten me. I will be back." Tossing her head defiantly, she turned toward the door.

Was it fate or just plain coincidence that the minute she decided to knock off a few pounds the doorbell would ring? With her luck, it was probably a cute little Girl Scout selling those mouth-watering mint cookies. *Ten boxes, please . . .*

Trish closed her eyes tightly for a minute and repeated the mantra, "I will be strong, I will be strong!" But her pep talk was interrupted when the blasted doorbell rang again.

"I'm coming," she yelled rudely. "Hold your horses!" Flinging the door open, she scowled at a tiny woman wearing jeans, a red sweatshirt, red tennis shoes, and a red bandana tied across her forehead, and another woman, immaculate in a turquoise sweatsuit, not a silver hair out of place. Definitely not Girl Scouts. "What do you want?"

"Good morning to you too," Millie Morrow, the lady in red, said cheerfully as she pushed her way inside, Edna Radcliff following close behind. "Got any coffee?"

Trish slammed the door shut. "It's eight o'clock in the morning. You know I have coffee," she said, rolling her eyes and following them into the kitchen.

"Not since you've gotten on this crazy health kick, I don't. Bet you don't have any doughnuts, though, do you?" Millie opened a cabinet and pulled out two coffee cups.

"Millie! You are going to undo all the good our walk did this morning if you keep eating junk in the mornings."

"Hasn't killed me yet." She peered at Edna through silver wire-framed glasses. Her message was clear: *Mind your own business!*

"It's a moot point because I don't have any doughnuts," Trish said breezily, sounding anything but sorry as she flopped into a chair, resigning herself to a visit with her friends whom she normally loved but would gladly kill right now.

Millie glanced in the living room and raised her eyebrows at Trish. "You know, you could go jogging with me in the mornings if you're so gung-ho on this exercise thing. Edna came this morning and she's already talking about how much better she feels."

Edna nodded eagerly and reached for the coffee Millie brought over to the table. "That's right, dear. I do feel better."

"Millie, you are eighty years old and—"

"And proud of it," she said, pulling out a chair and sitting down. "You should hope you look as good as I do when you're my age. Of course, I didn't wait until I was over the hill before I started jogging. Edna is sixty-five and you're forty-eight—not exactly spring chickens, if you know what I mean."

Trish sighed. "As I was saying, you're eighty years old, and you don't jog. You just walk fast around the block, and the only reason you do that is to snoop on all the neighbors. You don't need the exercise." Millie was a trim five feet flat and as energetic as a twenty-year-old baseball player, a fact that irritated Trish to no end. Millie was also the neighborhood gossip. Having lived in the area of Grand River, Texas, for most of her adult life, she knew everybody . . . and their business.

Grand River is a small suburb right outside of San Antonio, Texas. An exaggeration, really, because as Millie puts it, you can stand on one block in Grand River and spit, hitting an area legally taxed by the City of San Antonio. The main thoroughfare is a speed trap for the unsuspecting, chaning speed limits every few miles which provides most of the income for the small city.

Trish had moved there four years before with her now-ex-husband because she dearly loved the area. The street she lived on had older, huge southern-style homes and acre-size lots. Giant oak trees lined both sides of the street, their strong branches forming a shady arch that was magnificent in the summer, but a royal pain in the spring when the leaves fell.

Millie lived right across the street and was the first neighbor Trish had met when she'd moved in. Charmed by the older woman's independent personality, they had become fast friends. Millie was stubborn and opinionated, but loyal to a fault. She had proven that when Trish divorced her husband. And Millie was the one who'd introduced Trish to Edna and Joe Radcliff, the wealthiest—and sweetest—couple on the block; they were thoughtful and easygoing, always seeing the positive side of things and more than willing to offer a helping hand where they could.

Millie and Edna were as close as sisters, even though

Millie teased her unmercifully, calling her a Pollyanna. Yes, they were good friends with a lot in common, except when it came to national politics. In fact, the only time Edna ever lost her patience was when Millie would goad her into a discussion about a political issue. But Millie was a troublemaker—a loveable troublemaker, but a troublemaker just the same.

Millie stirred sugar into her coffee. "So what do you think about your new miracle inches-off contraption?" she asked, nodding toward the living room.

Trish shrugged. "I don't know yet. But it's not a *miracle-off* anything. It's still going to take a lot of hard work to get back in shape. The problem is that I'm scared to death of it. I just know I'm going to climb on the blasted thing and end up doing a back flip off it."

Millie chuckled. "I know what you mean. I got one of those stationary bicycle things a few years back. Thought I was doing great until the pedals started going so darn fast and I couldn't stop it. I must've lost a hundred pounds on that one occasion alone. I sold it at a garage sale the next month. But, hey, at least you're dressed for the part," she said, her lips twisting into a grin.

Trish looked down at her new exercise outfit the sales lady at Sears had told her was absolutely perfect, right down to the black leg warmers. "What's wrong with my outfit?"

"Nothing at all is wrong with it," Edna said, patting her arm comfortingly.

"Oh, come on, Edna," Millie scolded. "Trish needs to hear the truth. Do you really want her going out in public like that? You'd be as embarrassed as I would, and don't bother denying it.

"Trish, dear, you need to wait to wear those shiny leotards and that elastic belt until you're over the donelap disease."

"The what?" Edna asked.

"The donelap disease—you know, it's when your fat 'done lapped' over your waistline."

"Millie!" Edna exclaimed.

"It's okay, Edna," Trish said hurriedly before a full-scale war broke out. Edna must have missed the twinkle in Millie's eyes. "We know Millie is exaggerating. She doesn't embarrass that easily."

Millie laughed. "Of course I'm kidding. I know you want to get in shape and have more energy, but you don't have that big a problem. You've been carrying on like you're a two-ton Annie, and you're not. A little firming up here and there," she said pointedly, peering at Trish's butt over the rim of her eyeglasses, "and you'll be in shape in no time."

"You look just fine, dear," Edna said, slanting her eyes at Millie in warning. "Anyone who is trying to improve their health can wear whatever they please and I'm proud of you."

"Yeah, I want to look my absolute best when I'm lying in my coffin having died of exercising," Trish said wryly. No one spoke for a moment. "I'm sorry," she said. "That was insensitive."

Millie cleared her throat. "You didn't mean anything by it, honey. It's natural for the living to go on living. We say things that sometimes bring back sad memories, but we're human."

Edna looked down at her clasped hands. "I sure do miss her," she said softly.

Trish and Millie both nodded silently. Edna was referring to Susan Wiley, a neighbor down the street who had died two weeks before in a tragic accident. They hadn't seen much of Sam, Susan's husband, since the funeral. He had withdrawn into himself, completely devastated at the loss of his wife of forty years. They knew it was going to take time for him to deal with his grief, but they were concerned about him. All they could do right now was to provide enough prepared meals to help him get through this difficult period.

Sam and Susan had regularly participated in the barbeques, card games, and luncheons that Millie, Edna, and Trish organized. Only a week before her death, Susan had invited all three women over for lunch. She had been her usual happy and vivacious self, a joy to be around. Yes, Susan would be missed terribly.

"Joe saw Claire a couple of days ago," Edna said. "Evidently Sam is thinking about moving in with his sister for a while. He can't stand to be in the house where Susan died." Claire had been the Wiley's housekeeper for the last five years. Never married, she was a sweet woman who became more of a friend to the Wileys than an employee. Susan used to boast that Claire, at age sixty, was a true miracle worker around the house.

"I know I wouldn't ever be able to use that bathroom again, regardless of how gorgeous it is." Trish shuddered. "Can you imagine bathing in the same tub where your wife accidentally electrocuted herself?"

"I wonder if Claire will go with Sam if he decides to go to his sister's house?" Edna asked.

Millie shrugged. "She probably will. She's like a member of the family, after all."

Edna sighed deeply and rose from her chair. Carrying her cup to the sink, she said, "I think I'll run over and see how Sam is doing. If Joe comes by looking for me, will you tell him where I've gone? He took our car in for service this morning, and then we're meeting Stan and Lewis for lunch."

"How are your sons, by the way? I haven't seen them in a while," Trish said.

"I'm keeping my fingers crossed. I think Stan has a girlfriend. If those two boys don't get busy finding wives, I'll never get to be a grandmother."

Millie chuckled. "In case you haven't noticed, your *boys* are in their forties. They are considered men now."

"I don't care how old they are. They're still my boys. I just don't understand it. Both are successful in their jobs, both are very handsome, if I do say so myself, and they have never been in any trouble. What's wrong with them?"

"Marriage isn't for everybody, you know," Trish said sardonically. "Even though you have a fairy-tale marriage, that happily-ever-after stuff doesn't work for everybody."

Millie raised her eyebrows. "My, we're the cynical one, aren't we?"

"I am not cynical. I'm a realist."

"Well, then, you're a cynical realist."

"There's no such thing."

Edna threw her hands in the air, motioning for a time out. "You two can argue after I'm gone. I'll talk to you later."

"Give Sam our love," Trish called out to Edna's departing back.

Millie stayed a few minutes longer, finishing her coffee and talking about her own daughter and two grandchildren. Finally, she stood to leave. "I need to run to the grocery store. Do you need anything?"

"No, thanks. I went yesterday."

"Want to come over for dinner tonight? I'm fixing meatloaf, and that movie you've been wanting to see about the horse who rallied the country after the stock market crash is on."

Trish thought for a minute. The idea certainly held appeal, and she hated cooking for just herself. "Okay, that sounds good. I would normally bring a cake, but since I'm dieting I'll bring Jell-O and fruit."

"Yippee," Millie said apathetically. "My mouth is watering."

Chapter Two

Trish yawned and leaned against the opening to the living room, looking at her exercise machine. "What the heck," she muttered to herself. "Tomorrow is another day." She should start on the dessert for tonight, anyway. Grinning, she rinsed out the coffee cups and placed them in the dishwasher.

Maybe she'd surprise Millie and bake some cupcakes. The woman was a chocoholic if there ever was one. She'd have to make sure she took them all to Millie's, though, and more important, be sure she left them all. Otherwise, she'd be tempted to eat half a dozen in one sitting. Millie, she knew, could eat them all and not gain an ounce. It just wasn't fair.

Trish unfastened her new stretch belt. Her favorite sweatpants hung on a convenient hook on the back of the bathroom door, and they beckoned to her like a long-lost friend. She was halfway down the hallway when the doorbell pealed for the second time that morning. "Now

15

what?" she sighed and backtracked. But before she could even get to the door, the bell rang twice more.

She flung open the door, ready to give whoever was on the other side a piece of her mind when she saw the frazzled look on Edna's face. Edna pushed through the door with a hand on her chest. Breathing heavily, she said, "Oh my goodness! Oh my goodness! You are not going to believe what happened!"

"What?"

"They just took Sam away!"

"Who did?"

"The police did!"

Trish's eyebrows rose. "The police took Sam away? Why would they do such a thing?"

Edna walked into the kitchen on rubbery legs and sank down at the table. She appeared ready to jump out of her skin. Her face was pale, her hazel eyes opened wide in shock. Trish silently wondered if Edna had fallen and bumped her head, but that wasn't likely because her perfectly coifed silver hair was still in place.

Finally, Edna took a deep breath and leaned back in her chair. "I was having a cup of coffee with Sam when his doorbell rang. Claire went to answer it, and when she returned she had two policemen with her. They started all that mumbo-jumbo about his rights, and then they handcuffed him!"

Trish leaned over and grabbed the box of tissues off the counter and pushed them toward Edna. "You've got to be kidding!"

"I wish I were. You should have seen Sam's face," Edna sniffed.

"Were you able to talk to him? Did he say anything?"

"No. They rushed him into one of the patrol cars so

fast I was afraid there was a sniper around or something. Then the two officers drove off with Sam in the backseat. Claire was hysterical, so I stayed with her until she calmed down. I came here as soon as I could."

"I still can't believe Sam could be in any trouble, not with the law! Did you find out what the police are after him for?"

Edna nodded and the tears spilled over. "They say it's for murder."

Trish's heart stopped beating for a moment. "*Murder?* Are they crazy? Who in their right mind would think Sam was capable of murder?" Her mind couldn't comprehend this. There had to be some mistake. Then it occurred to her. "The police think Sam killed Susan, don't they?"

Edna nodded, the tears running down her face.

Trish drummed her fingernails on the table. Her mind was spinning helplessly as she tried to make some sense of what was going on. Finally, she said, "Okay, let's go talk to Claire. Maybe she knows if Sam has an attorney. First, we need to get him out of jail. I'm not sure the man can stand much more stress."

Edna drew a shaky breath and stood. "You're right. We need to take action. Crying isn't going to help anybody."

Trish put her arm around Edna's shoulders. "You cry all you want, sweetie. Get the shock out of your system— because when Sam does get out we're going to have to be strong and supportive."

Edna sniffed and nodded. "You're right, of course. We know Sam isn't guilty. We can't let him know how horrified we are that he's been charged with this. He'll think we may have our doubts. We need to show him, above all else, that we are there for him, that we believe in him." Edna's voice had gained strength and her hand was clenched in a fist where it rested on the table. Sam needn't worry about Edna's loyalty, that was a fact. The little lady looked like she was ready to punch somebody out just for suggesting he could do anything wrong.

Trish reached over and squeezed Edna's hand. "Let's go see Claire."

Sam's house was three doors down. It was hard to believe that the beautiful old home with the meticulous landscaping and the cheerful red door Susan Wiley had painted herself held so much recent tragedy.

They were almost at the house when they heard tires screeching. Both of them looked over their shoulders. It was Millie, turning onto their street. "Boy, I wish they would take her driver's license away," Trish said. "She's more dangerous than a carload of teenagers on cell phones."

"I know what you mean. She scares me to death." They watched as Millie pulled into her driveway and slammed on the brakes. It took a few seconds for the big car to stop rocking.

"You go fill in Millie on what's happened, and I'll go talk to Claire. You two can meet me over there."

Edna nodded and hurried back down the street while Trish walked up the sidewalk to Sam's house. She rang the doorbell and waited, then realized that she was still wearing her bright blue spandex exercise outfit. Hopefully none of the neighbors were watching, she thought self-consciously as she quickly glanced around. Down the street, Millie was scooting off the three cushions she used to help her see over the hood of her car just as Edna reached the driver's door. She didn't see Millie's reaction to the news because at that moment the front door of Sam's house opened.

Trish took one look at the face of the housekeeper and stepped inside to envelop her in a hug. "Oh, Claire, I'm so sorry." Claire's swollen eyes were red-rimmed, her lips trembling on her ashen face. Hopelessness seemed to shroud her as she clung tightly to Trish, her shoulders shaking. "Shh, shh, everything is going to be okay," Trish said soothingly, hoping she spoke the truth.

Claire stepped back. "Nothing will ever be okay again."

The sadness in Claire's voice broke Trish's heart. "Of course it will. You have to have faith, Claire."

Claire smiled slightly and ran her fingers through her short, thick hair. "I appreciate your coming over. I was just getting ready to make some coffee. Would you care to join me?"

"Coffee would be nice," she said, following Claire into the kitchen. The house was dark and quiet as if it, too, were in mourning. Sadness and worry permeated the air, seeping through the sand-colored walls and rich hardwood flooring. The kitchen, as usual, was spotless. She sat at the oval table while Claire started the coffee-maker and pulled cups down from the cabinet.

Trish had always adored this kitchen, coming over often during the remodeling that Susan had supervised from beginning to finish. The open spaciousness Susan had wanted to convey, while projecting a warm, comfortable atmosphere, was successfully achieved with a tasteful mixture of old-fashioned knickknacks and state-of-the-art appliances. The ceramic bread box sitting on the dark green granite countertop had been a gift from

Trish last Christmas. She smiled sadly as she remembered Susan's joy when she'd opened it.

There was a knock at the front door just as Claire prepared to sit down. Noticing the startled look on the other woman's face, Trish hurriedly explained, "That's probably Millie and Edna. I told them I would be over here." *Poor woman,* Trish thought to herself as Claire went to the door. *She has been through so much lately that she's afraid of even going to the door, afraid of the news the person on the other side is there to relate.*

As Trish predicted, Millie and Edna followed Claire into the kitchen. Millie's arm was wrapped protectively across Claire's shoulders as she led her to the table. Edna reached into the cabinet and pulled out two more coffee cups. They were all going to be bouncing off the walls with as much caffeine as they had consumed today—either that, or they should seriously consider purchasing stock in coffee beans.

Trish waited until they were all seated at the table. "Claire, do you know if Sam has an attorney?"

Claire shook her head. "I don't know. I wasn't involved in any of their personal business. I guess he must have, you know, to settle the issues regarding Susan's death and her will, but I never met an attorney or heard Sam mention one."

"That won't be a problem. As soon as I get home, I'll talk to Joe. He'll know who to call," Edna piped in.

"Yes, that's good," Millie said. "If Sam happens to call you, Claire, tell him we're working on busting him out of there. You tell him we are firmly behind him."

"Do you have any idea why the police would think Sam was involved in Susan's death?" Trish hated to ask the question but there was no point avoiding it.

"I have none whatsoever," Claire said vehemently, her earlier despair temporarily forgotten as she quickly defended the man who was her friend and employer. "This is absolutely ridiculous! The poor man is grieving for his wife, but then he's accused of her murder! You want my opinion? I think the police are bored with so little crime in our community that they're just looking for something to do."

"Oh, Claire, surely you don't believe that?" Edna said, clearly shocked at Claire's remarks. Trish wasn't about to criticize Claire. She had her own problems with the local police department.

"Why not? When I got home that day and found Susan, I immediately called nine-one-one, and then I had Sam paged at the golf course. The police got here first, and then the ambulance. They told me to stay downstairs while they went up to check on things. They wouldn't even let Sam go upstairs when he got home. Even after the ambulance carried Susan away, the police were still upstairs. They finally came down and asked both Sam and me where we were when the accident happened. They were so nice that I just figured it was part of the normal procedure, but now I wonder if they planted something to make Sam look guilty!"

Whoa! Trish might believe the Grand River Police Department was apathetic on domestic issues, but never would she think they were dishonest. Claire was obviously distraught, her reasoning powers off-kilter. They had better make sure that remarks questioning the police's integrity never left this kitchen.

Trish glanced at Millie, who was biting her lower lip, and at Edna, who appeared astounded at Claire's outburst. Good—she wasn't the only one who felt Claire was out of line. "Look, Claire," she said softly, "you need some rest. This has been a horrible, stressful situation all the way around. You're not going to do anybody any good if you fall apart."

"Look at it this way," Millie said. "If they don't really have anything on Sam, the charges will be dropped pronto-quicko." Millie had a habit of using quirky terms, but *pronto-quicko?*

"But the damage will be done. This isn't something Sam will be able to forget—arrested for his wife's murder, and only a week after her funeral! I feel so guilty."

"You? Why in the world would you feel guilty?" Trish asked.

"I wasn't here when Susan died." Claire's voice broke. "Oh, I know I couldn't have prevented what happened, but I hate the idea of her being here alone. I should have been here."

"Claire," Trish said, leaning over to squeeze her arm, "you couldn't have known while you were grocery shopping that something like this would happen. Goodness, look at how many times you've done the same exact thing. You've never had any reason to believe that Susan shouldn't be left alone, have you?"

"Of course not. It's just that if I didn't have that stupid car trouble, at least I would have been here when it happened. She wouldn't have died here alone in this house."

"I hadn't heard about the car trouble," Millie said, "but I can surely sympathize. There's something wrong with my brake system. It never happens at a good time. You can't blame yourself for that." Edna and Trish exchanged an amazed glance. For Millie, *car trouble* meant replacing brake pads, which she had to do much more frequently than most people, probably due to the fact that she waited until the last minute to apply the brakes, slamming her foot down hard on the brake pedal. She must have missed the class that taught a driver how to start slowing down before it was necessary to stop.

"If it had been the brakes, I could have made it home. Some kind of wire came off. The engine wouldn't even turn over."

"How did you get home?" Edna asked.

"This nice man was coming out of the grocery store, and he saw that I was having trouble. When he looked under the hood, he knew immediately what was wrong, but he said he couldn't understand how the coil wire had come off and simply disappeared. Anyway, he went over to that auto-parts place in the strip center across the street and got another one. I paid him for it, of course. He put it on, and the car ran perfect. If I hadn't have been delayed, I believe I would have been here when the accident happened." The tears Claire had been trying so hard to rein in slipped slowly down her face again.

Edna got up to wrap her arms around her. "It's okay, Claire. Everything is going to be just fine."

Trish wished she could be as certain. Not that she believed for one minute that Sam was guilty, but the cops had to have something to have arrested him. She wondered what it could be.

It was decided that Claire would go home with Millie that evening and spend the night. Even though Millie extended her previous invitation to Trish concerning dinner and a movie, Trish declined. She was exhausted from all the different emotions that had wreaked havoc on her system today. An evening alone sounded like heaven. All they could do now was wait until Sam came home to see how they could help him. This ordeal would probably warrant more than a few cooked meals.

Later that afternoon, Trish sat at her kitchen table waiting for Edna. The poor woman had sounded so tired when she'd called to say she was coming over. Trish made iced tea and set out a plate of chocolate chip cookies, the ones she had set aside for a special occasion. She could start her diet tomorrow.

Nervously, she strummed her fingers on the table and wondered if Edna had found out anything. She still couldn't comprehend the whole thing. Sam had been arrested for murder? The very idea was so preposterous it would almost be funny, except for the fact that Sam had been carried away in a patrol car. That was not a laughing matter.

Trish heard the front door open. "It's me," Edna called out. Nobody locked their doors until they went to bed at night in this neighborhood. Trish couldn't help wondering if that would change now that a "murder" had occurred.

"Well, Sam might get out late this evening or early tomorrow morning," Edna said, pouring herself a glass of tea before she flopped down at the table.

"That's great news! What happened?"

"Joe didn't know a criminal attorney, but he called our attorney and got a recommendation—George Mueller. He's supposed to be one of the best." Edna took a long drink and sat back in her chair. For the first time Trish could ever remember, Edna's perfectly groomed appearance was slightly askew. A lock of silver hair fell over her forehead and her sweatshirt was wrinkled and slightly smudged.

"Edna, you're a wonderful friend. I'm sure Sam appreciates all you and Joe are doing. If I'm ever in trouble, it will be good to know you're on my side."

Edna blushed and waved her hand. "Don't be silly. I haven't done anything more than anybody else. And you know I will always stand beside you." Edna then grinned impishly. "However, I'm hoping your trouble-making days are over."

Trish raised her eyebrows. "After all these years, you're not saying that you think I was to blame for that episode with my ex, are you?"

"Certainly not! Any man who sleeps with another woman in his wife's bed should have to hang. I must say, though, that you were a little . . . *aggressive* in how you reacted. That's why the police got involved."

"I disagree. Aggressive would have been to shoot Ed in the kneecap."

"Thank God you didn't have a gun!" Edna chuckled.

"You can say that again." Actually, the unfortunate incident Edna referred to was what had cemented her friendship with Edna and Millie. Trish and her husband, Edward Frisk, had lived in the neighborhood only a few months when Trish had come home from work early and found Ed dancing horizontally with his secretary in their own bedroom.

Looking back, Trish had to admit there had been signs of Ed's infidelity, but she had either been too afraid of leaving him, or her self-confidence had been so low that she never confronted the problem. Naively, she had hoped that the thrill of their new house would bring them closer together again. Ed had definitely grown closer, just not with her. Somehow, having Ed's unfaithfulness thrown in her face sparked the stubborn, independent streak she had grown up with but lost somewhere along the way. However, enough was enough. She deserved better than Ed Frisk.

Ed hadn't heard Trish enter the house that day, and only by a supreme effort of will had she been able to hold back the scream of outrage she'd felt upon witnessing Ed's betrayal. Very calmly, almost trance-like, Trish had walked back into the kitchen. She'd gotten two gallons of bottled water—Ed insisted it was much better, health-wise, than tap water—and a packet of matches. She'd set the water by the bedroom door. Then, in no hurry, she'd walked in and set the end of the bedspread on fire. With quiet dignity, shoulders thrown back, she'd walked out of her house, gotten back in her car, and driven down the street where she could still see what was going on.

She hadn't had long to wait. Soon Ed and his girl-friend had come running out of the house, smoke billowing after them. Ed had only his slacks on and the woman was wrapped in one of Trish's robes. Trish had heard the fire truck at the same time as most of the neighbors did. While they were spilling out of their homes, Trish had smiled grimly and cruised back up the street, noticing with satisfaction that the police were arriving also. The whole scene would have been perfect if there had been a television camera there. She'd parked in front of Millie's house and watched as the firemen began unwinding their hoses while Ed was yelling something about the fire being out, that everything was under control.

Well, there was one thing Ed had been right about: Bottled water *was* better for your health.

"I still can't believe you just walked up to the police

and calmly told them you had lit the fire." Even though Edna and Millie hadn't known Trish that well at the time, they had both stood right beside her when she'd confronted the police, and later, her husband. Their unquestioning support had given her the courage to do what she knew in her heart she had to do: Get rid of her lazy leech of a husband and get on with her life.

"Do you remember the look on Chief Espinoza's face? He didn't quite know what to do. Of course, I fudged the truth a little bit. I admitted walking in on my husband and his girlfriend and said that I was so upset I'd dropped my cigarette." Even after all this time, Trish still couldn't prevent laughing when she thought about that day. Her actions had been so out of character, but she knew that was the day she'd started getting herself back. And to this day she didn't regret any part of it. She called it "the day of liberation." No way was she ever again going to let a man control her the way she had allowed her ex-husband to do.

"What still amazes me is that Ed didn't speak up and tell him you weren't a smoker."

"I think Ed was in shock. Also, he knew if news about this got out he would probably be disinherited. His parents were strict moralists. Adultery was unforgivable. That was the only way I got to keep the house. I threatened to ruin his reputation."

"I still think if the chief had started investigating, you would have ended up in jail."

"Oh, he wanted to," Trish said wryly. "But I think he was slightly embarrassed about the whole thing. But I could tell he was itching to throw his weight around. Nothing really exciting ever happens in our neck of the woods, and he thought he was going to finally get to do some real police work instead of processing speeding tickets."

Edna's grin faded. Their reminiscing had been fun, but it had also brought them back to the current problem. "Do you realize that your remark very closely mimics Claire's?"

Trish winced. "Oh, wow, you're right. I was exaggerating, though. I'm just frustrated that the police let Ed come back to the house and take some things out when I wasn't home, even though I had warned them that we were getting a divorce and he no longer lived there. But to intentionally set someone up? No, that's ridiculous. We have to face the fact that they know something, or think they do."

Edna yawned. "Well, I guess we'll find out soon enough. I'm going to go get some sleep, and I suggest you do the same. Joe is over at the jail waiting for Sam's bond to post so he can bring him home. I'll call you when I hear something."

Trish rose to walk Edna to the door. "I hope you realize what a wonderful husband you have."

Edna smiled, a sweet, lovely smile. "Oh, I do," she said softly and then waved good-bye.

Chapter Three

It seemed as though Trish had just closed her eyes when the telephone rang. Rolling over, eyes still glued shut, she reached for the bedside phone. "Hello," she mumbled sleepily.

"Trish, it's Millie. Edna just called. Sam's home and Claire just left to go back over there. I'll meet you out front in five minutes."

"What do you mean, you'll meet me out front? What time is it?"

"It's eleven o'clock. Just throw on a robe and hurry up. Claire said she'd have coffee ready."

Great, Trish thought, trying to force her eyes open, just what I need. More coffee. "Why are we going over there tonight? Shouldn't we wait until morning?"

"According to Edna, Sam's packing up a few things and going over to his sister's tonight," Millie said impatiently.

"And we can't visit him at his sister's house tomorrow because . . . ?"

"We're going to see him tonight," Millie snapped before she abruptly hung up, leaving Trish to stare at the phone in her hand. "Oh, that's why," she muttered sarcastically.

Fifteen minutes later they were all seated around Sam's kitchen table, fresh coffee in front of them. Joe sat beside Edna, his arm braced casually against the back of her chair. Even though he had been at the jail most of the evening waiting for Sam to be processed and released, he looked fresh and alert. Maybe there was something to be said for regular exercise, after all, Trish thought to herself, as she tried to stifle another yawn.

The bright, cheerful atmosphere was in stark contrast to the mood in the room. Sam looked dangerously close to collapse, his eyes sunken with dark shadows around them. His jeans and polo shirt, obviously worn all day, were rumpled and his face showed the gray stubble of a full day's beard. He was holding onto his cup with both hands, nervously running his fingers over the rim. Claire was trying too hard to appear positive and confident as she flitted around the table in her cotton robe and slippers, pouring coffee and setting out sugar and creamer.

She started babbling something about the weather when Sam reached out and gently placed a hand on her arm. "Claire, sit down," he said softly. Swallowing, she did as he asked, but not before Trish noticed her eyes filling up with tears.

"First of all," Sam said into the silence, his eyes focused on his coffee cup, "I want to thank you all for showing your support for me, and for taking care of Claire during this . . . difficult time." He cleared his throat, then suddenly looked up, his eyes burning with indignation. "I did not kill my wife."

"Of course you didn't," Millie said firmly, breaking into the stunned silence. She looked like a Christmas tree that had definitely seen better days with her dark green robe, red tennis shoes, and a red bandana tied over her hair. "We wouldn't be here if we thought you were capable of such a thing."

"We don't know exactly why the police believe you are guilty," Joe said, his voice calm and reassuring. He had a way of soothing troubled waters with his anything-is-possible attitude. When he spoke, people generally listened, one important reason he had been such a successful stockbroker. "George Mueller is going to get all the information he can today. When we know what we're dealing with, we'll know how to fight it."

"Joe, I don't know how to thank you for all you've done," Sam said, his voice gruff with emotion. "I'll reimburse the fifteen thousand you put up for my bond tomorrow morning."

Joe shook his head. "Don't worry about it. You just get some rest. I know that sounds impossible under the circumstances, but if you wear yourself down you won't be able to help the attorney strategize. This could be a very long, drawn-out process."

Sam cleared his throat and nodded. "You're right, of course. I'm going to spend the next couple of days over at Shelley's. You all have her number, right?" Everyone around the table nodded. Shelley was Sam's younger sister and was always a welcome member of their get-togethers. She lived just a few blocks down with her husband and two dogs. "The attorney has the number too. Joe, I'll call you as soon as I hear from him, and you can spread any news if you don't mind."

"Of course I will. Claire, I understand you're going with Sam?"

"Yes. Shelley was kind enough to invite me too."

"Good," Millie said. "We'll get the newspaper and check the mail every day."

"Thanks, Millie," Sam said. "This is only temporary. I'm just having some trouble right now . . ." Sam's voice broke off as he struggled with his emotions, but they all knew what he meant to say.

"Is there anything else we can do for you, Sam?" Edna would move boulders barehanded if Sam asked her to. Her smile was tender and caring, her eyes full of compassion.

"No, but thank you. You've all done more than enough. I think Claire and I will go on over to Shelley's. You folks go on home and get some sleep. None of us are spring chickens anymore, you know." That was twice in one day that Trish had been compared to an old rooster.

"Speak for yourself, Sam Wiley," Millie said as she got up to give Sam a hug. "Besides, chickens are idiots."

Everyone said their good-byes and left Sam and Claire to finish gathering the things they'd need over the next few days. "It's just so sad," Edna said softly as she walked beside Joe, his arm wrapped around her shoulders.

"I know, honey. I know."

The night was clear and cool, one of those beautiful nights where you felt you could reach out and touch the moon. Millie sighed. "Those two lovebirds are so cute, aren't they?"

Trish looked at the couple walking in front of them. *Cute* usually didn't apply to mature, sixty-five-year-olds, but she had to admit the phrase fit.

"Tom and I used to take long walks in the evenings. It was so romantic, just us, the stars, and the moon."

"I wish I had known your husband," Trish said quietly. He must have been a saint to put up with Millie. He had passed away shortly before Trish moved into the neighborhood, but it was obvious that he'd been a well-loved and well-respected man.

"We had fifty-five years together. I still miss him, you know. But we'll be together again one day—just not yet," she chuckled. "I still have too much to do."

Grinning, Trish put her arm around Millie and squeezed her shoulders. "You bet you do. You still haven't taught me how to crochet."

"I've tried," Millie said wryly, looking up at Trish. "It's hopeless."

They reached Edna's house first. Joe stopped and turned to face them. "I'm going on inside. I'll let you ladies say good night and gossip a bit in private."

"Joe Radcliff," Edna exclaimed, "we do not gossip."

Joe laughed as he turned to walk up his front path. "Good night."

"Thanks, Joe, for everything," Trish called after him.

"Ditto," Millie said.

Trish raised her eyebrows. *"Ditto?"* Millie stuck her nose in the air, in silent reply.

"I just hope Sam can get some sleep tonight," Edna said. "He looked like he was about to fall on his face."

"Sam's a fighter, but he's been hit with too much at one time. I'm really worried about him." Millie wrapped her arms around herself to ward off the chill.

"What time are we going to get started in the morning?" Trish asked with renewed energy. She was worried about Sam too, and she'd be doggoned if she was going to sit idly by while a good man was destroyed. Edna and Millie stared at Trish as though she had lost her mind. "Look, we already agreed we were going to do everything we could to help Sam, didn't we?" They nodded slowly, not quite sure where Trish was going with this. "Fine. Then I think the first thing we need to do is check out the house while Sam and Claire are gone."

Millie placed one hand on her hip. "And exactly what do you think we're going to find, Sherlock Holmes?"

"Who knows?" Trish answered, warming to the idea. "I don't have a clue how to prove an accident, but maybe if we can realistically recreate what happened, or if we find something to prove there was no way Sam could have murdered Susan, then we could share that information with the attorney. He'll know what to do."

"Trish, I don't think that's a good idea. We should just wait to see what the attorney finds out. Besides, don't you think the police have already covered every angle?"

"Of course, I do, Edna," Trish replied sardonically. "That's why Sam has been charged with murder."

"Oh, I don't know, Edna," Millie said, considering the idea. "Trish may be on to something. Regardless, what harm can it do?"

"Joe would kill me if he knew I went snooping in Sam's house!"

Millie looked at her pointedly. "Do you tell him *everything?*"

"Yes, I do!"

Millie rolled her eyes. "Well, suit yourself. Count me in, Trish."

"Great. How about eight-thirty?"

"And just how are you two planning on getting into Sam's house?"

"With the gardener's key." Millie said. The previous year, Sam had spent a fortune landscaping his front and back yards. It had proven too much for him to care for on his own, and although Susan loved the gardens, she hadn't wanted to be tied down to yard work to preserve the intricate mixture of flowers and shrubs. Hence, they had hired a professional gardener who came once a week, just like clockwork, to maintain the magic.

"Last chance, Miss Chicken. Are you going to come with us, or not?"

Edna looked at Millie and chewed on her bottom lip. "Oh, all right, I'll join you. I still don't think it's a wise thing to do, though." She didn't know what she was going to tell Joe, but she couldn't sit at home while her friends worked to prove Sam's innocence.

Trish grinned and threw her arm straight out. "All for one—"

Edna giggled and clasped Trish's outstretched hand. "And one for all!"

Millie rolled her eyes and slapped at their hands. "Ditto. Okay, it's settled. We'll meet at Trish's in the morning. Now, we had better get inside before the neighbors think we're getting ready to streak or something. Three silver-haired cronies standing outside at midnight in their robes could cause severe indigestion."

"My hair is not silver," Trish smirked.

"It would be if you stopped putting color on it."

Unfortunately, Trish thought to herself, Millie had a point.

"Is this legal?" Edna whispered, definitely having qualms about what they were doing. She was crouched behind Trish, who was bending down and searching for the key Sam always left under the big rock by the back door that led into the garage.

"Got it!" Trish grunted as she pushed herself up.

"Did you hear what I asked?"

"Hush, Edna," Millie said, pushing her glasses up her nose. "This isn't breaking-and-entering."

"But we don't have permission, either."

"Who do you think is going to file a complaint—Sam?"

"Millie, you take a lot for granted, you old coot!" Those were strong words, coming from Edna.

"And you're a chicken!"

"Shh! Would you two stop arguing? Look, the door is already unlocked!"

"Hmm . . . I guess Sam forgot to check it last night. Oh well, it just makes our job easier. Come on." Pushing her dark sunglasses on top of her head, her effort at a disguise, Millie went through the door with Edna and Trish following. Immediately they were enveloped in complete darkness.

Edna gasped, her nerves clearly already stretched thin.

Trish said, "Millie, open that door again to let in some light until I get the door to the kitchen open." No one had thought to bring a flashlight since they would be doing their snooping in broad daylight.

"What if Sam locked the kitchen door?" Edna asked, probably praying that he had.

"He didn't," Trish said, pushing the door open. "Come on." She led the way inside the house. She wasn't going to admit it to Millie, and certainly not to Edna, but there was a growing unease in the pit of her stomach. She reasoned that it was a natural response, though. They were alone, uninvited, in a dark, quiet house where a woman had died recently. Nevertheless, the hair on the back of her neck stood up, goading her imagination to believe that evil lurked behind every shadow.

"Shouldn't we turn on some lights, or at least open some of the blinds to let in more light?" Edna whispered. The morning sunlight struggled in vain to cut through the barrier of the closed window blinds. There was just enough light to enhance the feeling of a deserted house breathing sorrow and misfortune.

"I don't think that's a good idea," Millie said. "We don't want to advertise what we're doing. You know, I didn't think of this at first, but they may even have police patrolling this area to keep an eye on Sam. And would you stop whispering, for goodness' sake?"

"Oh," Edna grimaced. "I didn't even know I was."

"You may be right, Millie. Regardless, we don't want to take a chance on getting caught in here. I think there's enough light to see by," Trish whispered, peering through the shadows. Then she shook her head. "Geez," she said in a normal voice. "You've got me doing it, too."

"It is kind of creepy, isn't it?"

Trish shot her an exasperated look. "Hush, Millie. We don't need any theatrics right now." They were still standing in the kitchen, almost huddled together. There wasn't any sign of their late-night meeting. The cups must have been washed and put away, the table wiped clean. Claire wouldn't leave a mess, even though she knew there wasn't anybody who would notice. The faint smell of lemon oil was achingly familiar.

Trish sighed deeply. She would have to take the lead. This had been her brainstorm, after all, but that eerie feeling persisted, making her wonder if maybe her mouth had overridden her common sense last night. She couldn't back out now, though. She'd never hear the end of it. Besides, Sam needed their help.

"What are we looking for, anyway?"

"To be quite honest, I'm not sure, Millie. I think, going by Claire's explanation of what happened to Susan that morning, we should try to recreate what happened. Maybe we'll get some sort of idea about what the police are thinking."

"Fine. Which one of us is going to play Susan?" Millie asked in a saucy tone.

Now, there was a dare if Trish had ever heard one. Squaring her shoulders, she said with false bravado, "I will. I'm more her size, anyway."

"Susan wasn't chubby."

"Ha ha, that's very funny. Come on, let's go upstairs." With Trish in front, they walked single file past the dining room with the elegant cherrywood furniture and into the front foyer where the stairs began. There were no windows in this area to let in even a sliver of light. Trish stopped, took a deep, calming breath, and said over her shoulder, "Edna, Millie, be very careful. It's impossible to see a thing. Let's hold hands and walk up very, very slowly, one step at a time."

"Trish," Edna said in a small voice, "why don't we come back tomorrow and bring a flashlight?"

Uh-uh, there was no way that Trish was coming back

into this house without Sam or Claire. But, her common sense nudged at her: what if Millie or Edna got hurt during this little investigative venture? She'd never forgive herself. Running a hand through her hair, she sighed, ready to call it quits for the day when Millie spoke up. "Girls, we can do this. We've come this far, and all we have to do is look around the bathroom. Let's just get it over with." Her voice was tinged with excitement. Trish couldn't help but admire her spunk, but she still wondered if it was the right decision. Just because she personally wanted this over with didn't mean it was a smart idea.

"Edna, what do you think?" Trish asked, giving her the opportunity to voice her opinion. Whatever Edna said, they would do.

Edna gave a very deep, audible sigh. "Okay, okay, okay—let's go. But, please go slow. I don't want to spend the rest of my day at the hospital because one of you broke your leg, or even worse, your neck."

"That's the spirit!" Millie exclaimed. "Trish, you go up first. Edna, grab her hand with one of yours and then hold mine with your other. That way, if one of us trips, we'll have help."

"No, wait a minute," Trish said, moving behind Millie. "Better yet, I'll bring up the rear. I'm younger and stronger. If one of you stumbles, I'll be able to break the fall."

"Well, that's a good point," Millie said.

"I'm not going up first!" Edna exclaimed.

"I will, then," Millie said, pushing Edna out of the way. "Get behind me and hold on tight."

Trish closed her eyes and prayed for patience. By the time they decided how they were going to navigate the stairs, Sam could be convicted.

"Okay, gals, are you ready?" Millie asked.

"I'm ready," Edna replied, almost breaking the bones in Trish's hand.

"Ditto," Trish groaned.

Slowly, leaning back against the stairwell wall, they walked sideways up the stairs, one step at a time. Edna started counting in time with their steps: one, two, stop; one, two, stop. While part of Trish's brain tuned in with the rhythmic chant, another part tried to deal with the ongoing feeling that something wasn't quite right. Faced with a clear problem, Trish was usually excellent at solving it, tackling it head-on, but this feeling wasn't something she could neatly classify. It was an aura, a sense of . . . what? That was the question. If only she could pinpoint the *what.*

Finally, after what seemed like hours, Millie announced that she had reached the landing. With a collective sigh of relief, they stood still for a moment, shaking out their numb fingers. It was brighter up here, sunlight slightly filtering in through the bedroom windows and faintly spilling out into the hallway.

Suddenly, Trish started to giggle. "What's so funny?" Millie asked, a little worried that the stress had gotten to her friend.

"As much fun as it was holding Edna's trembling hand and learning to count again, it would have been much simpler to have just held on to the banister."

"Oh, Lord," Edna chuckled, covering her face with her hands. "Thank goodness there aren't any witnesses to what we just did."

Millie was laughing so hard her side hurt. "If either of you ever tells anybody about this," she gasped, wiping a tear from her eye, "I'll deny it until the day I die!"

Their laughter finally subsided, the welcome relief from tension and fear spurring them down the hall. But then Millie stopped and held up a hand. "Why is this door open?"

Trish looked into the room and shrugged. "It's just a spare bedroom. All of the other bedroom doors are open, so why wouldn't this one be?"

"I thought you knew," Edna said nervously. "This bedroom door is always kept closed and locked. There's a . . . um, well, I hate to reveal secrets, but I'm sure Sam thinks you already know . . ."

"What does Sam think I already know?" Trish wished Edna would spit it out. What was the big secret?

"For goodness' sake, Edna, I'll tell her," Millie said impatiently. "There's a hidden safe in here. I've got the combination written down in my address book. Sam always said if there was an emergency we should open up the safe and give the contents to his sister."

"Well, then, Sam probably left the door open," Trish said. "He either emptied the safe, or he just checked it recently. Maybe Susan's will was in there. Who knows? But who else could have opened the door if it was locked? Let's don't invent problems, okay?"

"You're right, of course," Edna said. "Let's get on with this. Joe went to the hardware store this morning, but he should be home soon."

"So you didn't have to lie to him, did you?" Millie chuckled.

"No, thank God, but I want to be home when he gets there."

The elegant features of the master bathroom were shrouded in gloom. Trish wasn't prepared for the rush of emotion that ran through her as she surveyed the room. Her friend had died here, a horrible, tragic death.

The room was big enough for all three of them to move around. Trish wondered again if this was a terrible mistake, their coming into the house to try and understand the exact circumstances so that they could help Sam. Seeing the scene where the accident had happened felt like an intrusion into personal heartache, an unforgivable invasion of the most intimate moment in a person's life, the unwilling surrender of a heart and soul.

In the back of her mind, Trish heard Millie and Edna chatting about the gorgeous room, but their comments were choppy, agitated. They felt it too.

Trish took a deep breath. *Think about Sam. Remember that you're doing this for him. Do what you have to do, and then get out!*

Chapter Four

"**O**kay, let's walk this through," Trish said. "Susan would have walked in and probably started the bath water first." Millie and Edna moved closer and watched as Trish bent over the tub, pretending to turn on the faucet. She then acted out the steps she assumed Susan had taken next, placing a towel over the towel rack, pouring in bath oil, and, since there was no radio in sight—the police probably had it—she pretended to pull one from the cabinet. It was while she was trying to place it on the tub edge that her gut clenched.

Millie noticed the same thing. "There's no way a radio could have perched on the edge of the tub."

"What are you talking about?" Edna asked, coming to stand beside Millie.

"This tub doesn't have a normal ledge. Its edges are small and rounded. You couldn't even place a bottle of bath oil there," Millie said.

"Then, where was the radio before it fell in?"

Trish straightened and looked around. Where could Susan have placed a radio? The nearest electrical plug was above the medicine cabinet. The window sill was too high up, and both the commode and the wicker stand were too far away. If she had placed it on the vanity, it couldn't have accidentally fallen in. Suddenly she shuddered, that strange feeling of unease returning, but this time she felt as if they were being watched, that they were not alone. "There's an explanation, I'm sure. We'll just talk it through. But I think we can go now."

Millie and Edna didn't argue. They followed Trish out of the room and into the hallway, where once again they faced the dark stairs. "This time we'll use the banister. Edna needs to get home."

"That's right. I do," Edna said quickly, gripping the banister with both hands.

Millie and Trish were close behind.

Outside, on the sidewalk in front of Sam's house, the bright sunlight successfully chased away the lingering traces of fear. It was easy for them to relax now, even to giggle at their mad dash down the stairs.

"I don't ever want to do anything like that again," Edna said. "I don't think my heart can take it."

"Oh, pooh," Millie scoffed, "it wasn't that bad. Besides," she said conspiratorially, "we did discover something interesting. How did that radio end up in the bathtub?"

Trish crossed her arms over her chest. "I don't know," she admitted ruefully, "but I don't see how it could have *accidentally* fallen in." She looked back up at the house—and then did a double take. Had the curtains in the upstairs bedroom window just moved? Of course not! Still, she stared, praying that she could blame her imagination for the tingling along her spine.

"What's wrong?" Edna asked, noticing Trish's startled expression. The concern was evident in her voice as she placed a comforting hand on Trish's arm.

Trish shook her head and pulled her gaze from the window. "Nothing," she croaked, cleared her throat, and said again, "nothing—I was just trying to figure out what could have happened." There was no need to elaborate that she was talking about the curtains moving. That would really send Edna over the edge. Anyway, it had to have been her imagination. Trish definitely, one hundred percent, categorically, did *not* believe in ghosts.

"Well, it's a cinch to see what the police believe," Millie said with a grimace as she started to walk away from Sam's house. "How do we tactfully tell them that they're idiots?"

"Millie!" Edna exclaimed as she and Trish fell in beside her.

"I know, I know," Millie said too sweetly, "I usually don't care about being tactful, but Sam's life is at stake here."

"Millie Morrow, you know that is not what I was talking about," Edna said impatiently.

Millie's lips twitched as she peered up at Trish and winked.

"You're a pig-headed old lady," Trish whispered to her. Aloud, she said, "Let's calm down. We have to admit it does look bad, but that doesn't mean Sam is guilty. If this was, indeed, a murder"—a shudder ran through her as she forced herself not to look back at the house—"then who could have done it, and why?" Nobody had the answer to that question. "What's even more curious is why they're charging someone with the crime now. This happened almost two weeks ago, and there hasn't been any hint at all that they've been investigating anything."

They had reached Edna's house, where Joe's car was parked in the driveway. "Since Joe is home now, I'll find out if he's heard anything from Sam or the attorney. I'll call you if there's any news."

Millie nodded. "Please do that."

"We'll see you later, Edna," Trish said. "Tell Joe 'hello' for us."

"I need to do some house cleaning," Millie said as she and Trish continued walking. "Michelle is coming by today for lunch."

"Is she bringing those two adorable grandkids of yours?"

"Of course—my daughter knows better than to come over without them. I have to get my fair time to spoil them, you know."

"You enjoy your visit, then. I think I'll try and get some work done, myself." Trish operated an accounting service from her home office. The work was fulfilling, the hours were great, and the pay was quite good, but it was entirely too easy to let outside influences keep her from putting in the necessary time to complete a project—like now. If Trish wasn't careful, she'd get so wrapped up in Sam's tragedy that she'd be pulling an all-nighter just to get caught upon her work—and the older she got, the harder it was to work all night.

Millie took a deep breath. "Now that the ol' scaredy-cat isn't around, what do you think really happened to Susan?"

They were in front of Trish's house now, and she

stopped, shaking her head. Leave it to Millie to center all the blame on Edna when she knew good and well that they had *all* been scared silly. "First of all, Edna isn't a scaredy-cat. She's just cautious"—Trish ignored Millie's inelegant snort—"and there's nothing wrong with that. But, to answer your question, I can see how murder could be a possibility. If it wasn't Sam we're talking about here, I'd even say it was likely." Trish's voice had lowered to barely above a whisper.

Millie nodded, her lips drawn in a tight line as she bent to pluck a stray weed from Trish's yard. "I think we all agree. So, what do we do now?" she asked as she straightened, the offending weed still in her hand.

Trish's eyebrows rose. They were talking about murder, and Millie acted like it wasn't any more serious than deciding whether it was too early to eat dinner or not. She reached out and knocked on Millie's head. "Hello, is anybody home in there?"

Millie's mouth popped open and she took a step back. "What did you do that for?" she asked indignantly.

"I did that because I think you've lost your marbles! What do you mean 'What are we going to do now?' "

Millie placed her hands on her hips. "Whose idea was it to help Sam in the first place?"

"That was when I thought we were trying to prove Susan's death was an accident . . . not the result of murder!"

"So now he doesn't deserve our help?"

"I never said that, Millie," Trish said, her eyes narrowing at the short fireball standing in front of her. Both of them had raised their voices by now. Trish just hoped the neighbors didn't hear and come rushing out of their homes like kids gathering around a schoolyard fight. If Millie threw the first punch, Trish knew she could take her, but Millie didn't appear to be concerned at all. She was going to have to work on her threatening skills.

"Then, what *are* you saying?"

Trish counted to ten, slowly. "Do you realize how dangerous it could be to get involved in this?"

"Ah . . . you were right," Millie said, her eyes twinkling. "Edna isn't the scaredy-cat—sorry, my mistake."

It was the twinkling eyes that saved her. Otherwise, Millie might have been sitting on the ground by now. "You're a brat, Millie." The smile in Trish's voice added sincerity to the endearment.

"I know," she chuckled, and then sighed deeply as her forehead creased in worry. "We have to do something, though, and you know it."

Trish sighed. "I'm not having any brainstorms right now."

"That's it!" Millie exclaimed. "We'll have a brainstorming party tonight. When Michelle leaves, I'll come over. You get in touch with Edna and let her know. And," Millie said dramatically, "I'll bring dessert. Jell-O and fruit, my rear end!"

Before Trish could close her mouth, Millie was halfway across the street.

When Edna called that afternoon to tell her that the attorney had not yet received copies of the arrest warrant and official report, Trish related what Millie had suggested. To her surprise, Edna willingly agreed to the meeting later that evening. As she had so eloquently put it, "We're Sam's only hope."

A few hours later, Trish turned off her computer and

stretched. She would mail the financial statements she had just completed, along with her bill, to the construction company that used her services, and she'd be free for a few days. Yawning, she glanced at the clock. Four o'clock! My, how time flew when you billed by the hour.

At least the tedious work had kept her mind off Sam for a while. Speaking of which, she only had a couple of hours before Edna and Millie were due to arrive. She'd need to make a snack tray—they were all incurable munchers—and there was one other thing she wanted to do before her friends showed up.

A few minutes later, Trish stood in front of the exercise machine, sans the spandex outfit. She was wasting her time trying to intimidate this cold chunk of metal by dressing like an experienced, professional exercise person. Nope, this afternoon it was sweatpants and tennis shoes.

With a determined attitude she lowered herself onto the black leather seat at one side of the machine and placed her feet on the pedals. Her knees were bent almost to her chest, but evidently that was the way it was supposed to work. Grasping the two handles on each side of the seat, she took a deep breath and pushed with her legs, and . . . pushed! Nothing budged. Trish took a deeper breath and pushed harder. Still nothing happened, except that she now had a purple face and a headache. Puzzled, she sat for a minute reviewing the picture in her mind of the tiny, slim woman in the manual easily pushing the pedal as she smiled a movie-star smile, not even breaking a sweat.

Hmm . . . something had to be wrong. Trish got up and slowly walked around the machine. Then she saw it. The little lever that controlled the amount of weight to be used was stuck in the hole marking two hundred pounds. Rolling her eyes heavenward, she pulled it out and stuck it in the twenty-pound hole. She wasn't Wonder Woman yet.

This time the pedal moved with relative ease. Push . . . release, *clang!* Push . . . release, *clang!* Trish could feel the pressure, but it wasn't too bad. Soon she was into an easy rhythm. Smiling with satisfaction, she let her mind wander. And since there wasn't much else going on in her life right now, her mind wandered right over to the dilemma Sam was in.

The thought that Sam had killed Susan was ludicrous. So, the question became: Who had? Claire? But that thought was even more ridiculous than thinking Sam had done it. What possible motive would Claire have for killing her employer? There was absolutely none, as far as Trish could tell.

It was back to square one. As far as she knew, Susan didn't have any enemies, burglary was ruled out, and the two people closest to her, Sam and Claire, had both been out of the house when it had happened. What was she missing here? There had to be a reasonable explanation, and yet, was murder ever reasonable?

Trish felt the slight burning in the muscles of her thighs, but she didn't pay it any attention. Her thought process was on a roll. She blew the hair out of her eyes as she concentrated. Suddenly, as though a lightbulb had just flashed on in her mind, she knew this had to be tied to Sam, somehow—either intentionally, to make him look guilty, or just to plain hurt him. Either way, Sam was as much a victim of this as Susan had been. She was sure of it.

Trish stopped pedaling and glanced at her watch.

There was just enough time to take a quick shower and lay out some snacks before her cohorts would be over. Feeling both physically and mentally invigorated, she stood. Evidently, she'd stood too fast. Her rubbery legs barely held her up long enough to allow her to sink back onto the seat. Might have overdone it just a bit, she thought with a grimace. It took a few minutes before she felt steady enough to try standing again. Biting her lower lip, she wobbled down the hallway.

As scheduled, Millie and Edna arrived promptly at six, Millie carrying a plastic dish containing a beautiful chocolate cake. Trish dreaded the thought of how much exercising she would have to do to work it off tomorrow . . . or the next day, she hastily amended, as her legs protested at the mere thought of another workout. It never crossed her mind that she could just say no to the rich dessert.

Armed with crackers and cheese, pickles and olives, coffee and cake, the three women sat at the table and immediately started discussing Sam's plight.

"Sam is the reason behind this crime," Trish blurted, popping an olive in her mouth.

Edna's eyes opened wide. "You'll never make me believe Sam killed Susan!" Her hand shook slightly as she put down her coffee cup.

"Oh, Edna, I didn't mean Sam is *guilty,* but I do believe this happened *because* of him."

Millie mumbled through a huge bite of rich, chocolate cake, "Go on."

"I'm convinced that someone is out to get Sam. They've successfully framed him for the murder and devastated him at the same time."

Edna frowned. "What makes you so sure?"

"Let's look at this objectively." Trish leaned forward in her chair and crossed her arms on the table. "Nothing was stolen, so it wasn't a robbery. Susan never met anybody who didn't like her and vice-versa, so it's not a secret enemy. There's no sign of breaking and entering . . ."

"We got in the house, and we didn't have to break anything," Millie pointed out.

"That's exactly my point! Whoever did this knew how to get in, or maybe when Claire and Sam left that morning they didn't lock the door. Regardless, someone knew Susan would be alone."

Millie leaned back in her chair and patted her stomach, her gaze settling on the far wall as she contemplated Trish's theory. Edna was silent as she broke off a square of sliced cheese and placed it on a cracker. While they pondered the idea, Trish got up to refill their coffee, noticing that the muscles in her legs were really starting to tighten up. Making her way very slowly to the coffee pot, she hoped neither of her friends would notice. She'd never hear the end of it.

Finally, Millie broke the silence. "For argument's sake, let's say you're right. That still doesn't bring us any closer to figuring out who could have done it and why."

"Well, that's not necessarily so," Edna said slowly. "Sam can help us."

Trish sat back down and bit her bottom lip to keep from crying out as her muscles protested. She gave Edna two thumbs up on her suggestion, afraid her voice would come out in a squeak if she tried to talk right at that moment.

Millie nodded. "I think your theory is a possibility we need to investigate. So, what do we do now?"

"We start by going to the police," Trish said firmly. Her legs were settling into bearable pain as long as she stayed absolutely still.

"Why don't we just tell the attorney what we suspect?" Edna asked.

Trish finally gave in to temptation and cut a piece of cake. "He hasn't even gotten the information on Sam's arrest yet," she answered. "Our suspicion at this point will mean nothing to him. He'll just file away our theory until he has the whole case against Sam laid out. In the meantime, Sam is living with this horrible charge against him. Maybe the police can do something."

"In your dreams," Millie said wryly.

Trish licked a dab of chocolate from her finger. "Do you have a better idea?"

Millie hesitated and then shrugged. "I guess not. But don't be disappointed if the police don't jump for joy and announce that the case is solved."

With its white rock exterior and natural, understated landscaping, the outside of the Grand River Police Department looked like any other house in the area, except, of course, for the two official cars parked in the wide circular driveway—one of them must be out on patrol since the city owned only three—and the sign above the front door announcing the official establishment.

Trish had never been there before. Were they supposed to knock on the door? Millie answered that question when she walked up the front steps and marched right in.

The interior of the place was in sharp contrast to the homey atmosphere of the exterior. The tile flooring and painted beige walls were done with the normal imaginative flair of an administrator on Valium. On the wall across from the door was a large framed photograph of the chief and three other uniformed officers standing in front of the building. Trish wondered how many speeders had gotten away with their vicious crimes while the entire Grand River Police Department had been otherwise occupied.

Nobody sat at the desk in the corner of the entryway, but a full cup of coffee suggested that someone would be there soon. Evidently, Millie had decided that she didn't want to wait. She walked right past the desk, down a long hallway with closed doors on either side. There were more pictures, but they were of former officers long retired by now.

Trish and Edna followed Millie at a safe distance. If she was shot for trespassing, they didn't want to be anywhere near the flying bullets. Millie found the door she was looking for and knocked loudly before opening it. Geez, did the woman have any manners at all? Trish bit her bottom lip to keep from laughing as the expression *hell on wheels* came to mind.

A gruff, male voice, a *surprised* gruff, male voice, had started to respond to the knock, but stopped when Millie walked in. Edna turned slightly toward Trish and rolled her eyes before she followed Millie. Trish just shook her head and walked through the doorway.

Next time, if they were ever allowed back in the police department again, they would find a way to leave Millie at home.

Chapter Five

Police Chief Henry Espinoza sat behind a large, black metal desk. He rose slightly from his seat when they walked in and then sat back down with a large sigh. Not a good sign, Trish thought.

"Is there something I can do for you ladies?" he asked in a voice that made it clear he didn't appreciate unannounced visitors. His brown eyes were sharp and he was obviously intelligent, but everybody knew he was as cantankerous as a rattlesnake when somebody invaded its territory.

"Hi, Henry," Millie said, unperturbed, plopping down across from the desk in the only other chair in the cramped room. "You remember my friends, Edna Radcliff and Trish Anderson, don't you?"

I hope not, Trish thought to herself as she smiled slightly and leaned against the door frame. She really didn't want him remembering the burning mattress episode.

Edna, always the perfect lady, smiled brightly and held out her hand. "How are you, Chief?"

Henry leaned forward to shake her hand, nodding at both her and Trish before leaning back in his chair. "Again, what can I do for you? Are you having another problem with your neighbor, Mrs. Morrow?"

Millie waved her hand. "Call me Millie. And, no thanks to you, I took care of that problem myself."

Trish groaned silently. *Great, make the chief mad and let's see how willing he is to help us.*

Henry cocked his head. "We talked to Mr. Greenburg several times, and he swore he wasn't looking in your windows. He said he was only working in his garden."

"I know what he told you, but he didn't plant that garden until *after* his wife died, and isn't it coincidental that it's on the side of his yard facing my bedroom window?"

"I don't see anything strange about that at all."

Trish listened to the conversation with interest. Sweet, old Mr. Greenburg was a Peeping Tom? Of course, she knew his wife had died many years before and he lived in the big house alone now, but he had always worked outside in his beloved gardens. She agreed with Henry: it didn't seem strange at all. But why had she never heard this story before?

"Well, I think it was strange that every time I walked into my bedroom I could see him right outside, and several times I caught him turning suddenly when he realized that I saw him."

Henry sighed deeply. "So, how did you solve the problem yourself?"

"I stood my husband's old shotgun in the window and placed a full box of shells on the window sill," Millie said smugly.

Henry's eyebrows shot up. "You did what?"

"I refuse to close all my blinds during the day and live in darkness because a dirty old man is getting his kicks by watching me. So I sent him a message that he evidently understood. That particular garden bed is now full of cactus that needs very little care."

"The gun wasn't loaded, was it?" The chief's voice was stern, but there was a twinkle in his eye.

Millie ignored the question and plunged into the reason they were there. "Chief Espinoza, we're here to help you."

"You all want to *help* me? With what?"

"You recently arrested a friend of ours, Sam Wiley, and we need to talk to you about it," Edna said with a gentle smile.

Thank you, Edna, Trish thought to herself. It was much too dangerous to let Millie keep babbling on.

The twinkle disappeared from the chief's eyes. "Ladies, that's really none of your business."

Millie jumped up angrily. "That's where you're wrong, Chief Espinoza! But I can see we're not going to get any help from you. Let's get out of here, girls."

Edna grabbed Millie's arm to keep her from storming out of the office. "Chief Espinoza," she said calmly, "we don't want to interfere, but I think we have special insight as to what could have happened. We would really appreciate it if you would just hear us out."

Henry paused. All he needed was a group of old ladies telling him how to do his job. But Sam Wiley was their friend—a friend they were willing to defend to him. Maybe if he just patronized the women and listened to their story, he could prevent his name from being dragged through the mud.

His glance settled on Millie Morrow. Scratch that, he thought with resignation. His name was mud. "You've got three minutes," he said, settling back in his chair and crossing his arms over his chest.

With a huff, Millie sat back down. "Okay, Trish, tell him what we think."

Trish coughed to hide her sudden discomfort as the chief's gaze fell on her. Her theory had sounded so commonsense, so cut-and-dried last night in the protection of her home, but now she had probably one shot to convince this hard-nosed lawman that there was some merit to their belief that Sam had been set up.

Pulling away from the door frame, she moved closer to the desk, her arms imitating his as she crossed them over her chest. She took a deep breath. "Chief Espinoza," she began, hoping a show of respect for his position would change the bored expression on his face, "we believe firmly that Sam Wiley was either set up to make it look like he killed his wife, or that someone was out to just plain destroy him."

"Oh, you do, do you?"

Trish cleared her throat. "Yes, we do. There could be a convincing argument made against any evidence you think you have . . ."

"You don't even know what evidence I have."

"That's true, we don't," Trish continued, not appreciating being interrupted one bit, "but I'm sure you've wondered why there wasn't a broken window or a jimmied door, and—"

Henry gave a small laugh, causing Trish to grit her teeth. There he went again. Was it possible to get out a full sentence around this man?

"Outside of there having been no *forced* entry,"

Henry said pointedly, pinning Trish with an impatient look, "there is also the fact that, according to his buddies, Sam was late for his golf game that morning—first time ever. He *claimed* he had car trouble. Add to that the fact that the radio found in the bathtub had never been seen before by either Claire or, supposedly, Sam. What did the killer do, carry around an electric radio just in case Susan Wiley happened to be taking a bath? And, of course, there is the usual motive for murder—money. He was the beneficiary of her life insurance policy."

"But that's not unusual between married couples, Chief," Edna pointed out. "Joe and I are the beneficiaries of each other's life insurance policy."

"I agree that it's not unusual. But neither one of you has been murdered. Maybe Sam had the hots for his housekeeper and wanted his wife out of the way."

"That's a vulgar thought, Henry, even for you," Millie snapped.

Trish opened her mouth and then closed it. Sam had car trouble that fateful morning too? Did Chief Espinoza know that Claire had had car trouble that same morning? He probably didn't, or he would have mentioned it . . . gleefully. She opened her mouth to tell him what they had learned when a thought stopped her: How difficult would it have been for Sam to rig Claire's car for trouble that morning? It would have guaranteed that Claire would be away from the house longer than usual. If Sam had, indeed, planned the murder of his wife, which Trish didn't believe for one minute, then the fact that both he and Claire had had car trouble on the same morning could very possibly be construed as premeditation in the eyes of the police.

Trish closed her mouth. She decided it would be

better not to mention Claire's car trouble. This information would be better analyzed by Sam's attorney, but she had to get Edna and Millie out of there before they innocently mentioned the strange coincidence. "Well, it seems as if your mind is made up, Chief," she said in a rush. "I still feel like you're barking up the wrong tree, and I believe Sam's attorney will prove it."

Henry ran his hand through his gray-streaked dark hair and sighed, pushing himself up from his chair to signal that the meeting was over. "Believe it or not, I hope you're right. I've always liked Sam, but I can't ignore the evidence. Unless something else is discovered that could prove his innocence, then I'm afraid we've got the right guy."

Trish's eyes narrowed as she looked at Henry. He sounded sincere enough, but he had not let them present their suspicions at all. He must truly believe Sam was guilty and just be paying them lip service.

Millie evidently felt the same way. "Henry, you're just afraid that we may be right." Abruptly, she got up from the chair and glared at him. "You just remember, when someone besides Sam Wiley is arrested and found guilty for Susan's murder, it should be our collar, not yours!"

Trish reached over and grabbed Millie by the arm, propelling her out the door with Edna following. Millie really needed to stop watching so many of those cop shows she loved so much. *Their collar . . .?*

Once they were in her car, Trish reached for her seatbelt and yanked it across her lap. "Well, that was a waste of time."

"Not necessarily," Millie said with an impish smile. "We now know what the evidence is against Sam, and it's nothing. Their case hinges on car trouble? Give me a break."

Slowly, Trish smiled. Millie was right.

"Does either one of you remember Sam mentioning that he had car trouble that morning?" Edna asked from the backseat.

"No, I don't," Millie sighed. "That doesn't look good, does it?"

"Not really," Trish agreed, her voice somber. "I'm sure there's a good explanation, but what a strange co-incidence that both Claire and Sam had car trouble on the same morning."

"Well, let's go ask him about it," Millie said.

After a moment, Trish nodded. "We probably should. It could be an important piece of the puzzle, but where it fits, I don't have a clue."

Edna leaned forward. "If we're going to Shelley's, we need to stop and pick up something to take over there. We can't go empty-handed."

"Okay, Ms. Manners," Millie said sarcastically, "we certainly can't let the social graces fall by the wayside just because of something as silly as a murder."

Trish looked in her rearview mirror. Edna didn't say anything, but her lips were set in a tight line as she looked through the side window. Uh-oh, Millie might have gone too far with her teasing that time.

Trish nudged Millie and tilted her head back slightly toward Edna. Millie's eyebrows rose in question, but when Trish motioned again with her head, Millie turned around to see what was wrong. "Cat got your tongue, Edna?"

Terrific, Trish thought as she rolled her eyes. *That's one way to smooth over hurt feelings.*

Edna ignored Millie, keeping her gaze locked on the passing scenery. Millie grinned and cocked her head. "Are you upset with me?"

Edna still didn't reply. Trish racked her brain for something to say that would ease the tension, but before she could come up with anything, Millie unlocked her seatbelt and pushed herself up on her knees.

"What are you doing?" Trish demanded. "Sit back down before I get a ticket!"

"Stop worrying. I'll just be a minute." Millie grunted as she turned herself around and started to scramble over the seat. Her rear end hit Trish in the arm, causing her to jerk the steering wheel slightly.

"Millie," she yelled, "get back in your seat!"

"Don't be silly. I'm halfway over." And she was, but the heel of her foot caught the rearview mirror, knocking it off balance as she crawled head-first into the backseat beside Edna.

"Are you crazy?" Edna shouted as she reached up to pull Millie's legs over the seat.

Trish hurriedly straightened her rearview mirror. Any minute they would be surrounded by the police. "If we live through this, Millie, I'm going to kill you!"

"Right, another murder is just what we need." Millie sounded out of breath, but at least she was sitting upright now with her feet on the floor instead of pressed against the roof of the car.

Trish glared at her reflection for a moment. "Your hair is messed up," she said tightly.

"That's nothing," Millie said with a grimace as she reached under her shirt and rolled her shoulders back and forth. "You should see my bra."

Edna looked at her incredulously. "What in the world did you do that for? You could have caused us to have a wreck!"

"I just wanted to say I was sorry," Millie said mildly.

Edna's mouth popped open and then closed. She peered closely at Millie sitting beside her. "You could have done that from the front seat."

"Apologies need to be made face-to-face, not behind a head rest. Besides, I didn't think you'd believe I was serious. But I am. I was just teasing you, Edna." Millie turned slightly and reached for Edna's hand. "One thing I admire about you the most is that you always think of other people first—what will make them feel better, what they might need, and you jump right in to fill that need. You're amazing. I was teasing you because I knew the proper thing to do was take something over with us. I wish I had thought about it," she said, smiling wryly. "Forgive me?"

Edna stared at Millie for a moment. Then Edna reached over with her free hand and smoothed Millie's hair. "You are one crazy old lady," she said softly, "and I love you. Of course I forgive you. I'm sorry I was wearing my feelings on my sleeve. I guess all of this worrying about Sam is getting to me."

Trish drove straight ahead with her eyes opened wide in shock, afraid she'd ruin the moment if she so much as tried to sneak a look in the mirror. That was the most tenderhearted, sincere statement she had ever heard from Millie. She had owed Edna an apology, no doubt about it, but Trish never would have expected Millie to be so successful at it.

"Okay, that's enough of this mushy stuff," Millie said briskly. "Do we take doughnuts or cupcakes?"

Twenty minutes later they sat in Shelley's spacious kitchen eating melt-in-your-mouth coffee cake with Sam and Claire—with Claire, anyway. Sam wasn't eating.

While Claire had gone to tell Sam they were there, Shelley had confided in them how worried she was about her brother. He wasn't himself lately, not that anyone could blame him, she admitted, but she hoped their visit would help to cheer him up some. Then she excused herself, giving Sam's friends and neighbors some privacy for their visit.

Edna, bless her heart, did her best to carry on a normal conversation about the weather, about the roof leak she and Joe had just discovered, about anything that popped into her mind. Claire dutifully participated, but it was clear that her heart wasn't really in it. Sam, on the other hand, didn't even try.

Millie's eyes had just about popped out of her head when he'd come into the kitchen, but for once she had held her tongue. Shelley's concern about her brother was well-founded. Still in his bathrobe, Sam had aged at least ten years since they had seen him last. Shuffling to the table, he had accepted a cup of coffee but declined anything to eat.

While Edna tried to engage him in conversation, Trish cast covert glances at him. His smile was stiff and forced, and his eyes were dull and shadowed—not a good sign. Sam would have to learn how to manage the stress and grief he was under, or he would soon be facing serious health problems. But how did you say that to someone who had been through the traumatic events Sam had? She couldn't even begin to imagine what he was going through.

Claire gathered the empty plates and refilled coffee

cups, then said she wanted to clean the upstairs bed-rooms before Shelley came home. It was the least she could do, she explained when Sam protested halfheart-edly, since Shelley had so kindly invited her to stay in her home for a while.

After Claire left the room, Millie interrupted Edna's cheerful chatter. "Edna, you've given it your best shot, now hush. Sam doesn't want to talk about blooming azalea bushes."

Trish had wondered how long Millie would be able to stay quiet. Actually, Trish was pretty sure Millie had just set a new record. But she was right; Sam wasn't inter-ested in mindless chit-chat. Millie leaned forward and pointed her finger at Sam. "You're letting yourself fall apart."

Sam didn't appear to be offended by the remark. He leaned back in his chair, crossed one knee over the other, and smiled slightly at Millie. "No, I'm fine, really—just a little tired."

"No, Sam, it's more than just being tired, and you know it. But you have to snap out of it because we need your help."

"You need *my* help?" Sam chuckled bitterly. "I'm not in a position to help anybody right now."

Edna's smile was gentle. "Yes, you are. You're the only one who can."

"Okay, I'll bite. What do you need help with?"

"Proving your innocence," Millie said, looking straight into his eyes.

Sam's face became devoid of all expression. "I have an attorney to do that, Millie. I appreciate the thought, but I'm going to let him take care of this."

"In other words, you're just going to sit on your butt

while you're being railroaded for murder? That's not the Sam I know."

"My attorney will prove I didn't do this. It's just going to take time."

Trish placed her hand over his. "The police have a lot of circumstantial evidence, Sam, but sometimes that's all it takes to get a guilty verdict. We've all seen enough real-life court shows to know that."

Sam sat up straight and pulled his hand away. "What circumstantial evidence? What are you talking about? And how do you know all this?"

"So the old man does have some life still in him," Millie muttered. "Go ahead and tell him, Trish."

As Trish told Sam what they had found out from Chief Espinoza, she watched his expression change from a total lack of concern, to disbelief, and then to unease. "You need to let your attorney know this, Sam. That way he'll be prepared when he gets the report. But I wanted to ask you what kind of car trouble you had that morning. Did you know that Claire also had trouble with her car that same morning?"

Sam looked up and nodded. "Yes, she told me. I didn't think too much about it at the time because she easily had it taken care of. I never made any connection to my own car trouble, but I can see now how strange it looks." Sam shrugged his shoulders. "I just had two flat tires in the rear. I must have driven by a construction site or something. The tires weren't flat when I left the house, but by the time I got about a mile away I could feel something wrong. Fortunately, there was a tire shop close by, so I simply pulled in and bought two new ones. Sure enough, there were roofing nails in each of the tires. It's just a coincidence, not a conspiracy. The police will realize that when they start investigating."

But the police had already started the investigation and may very well be finished, Trish thought. It would be up to Sam to prove his innocence.

"Sam, the police have already started investigating, but I'm not sure they've given any significance to the two incidents with the cars," Trish said. "They do consider your car trouble significant, though—a cover-up for the crime, so you would have an excuse for being late to your golf game."

"Well, they're wrong."

"We know they're wrong," Edna said, "and we're going to prove it."

Trish coughed. Edna should have said, "and we're going to help your attorney prove it." It seemed they were all getting a little loose with this Sherlock Holmes talk.

"You've been set up," Millie said bluntly.

Sam laughed, but there was no humor in the sound. "Don't be ridiculous, Millie. It was an accident."

"I'm afraid we all agree, Sam," Edna said quietly. "It's the only thing that makes sense. Neither you nor Claire had ever seen that radio before, it couldn't have fallen into the tub accidentally, nothing was stolen, and now we discover that both you and Claire had car trouble on the very same morning that Susan died."

"Okay, everything may look suspicious, but it still doesn't prove a murder was committed," Sam argued. "Besides, who in the world would want to set me up for murder? If you're right, this crime took a lot of planning. Don't you think I would have realized that someone was out to get me?" He answered his own question.

"No, the idea is too far-fetched to even consider seriously."

"Humor us," Millie said. "We're a bunch of old ladies with nothing better to do, so humor us and answer our questions while we play detective."

Sam lifted an eyebrow. "What kind of questions do you have?"

Millie thought for a moment. "First of all, we want a list of everybody you've been in contact with over the last couple of years."

Sam's eyes opened wide. "I'll do nothing of the sort! You are not going to start harassing innocent people and causing trouble just because you're bored!"

Trish sat back and listened to the exchange between Sam and Millie, thoughts careening around in her head. Millie was taking charge of the situation very nicely indeed. Not only was she irritating Sam, but now she was telling him that they were going to solve this mystery, if there even was one, because they were old and in a rut. And Edna just sat there, her silence expressing her agreement with the plan. This situation was getting out of hand fast.

Millie leaned forward. "What have you got to lose, Sam? Your reputation and your freedom are all you have left to begin picking up the pieces of your life. If you lose those two things because you're too stubborn to admit that maybe, just maybe, we're on to something here, then you'll be letting everybody down, everybody that loves you and believes in you."

"She's right, Sam," Edna said. "And, most of all, you'll be letting down Susan."

Sam opened his mouth to say something but then closed it again. Finally, after several agonizingly quiet moments, he sighed deeply and nodded. "I still think you all are barking up the wrong tree, but to satisfy your minds and to say that at least all possible scenarios were explored, I'll cooperate with you. I'm warning you, though," he said with a stern look at all of them, "if you hurt any of my friends' feelings, then you stop this charade immediately. Is that understood?"

Millie grinned broadly. "We'll be the model of decorum. Don't worry."

Edna clapped her hands together and smiled. "I think you've made the right decision, Sam."

Trish tried to smile—she really did—but it came off as a grimace. Were they getting Sam's hopes up for nothing? And what happened to just throwing out some suggestions to the police or the attorney? She glanced at the pleased expressions on Millie's and Edna's faces. What had they—or, more precisely, Millie—just gotten themselves into?

For the next hour, Sam talked about his friends and his past business associates while Edna furiously scribbled notes. It was a frustrating process. Every time one of them would ask about a possible hidden agenda by a person on the list of names Sam was giving them, he would become defiant and defensive. He finally called it quits altogether. "That's everybody I can think of. Not one of those people would have a reason to hurt me, but I've done what you've asked." He leaned back in his chair and crossed his arms over his chest. "So, what are you going to do now?"

Millie looked at him. "We're going to find out who set you up, of course."

Chapter Six

"There's Charlie," Edna exclaimed as soon as Trish turned onto their street.

"That's perfect," Millie said. "He can be the first person we interview. Pull up in front of Sam's house, Trish."

Trish sighed, but did as she was asked. She had to admit that she was more than a little curious about the people on the list Sam had given them, but she still wasn't convinced that conducting secret interviews on their own was the right thing to do. What if they inadvertently ruined any chance the person's words could be used as evidence pointing to Sam's innocence?

Trish had argued the point tirelessly on the way home from their visit with Sam, but her comments had fallen on deaf ears. Millie was certain the police would do nothing more to investigate this case since they were so sure they had the guilty man. Edna had agreed, but her opinion was different. She felt the reason they wouldn't be taken seriously was that Millie had angered the chief.

Still, it wasn't as though they were trained in detective work, Trish had pointed out. However, one thing she was pretty sure of was that you never ruled out anybody as a suspect, regardless of your instincts. And her instincts were laughing outright at the idea that Sam's gardener, Charlie Simms, could have killed Susan Wiley.

Millie climbed out of the car as soon as it stopped. "Follow my lead," she whispered as she slammed the door and waved at Charlie.

Trish shook her head. "Lord, help us," she muttered in sincere prayer.

"And all His angels," Edna added fervently as they followed Millie.

Charlie turned off the riding lawn mower and climbed down as he nodded respectfully at the three women. "Good afternoon," he said as he pulled a handkerchief from his back pocket and wiped his brow.

"Hi, Charlie," Millie said as she approached. "Sam's yard looks just wonderful."

"Thank you, ma'am. I wasn't sure if Mr. Wiley wanted the lawn done this week or not, since . . . well, you know."

"I'm sure he'll appreciate it," Edna said, patting Charlie's arm.

The old gardener cleared his throat. "Well, he isn't home right now, but I did it anyway. I sure hope you're right."

"Yes, I think Sam had to . . . um, run an errand," Millie said. "He should be home soon. Charlie, the reason we stopped is because Trish is thinking about having her yard done on a regular basis. You know her house, the one three houses from the corner? Would you be interested in taking on another yard?"

Trish fought to keep her smile in place even as her hands itched to wrap themselves around Millie's neck. A gardener was definitely not in her budget, and Millie darn well knew it.

"Sure, I'd be glad to. What exactly do you want done?"

"Well, I'm not quite sure," Trish said truthfully with a sideways look at Millie. "To start with, I'd probably just need basic mowing and edging."

Charlie rubbed the back of his neck. "Would you want it weekly or monthly?"

"What about once every two weeks?" she asked, crossing her fingers that the expense wouldn't be too bad. The choice between food and a beautiful lawn was a given. Food would win hands down, regardless of whether Charlie was a viable suspect in Susan's murder or not.

Charlie nodded. "If I'm still going to be doing Mr. Wiley's yard, I can do yours the same day that his is scheduled." When Charlie quoted a price, Trish breathed a sigh of relief. She wouldn't starve after all.

"That's wonderful," Millie said. "Does Trish need to leave a key out for you somewhere, like Sam does if he's not at home?"

Trish exchanged a quick glance with Edna. So far, Millie was surprisingly smooth at this questioning thing. Unless Millie planned on hiring everybody they talked with to do some work for Trish, they just might get some important information, after all.

Charlie shook his head. "No, that won't be necessary. If all you need is mowing and edging, I can use my own equipment. Mr. Wiley uses special fertilizers and stuff that he keeps in his garage. That's why he always leaves a key out."

"We all know that he trusts you completely," Edna said. "How long have you been doing Sam's yard, five years?"

"That's right. I started out just mowing, but gradually it progressed to more-detailed landscaping. I've helped him transform his lawn from just a single flower bed to this." Charlie waved his arm to indicate the beautiful gardens and shrubs. "Mrs. Wiley did a lot of research on what she wanted, and Mr. Wiley planted, trimmed, dug out, and transplanted whatever she wanted until it was just right."

Sam's yard really was quite breathtaking, especially at the time of year when the artfully decorated lawn burst into color, proclaiming its majesty for anybody who wanted to see it. A local newspaper had even featured the Wileys' yard a couple of years back in its special gardening section, causing quite a lot of traffic through their quiet neighborhood.

Realizing that Charlie thought Edna had been referring to Sam's trust in his gardening abilities instead of his trust in leaving a key out, Trish angled for another approach. "To be honest, I'm glad I don't have to leave a key out like Sam does. Even though I'm sure it's a well-kept secret, I'd constantly be worrying about somebody finding it."

"It's not a secret," Charlie chuckled. "I think everybody who knows the Wileys knows about that key. I used to worry about it myself, since it was originally left out for me. Not many people are that trusting."

Millie's ears perked up. "Yes, he does trust every-body," she said, remembering how reluctant Sam had been to disclose the names of his friends and associ-ates. "You think other people used that key also?"

"I know they did. I saw it all the time. It was mainly people that worked for him, you know. They'd come by to pick up something for Sam, and if Susan wasn't home, they'd just use the key. None of them were sneaky about it, though. They'd tell me outright what they were doing. It probably happened all the time. I wasn't here that of-ten, you know."

Trish wanted to ask specifically who Charlie had seen using the key, but she sensed that he was becom-ing curious as to why they were so interested in who used the key. Charlie didn't know that Susan's death was now considered murder. Let him continue to think it was a horrible accident—at least, for a while longer.

After agreeing that Charlie would start Trish's yard in two weeks, the women said good-bye and drove back to Trish's house. By unspoken agreement, they piled into her kitchen and poured fresh coffee.

Edna covered a yawn with her hand. "I don't know about you two, but I'm exhausted."

Trish glanced into the living room at her exercise ma-chine and then purposely looked away. Her legs were still tingling from her recent workout. "I could use a nap, myself."

"Wimps," Millie muttered as she pulled a pen and the list of names from her purse and spread it open on the table. "We've got work to do." She placed a check mark beside Charlie Simms' name and wrote "no" be-side it.

"I'm glad we all agree," Trish said dryly.

"What? You think there's a possibility that Charlie's guilty?"

Trish rolled her eyes. "Of course not, but before you go checking anybody off that list we should all voice an opinion, in case one of us picked up on something the others missed."

Edna nodded. "That's a good point. So, do we all agree that Charlie is off the list?"

"I should hope so. I'd hate to think Millie just hired a murderer to do my lawn."

"Don't worry. You've never made me that angry. Okay, I think it's safe to say Charlie is not our man. He looked me straight in the eye."

"What do you mean?"

"A guilty person never looks you straight in the eye when they talk to you."

"That's true," Edna said. "I've heard that all my life. In fact, just the other day, this remodeling company was trying to sell me new flooring—"

"Edna, we get the point!" Millie snapped.

Trish hid a grin. "So, who do we check out next?"

"Maybe we should turn this list over to the police," Edna suggested.

Millie frowned. "Do you really think Chief Espinoza is going to check all these people out? Of course he isn't," she said before Edna could reply. "We need to have some concrete dirt on someone before we say a word to the police. We need motive and opportunity. You saw the way he acted today. He isn't going to take us seriously unless we can raise some doubt in his mind that Sam is guilty."

Trish sighed. "As much as I hate to admit it, Millie has a point. You both realize, though, that this could have been done by a complete stranger, don't you? This could be a waste of our time."

Millie leaned back and crossed her arms over her chest. "I don't think so. I have a gut feeling the guilty person is on this list. I just wish it wasn't such a long list. Sam sure has a lot of friends."

Trish looked at both Edna and Millie. "They could be friends—or enemies. Look, girls, there's something we need to consider before we go any further. If, as we suspect, Susan's murder is the result of someone out to get Sam, then that person isn't going to take our interference lightly. Actions have consequences, and we need to be sure we're willing to face those consequences, because this could be very dangerous."

There was complete silence at the table. The looks that passed between them were serious and focused, and Trish was pleased that finally her friends seemed to understand her fears. They weren't getting ready to embark on a game of Clue, where all they had to do was move game pieces around a board and declare Colonel Mustard the murderer. Someone had killed Susan Wiley, and they probably wouldn't think twice about killing again.

Millie leaned forward and picked up the pen. "Okay, now that Miss Paranoid has had her say, let's get back to work. Now, who's next on the list?"

Trish sighed. It was good to know that she'd gotten her point across.

Millie wanted to drive the next morning, but Trish flatly refused. Their self-imposed mission was dangerous enough. So they piled into Trish's car and drove to Bennie's Remodeling Company. Bennie Johnson had bought Sam's company a few years ago, and according to Sam, the two men had become—and still were—good friends.

Millie had once again surprised her friends and come up with a brilliant plan. Since none of them had ever formally met Bennie, it should be easy enough to gain information, they figured. Bennie would be ignorant of their close friendship with Sam. At least, that was the idea.

A tinkling bell over the door announced their entrance into the main office. A young girl looked up from the computer on her desk with a smile. "Can I help you?"

"I'm afraid we may have the wrong place, dear," Millie said in her best old-lady voice. "Is Sam Wiley here?"

The girl grimaced. "I don't know. I've only been here a couple of weeks. But if you don't mind waiting, I'll find out for you."

"Not at all. We'd appreciate it," Millie smiled.

"Just have a seat and I'll be right back."

"Thank you." Millie turned and winked at Trish and Edna, and then she sat in one of the chairs alongside a wall of windows facing the parking lot.

Edna sat down beside her, primly holding her purse in her lap as she leaned over and whispered, "You're doing great."

"I know," Millie chuckled. "Once you're past seventy, you can get away with anything. You can even make bodily function noises and no one will say a word. Just wait," she said, patting Edna's knee as though she was sixteen instead of sixty-five, "and you'll see for yourself someday."

Trish grinned and turned away to glance around the office. It was small, clean, and looked amazingly efficient. This wasn't the average fly-by-night contracting company that gave construction workers a bad rep, but Sam's business hadn't been, either. Evidently, when Bennie had bought Sam out, he had adhered to the same high quality standards.

A large picture window gave a full view of the parking lot with *Bennie's Remodeling Company* painted across it in big, bright yellow letters. A tan leather sofa sat under the window next to a small table covered with popular remodeling magazines. On the other wall were the chairs Millie and Edna were sitting in, and a huge potted plant sat in the corner, perfect for catching the morning light. The desk, covered with the latest technological gizmos, centered the remaining wall and faced the sitting area. Awards of every kind, from Remodeler Of The Year to Best Design graced the walls in wooden frames that were subtly elegant. The air even smelled fresh and clean, certainly an oxymoron for the type of business conducted here.

The swinging door the girl had passed through earlier swung open, and a big man with a big smile and a big handshake came into the office. He appeared to be in his mid-fifties, but he had such a friendly, boyish face it was hard to tell. He greeted them all individually in a loud boisterous voice and introduced himself as Bennie Johnson. "What can I do for you?"

Millie smiled a perfectly innocent smile. "You'll have to forgive a bunch of old ladies. We were actually looking for Sam Wiley. I'm afraid we must have gotten lost."

Bennie shook his head. "Nothing to forgive, and you're

not lost. This used to be Sam's place. I bought him out a few years ago so he and his wife could enjoy their retirement." Bennie suddenly looked uncomfortable. "Are you friends of his?"

"In a way, I suppose we are. He did some work on my house several years ago. Now Trish here needs a new patio cover. Naturally I recommended Sam, but I didn't know he had closed his business."

Trish froze. Their original plan had been to discuss exterior painting, something she was somewhat familiar with, not a patio cover! She smiled, but the look she gave Millie would stop a freight train. Millie must have picked up on her mistake because she added quickly, "And she wants it painted."

Bennie nodded. "Sam's a good man. I was proud he decided to sell his business to me. He comes by every now and then just to say hello, and I'd be glad to let him know you were thinking about him." Then he looked down and cleared his throat. "Unfortunately, Sam's wife passed away recently. I don't know how long it will be before I see him again."

"Oh, my goodness," Millie said, her eyes round as she daintily covered her mouth with her hand. "You know, I remember reading something in the paper, but I didn't make the connection. She accidentally electrocuted herself, didn't she?"

Bennie nodded sadly. "Mrs. Wiley was one of the best. She'd always bake a cake or some cookies and send them along with Sam when he came by. And she never forgot the anniversary of the day we bought Sam out. Without fail, we'd get a huge basket of sausage and cheese with a congratulations card."

Trish felt the air leave her lungs as a sudden thought

entered her mind: Susan's funeral. She racked her brain trying to recall if Bennie Johnson had been there, but she just couldn't remember. There had been so many people there and the sadness and grief had kept any socializing down to a minimum at the gathering afterward, but Trish, Edna and Millie had all helped out with the food and drinks. If Bennie had been there, it would only be a matter of time before he realized that not only were they good friends of Sam's, but they were also his neighbors.

Professional sleuths they weren't, Trish thought to herself ruefully. Why hadn't they thought about this possibility before now? Well, it was too late to change their story, but Trish had to do something before Edna or Millie put their foot in it any further. "I think that says a lot about you, Bennie, that you became such good friends with the Wileys," she said in her most charming voice. "I've heard nothing but good things about Sam. I imagine he took the loss of his wife very hard. Were you at the funeral?" It wasn't a great segue, but it would have to do.

Bennie shook his head. "No, I was out of town. Mark, who worked for the Wileys as a driver and stayed on with me when Sam sold out, called and told me. I immediately called Sam, but he wasn't able to talk much, just thanked me for taking the time to call. Mark went to the funeral to represent us and express our condolences. I figured I'd give Sam some time to deal with the tragedy and then I'd get back in touch."

Trish's relief that Bennie had not been at the funeral was short-lived. Mark *had* been there, and she remembered seeing him there. He was hard to miss—over six feet tall, long and lanky, with a head full of salt-and-pepper hair. He had been at Sam's house several times during the years he had worked with him, a trusted and loyal employee, according to Sam. She didn't realize he was working for the company that had bought Sam's business, though. But that was beside the point. He would recognize them instantly.

Chapter Seven

Bennie straightened and seemed to shake himself mentally. "I'm sorry to get off on such a depressing subject, ladies," he said, his voice once more friendly and cheerful. "Now, about that patio cover, I'd be glad to give you an estimate if you'd like."

Trish reached down and grabbed Millie's hand, pulling her up. "I just remembered that I have an appointment," she said apologetically. "Can I call you and schedule an appointment for an estimate later this week?"

Millie, of course, didn't take the hint. "What appointment are you talking about? You didn't say anything earlier."

It would have been too obvious to kick Millie in the shin, so Trish squeezed her hand instead, painfully. "It's my hair appointment. I completely forgot, but if we don't hurry I'm going to miss it."

Millie raised her eyebrows and looked at Trish's hair.

Trish very seldom ever went to a salon, something Millie considered downright neglectful, and her tone of voice said it all. "It's about time."

Bennie walked over to the front desk and grabbed a business card while Trish glared at Millie behind his back, a silent message demanding she keep her mouth shut. "Here you go, ma'am," Bennie said. "You call me whenever you're ready."

"Thank you. I'll do just that. I appreciate your time."

Bennie shook all their hands and walked them to the door. Here was another suspect they could cross off their list, Trish thought. There was nothing sinister about him at all that she could see. He appeared to be a kind, considerate man running a legitimate business, and he seemed sincerely upset about Susan's *accident.* Positive that Millie and Edna would agree, she ushered them into her car and backed out of the parking lot.

"Where are you going to get your hair done?" Millie asked. "Lynette over at Marsha's Beauty Salon does a great job. She could get rid of some of that gray."

"I am not getting my hair done!" Trish snapped. "Millie, you have got to learn to pick up on hints without blurting out whatever is on your mind! Edna was as surprised as you were at my announcement, but you didn't hear her voicing any arguments. If we're going to secretly investigate people we think may have committed *murder* you're going to have to learn to zip your trap!"

"That man is no more capable of murder than you or me," Millie said in a huff.

"That's not the point!" Trish said in exasperation. "The next person may be. And, if he's not, I may just pay him to do it!"

"What's that supposed to mean?"

"Nothing, it means nothing." Trish sighed deeply. "The reason I was so anxious to get out of there was that Bennie said Mark worked for him now, and Mark was at the funeral. It would have looked mighty suspicious if Mark had walked in and mentioned that we're Sam's neighbors and friends."

Millie sat quietly for a moment. "Oh."

Trish glanced over at her. "Well, I think the meeting was productive, anyway. We seem to agree that Bennie is not our man, and we found out one of Sam's former employees works for him now."

"Girls, I hate to change the subject," Edna interrupted, "but there's a strange car in front of Millie's house."

Sure enough, a dark, four-door sedan sat parked beside the curb. They drove by the car slowly and tried to peer in the tinted windows before Trish pulled into her own driveway.

"That's an unmarked police car," Trish said and glanced at Millie.

"Don't look at me," Millie shrugged and opened the car door. "I haven't done anything."

"Somehow, I find that hard to believe," Trish muttered as she and Edna climbed out of the car.

The first thing Trish noticed was how extremely handsome the young man was who climbed out of the car in front of Millie's house. Probably in his mid-thirties, she thought as she took in his appearance, tall, muscular and slim, with jet black hair and dark eyes, he wore khaki pants with a white open-necked shirt and brown loafers, and he wore it all well—very well. He waited beside the car with a warm, friendly smile while they crossed the street.

"Hello," he said, his voice rich and deep, "I'm Larry Thompson."

"You're also a cop," Millie said, her chin jutting up as she placed her hands on her hips.

Trish coughed and hurriedly stuck out her hand. "I'm Trish Anderson." While her hand was engulfed in Mr. Thompson's firm grasp, she nodded over her shoulder and said, "This is Edna Radcliff, and the feisty one over there is Millie Morrow."

Edna smiled and shook hands with Mr. Thompson, but Millie eyed him suspiciously before she grudgingly held out her hand. "What do you want, Mr. Thompson?" she asked bluntly.

He grinned, clearly not offended. "Please, call me Larry. And, yes, I'm a cop. Actually, to be specific, I'm a detective." His voice was rich and deep with a sincere, friendly tone. "Chief Espinoza mentioned you came by the station concerned about your friend, Sam Wiley, and since I was in the neighborhood, I thought I'd stop by."

Millie's eyes narrowed. "Why?"

Edna gasped. "Millie! Stop being so rude!"

But Larry just threw back his head and laughed, his eyes dancing with amusement. "I wanted to meet the women who believe so strongly in their friend's innocence that they would threaten the chief of police."

Trish groaned and grabbed Millie's arm, propelling her toward the front door. "Let's go inside before the neighbors think we're being arrested or something. However, if there's a reward for Millie, then I'll gladly hand her over." Edna hurried after them, motioning for Larry to follow. Millie huffed, but she dutifully unlocked her front door.

Once inside the house, Trish looked over her shoulder at the detective. "By the way," she told him quietly, with wide, innocent eyes, "*we* didn't threaten the chief. Millie did."

"I heard that," Millie snapped as she led the way into the kitchen.

Millie's kitchen was comfortable, cozy and cluttered. Every imaginable appliance, ranging from turkey roasters to watermelon scoops, perched on the yellow tile countertops. When Trish had asked Millie why she kept all of her cooking tools out, Millie had replied, "They give me inspiration. You've heard of writer's block? Well, I get cooker's block. When I can't decide what to fix, I just look around, and *wham!,* I get an idea."

Yellow and white frilly curtains covered the kitchen window facing the front of the house and the bay window facing the back yard. The white cabinets sparkled, and the hardwood floor was clean enough to eat off of, according to Millie. Everybody just took her word for it.

Millie poured iced tea while everybody else sat down around the oak table. "Your home is beautiful," Larry said to Millie's back.

"I bet he told you to say that," Millie muttered.

Larry looked puzzled. "Who?"

"Don't play innocent with me, young man," Millie said as she carried the glasses to the table, her lips pinched in a tight line. "Henry told you to come over here and make us back down, didn't he?"

"The chief? No, of course he didn't. Why would he?"

"Maybe he's afraid we might be right about Sam's innocence, and that would be pretty embarrassing for him. Arresting the wrong man wouldn't look too good on his record, now, would it?"

Larry coughed and reached for his tea, obviously trying to hide a smile. Trish felt sorry for the detective. Until you got to know Millie, she could be quite overwhelming, but Larry appeared more amused than flustered. Trish bit her bottom lip and glanced at Edna, who was staring down at her hands. Poor Edna, always the peacemaker, she was probably trying to think of something to say to diffuse Millie's outburst. Sometimes there just aren't enough words, Trish thought wryly.

Larry sat back in his chair and crossed one leg over the other. "All the evidence so far points to Sam Wiley," he said gently, "but this is still an open investigation. Chief Espinoza relayed your concerns to me and said I might want to talk with you. That's it, I promise." He held up his hand in the traditional boy scout salute, his expression completely guileless.

Trish found that she believed him, and by the pleasantly surprised expression on Edna's face, it seemed she did, too.

Millie, on the other hand, might need more convincing. She glared at him suspiciously as she pushed her glasses up her nose. "What did Henry tell you?"

"He told me that if Susan Wiley didn't die from an accident, then you believe your friend has been set up to take the fall for murder."

And that's all it took. Millie's face broke into a huge smile. "You may be all right, after all, Larry. Would you care for some more tea?"

"Yes, please. Thanks, Mrs.—"

"Call me Millie. And the same goes for Edna and Trish. We don't stand on formality here."

"Thank you, Millie." Larry grinned and then suddenly winked at Trish and Edna, causing Trish to choke on her tea. He had been warned, obviously by Chief Espinoza, about Millie. What a good sport he was, she thought with a smile, to let Millie air out her suspicions so rudely as he tried to gain their trust. Not many men had the self-confidence to sit back and let a woman jump all over them, but Larry seemed to take it all in stride.

"Does this mean that you agree with us?" Edna asked, interrupting Trish's thoughts.

"Of course it does, Edna," Millie said, placing Larry's glass in front of him and sitting down. "Why else would he be here?"

Larry scratched the back of his head and grimaced. "Well, I can't say definitively either way. My job is to keep an open mind and investigate all possibilities. Since your assumption is not out of the possibility range, I'd like to hear more."

Millie's smile faltered, but after a moment she nodded. "Okay, I guess that's fair enough."

"The first thing you need to know, Larry," Edna said, leaning forward intently, "is that we don't think Susan's death was an accident. We believe she was murdered, but not by Sam. And, with or without your help, we're going to prove it."

Trish blinked and then looked at Millie, who was staring at Edna as if she had just sprouted two heads. Edna *never, ever* spoke that firmly to anybody.

Then, as if to prove the point, Edna said apologetically, "I hope you don't think I'm being adversarial."

Trish relaxed. That was more like it.

"Of course not, Mrs. . . . . Edna. I think you care deeply for your friend and want to help him." Larry leaned forward and looked each of them in the eye, in turn. "But let me ask you this. What if you're wrong? What if Sam Wiley wasn't set up, that the evidence does convict him? Will you be able to accept that?"

Millie sent him a piercing look. "That ain't gonna happen."

Trish raised her eyebrows. "I would completely lose faith in all mankind—not to mention in the entire legal system."

Edna shook her head. "There's nothing that could convince me Sam is guilty."

Larry sighed deeply and settled back in his chair. "Well, as long as we all keep an open mind . . ."

For the next half hour, the women discussed their ideas about the evidence the chief had told them pointed to Sam. Larry listened attentively, jotting a few notes in a small notebook he pulled from his back pocket. He remained basically noncommittal, but it didn't appear as if he was simply placating them, more like he was digesting their opinions for further analysis. By unspoken agreement, none of them mentioned that Claire had had car trouble on that fateful morning, also. It was a piece of the story that only they knew so far, and besides, it would only make Sam appear more guilty.

Trish shifted her weight in the chair. "Larry, I know you can't discuss the particulars about this case with us, but what happens if we get some new information that could poke holes in the case you have against Sam?"

Larry's eyebrows shot up. "You're not planning on investigating this on your own, are you?"

"We've already started," Millie said proudly. "We've ruled out—"

"Whoa, whoa, whoa," Larry said, holding up his hands and shaking his head, "this isn't a game, you know. This could be very dangerous. I can't allow it."

That was definitely the wrong thing for him to say.

Millie's eyes narrowed. "You can't *allow* it?"

Larry tried another tactic. "What you're planning on doing could interfere with a police investigation. That's against the law. I'd hate to see any of you end up in jail just because you think we're not doing our job," he said.

Unfortunately, none of the ladies appeared frightened at the prospect of a night behind bars. He sighed, running a hand across his face. "I'll make you a deal," he said resignedly. "*I* will do any investigating, and I promise that I'll keep you informed with as much information as I can. You ladies keep on brainstorming, and if you think you have an idea on a lead, you just tell me and I'll do the follow up. So, are we agreed?"

"Nope."

Larry looked at Millie, but it soon became obvious to him that she wasn't about to change her mind. He quickly glanced at Edna, who just shrugged and shook her head. With an imploring look, he turned to Trish.

"I'm afraid we're not in agreement with you on that, Larry. We're going to do whatever we can to help clear Sam. From what we've seen so far, the authorities believe they have their man. I can't see them aggressively pursuing other leads when they have so much else to do.

People ignoring our speed trap are running rampant on our streets."

"It is absolutely unconscionable," Millie stated. "And to think I used to feel safe in this community."

Larry's look spoke volumes. The ladies' sarcasm wasn't lost on him. "You honestly believe that we would prefer to convict an innocent man of murder, instead of the real criminal?"

"I wouldn't say that," Edna said sweetly, reaching over to pat Larry's hand. "We just feel that Chief Espinoza believes he already has the real criminal."

"Why would he suggest I speak with you ladies, then?"

"Isn't he up for re-election soon? We're all at the legal voting age, you know."

Trish cleared her throat. "Millie, the Chief of Police is appointed by the City Council. Henry won't be running in an actual election. But she does have an interesting point, Larry. Is he only trying to protect his reputation?"

Larry sighed deeply, drumming his fingertips on the table. "You're just going to have to trust me on this. Nobody has slammed the door shut on this case, but unless somebody else confesses or new evidence is brought forward, Sam Wiley will be standing trial for the murder of his wife. As I've said before, all the evidence points directly at him."

Millie slammed her hand down on the table. "Prove it!"

Larry looked at her warily. "Prove what?"

"Prove we can trust you."

"How do you propose I do that?"

Millie didn't answer right away. Getting up, she walked over to the counter and reached into her purse.

Turning, she walked back and placed a folded piece of paper in front of Larry. Edna's eyes widened, and she looked at Trish. Millie was handing over their list of suspects!

"What's this?" Larry asked as he unfolded the paper and laid it flat on the table.

"We believe the killer is on that list," Millie said dramatically.

Trish groaned and dropped her head in her hand. "Millie . . ."

After he had skimmed the twenty-odd names on the list, Larry leaned back in his chair and very slowly let his gaze fall on each woman. He would have made a great school principal, Trish thought as she squirmed in her chair. Edna very wisely kept her own eyes directed at her hands in her lap. Millie, naturally, appeared totally unfazed as she stared right back at him.

Larry flicked the edge of the paper with his finger. "Where did you get this?"

Millie shrugged. "We asked Sam who he had associated with in the last few years, and we came up with that list of names."

"And what makes you think one of these people killed Susan?"

"Because," Millie blurted impatiently, "whoever did this *intentionally* made Sam look like the guilty party. That means it was someone who knows Sam."

"What motive would someone have to murder Sam's wife and do it in such a way that Sam looks guilty?"

"We won't know that until we know who did it!" Millie snapped. "Are you going to help us or not?"

Larry looked at her incredulously. "You want me to bring in all these people for questioning?"

"Of course not," Edna said evenly. "That would tip off the real killer."

Larry looked like he was about to explode, but to his credit, his voice remained calm and respectful. "Then what is it that you expect me to do?"

Millie leaned across the table and grabbed the paper. "We've already ruled out a couple of people on this list."

Edna leaned forward eagerly. "Yes, but we ran into a snag this morning. One of the people we were trying to get a feel for has a man working for him who used to work for Sam and, unfortunately, this man knows us."

Millie nodded toward Larry's notebook. "Write this down: Mark Wilson. Find out where he was the day Susan was murdered. See if he has an ax to grind with Sam, you know, or any stuff like that."

Trish nodded. "It would be too risky if we tried to check him out. Mark worked for Sam a long time. I really don't think he's involved, but he may know something about somebody else on our list."

Larry's eyes were dancing, amusement clearly on the verge of bubbling over. "I'm glad to hear you're not willing to take any risks," he said, tongue-in-cheek. "Are you going to give me the list?"

Millie chuckled. "Nice try. No, we'll keep the list. You said you wanted us to trust you. Get us the information we want on Mark and we'll see where we go from there. Personally, I'd like to know just how good you are at your job."

Larry grinned. "I'm good at what I do, Millie, very good." He fell silent for a moment as he flipped his pen back and forth through his fingers. "I'll tell you what, I'll see what I can find out about Mark Wilson, and I'll let you know if I discover anything interesting, but I won't divulge anything concerning privacy issues, you understand. In return, I expect to be kept informed on what you three are doing—preferably *before* you do it. As exciting as playing detective sounds, I can't stress enough how dangerous this could be." Larry paused for a moment and let his gaze fall on each of them. "Do we have a deal?"

The three women looked at each other. Finally, Millie shrugged. "Do you have a cell phone?"

Larry left a few minutes later, after promising to get back to them soon and warning them once again about the dangers of amateur investigating. "I think we can trust that young man," Millie mused as they watched him drive away.

"I hope you're right," Trish said. There was comfort in knowing an experienced professional was going to help them, but they would still need to be careful. Was Larry's true agenda to help them prove Sam was set up, or was it to further cement Sam's fate as a convicted murderer?

Trish had trouble sleeping that night, and for no apparent reason. She was tired, she was comfortable . . . and she was wide awake. Finally, she rolled over and glanced at the bedside clock. It was all of two A.M. Groaning out loud, she gave it up. She slipped into her house shoes and plodded down the hallway. A nap would definitely be in order later today, but, for now, she might as well get started on some much-needed housework. Coffee cup in hand, she headed toward her office to make a list of what she wanted to accomplish. Trish was big on lists.

Suddenly, a loud pounding at her front door accompanied by several shrill rings of the doorbell caused her to jump, spilling hot coffee down the front of her night-gown. With her heart banging in her chest, Trish felt rooted to the floor as she stared at the door. Who could be there at two o'clock in the morning?

Chapter Eight

"Trish! Trish, open the door!" Finally, Trish pulled air through her lungs and raced to pull the door open. Millie stood gasping, eyes wide behind glasses that sat slightly askew on her face. Her hair was pulled up in pink sponge-rollers, and she was grasping the bottom of her purple nightgown in one hand, revealing one bare foot and one slippered foot. Trish gaped at her.

Millie pushed inside, slammed the door, and then leaned against it. "Call the police!"

"Wha—?"

"I've been broken into! Somebody was in my house!"

"Are you all right?"

"I'm fine. Just call the police, please!"

This was serious. Millie never said "please." Trish ran to grab the phone and dialed nine-one-one. Hurriedly, she explained the situation to the emergency dispatcher, and then gave the address. She replaced the phone and rushed back to Millie, who was peeking through the front windows at her house across the street.

"What happened?" Trish demanded as she, too, peered out into the darkness.

"Something woke me up, a noise or a feeling, or . . . something. I don't know," Millie answered, her voice calmer and even a little angry. "After a while, I thought it had just been my imagination, or maybe a storm was approaching. Since I was awake, I got up to get a drink of water. That's when I saw my back door standing wide open. It still didn't register that somebody had broken in until I stepped on the glass. Somebody busted out one of the panels on the door and unlocked it. All I could think about was that somebody might still be in the house. I hightailed it out of there, and when I saw your lights on, I came over here."

What a scare she must have had, Trish thought as she squeezed Millie's shoulder. An eighty-year-old woman living alone was easy prey for an unscrupulous character. Thank goodness Millie wasn't hurt. Material things could be replaced, but the life of her friend was much more valuable than any *thing*.

Trish stared out the window looking for some kind of movement, a shadow crossing under the moonlit sky, or something else that would give them a clue as to the person, or persons, who had done this to Millie. But there was nothing. The branches in the trees weren't even stirring in the calm night air.

Suddenly, the hair stood up on the back of her neck. What was happening to this neighborhood? First there'd been a murder, and now a break-in, both incidents serious crimes, not the work of bored adolescents. Trish shuddered and glanced sideways at Millie, who was single-mindedly staring across the street at her house, her lips drawn into a tight, thin line.

They say everything happens in threes. Trish turned again to look outside, a sense of dread coming over her.

What would happen next?

The police siren sounded in the background. "The police will be here soon," Trish said unnecessarily. Millie was obstinate, Trish reminded herself, not deaf.

"Good. It's about time."

Trish looked at her quizzically. It had been what, maybe five minutes, since she had hung up the phone. It had been a pretty good response time by any standards—except, of course, by Millie's. Before she could stop her, Millie dropped the curtain and raced out the front door, while Trish rushed to catch up. For a little old lady, Millie sure could move fast.

Millie was standing out by the curb, practically hopping from one foot to the other in her impatience for the police to arrive. The noise from the siren was louder now, and several porch lights up and down the block flipped on as concerned neighbors peeked out their front doors. This was probably the most excitement any of them had witnessed since living in this neighborhood, or, at least, since Susan Wiley's untimely death.

Just then a patrol car rounded the corner and stopped in front of Millie's house, the red and blue flashing lights lighting up the whole street. Trish was surprised to see Henry Espinoza step out of the car. Surely the chief had enough seniority that he didn't have to work the graveyard shift!

Millie charged across the street, obviously unconcerned about the fact she was only wearing one slipper. Trish followed, uncomfortably aware that her soft pink nightgown, wet with coffee spills, had definitely seen better days. She caught sight of Edna and Joe coming up the sidewalk with worried frowns on their faces. "Millie's fine," she assured them as they drew closer, "but her house was broken into. She ran over here and we called the police."

"Oh, dear," Edna gasped. "Was anything taken?"

"I don't know. I don't think she looked around before she fled."

"Poor Millie." Joe shook his head and sighed deeply. Was he wondering, too, about the sudden rash of crime invading their quiet little neighborhood? "You two stay here, and I'll see if I can help." Joe walked over to where Millie was talking to Henry—well, more like arguing, if the sound of Millie's raised voice was anything to go by. It sounded as if the chief was demanding that she stay put for a minute, and she was refusing, wanting to go inside with him.

Trish and Edna moved closer, ready to tackle Millie if the need arose. It wasn't safe for her to go into the house before Henry had a chance to thoroughly check it out and make sure the intruder was gone. They were spared having to perform any heroics when Joe, in his usual calm way, wrapped his arm around Millie and pulled her to where Edna and Trish stood. The sight of Joe, over six feet tall, having to bend down to comfort tiny Millie would have been humorous if the situation hadn't been so serious.

"Millie," he said, his voice deep and soothing, "it could be dangerous for you to distract Henry right now.

Let him do his job, and then we'll all go in with you to see what damage there is and find out if anything has been taken. But first, Henry has to make sure it's safe to go in the house. Someone could get hurt if the guy is still in there." While Joe had been talking, Henry had walked up the driveway and circled around to the back of the house. Trish noticed that he had his gun drawn, and a shiver ran down her spine.

Millie snapped her mouth shut, and after a moment she nodded. "You're right, of course. I was hoping the guy *was* still in my house so we could catch him, but I wasn't thinking about how dangerous that could be." She reached up and patted Joe's hand, which was still resting on her shoulder. "Thank you, Joe."

Edna reached over and tightened one of the curlers that had loosened from Millie's head. "I'm just so sorry this has happened to you."

"I'm not."

Trish blinked, sure she had heard wrong. "What did you say?"

"I said, I'm not. It seems to me that we're making somebody nervous." Millie smiled an impish, satisfied smile as she turned to look at her house. It was fairly easy to follow where Henry was in the house as rooms lit up, one by one.

"What in the world are you talking about, Millie?" Joe raised his eyebrows in confusion. "Who are you making nervous?"

Millie clamped a hand over her mouth at the same time Trish groaned. Edna took a deep breath and cleared her throat. "Joe, dear," she said sweetly, placing a gentle hand on his arm, "you're intimidating poor Millie. I think it would be best if you'd leave your questions for later."

"You think I'm intimidating her? I just asked a simple question!"

"Not in front of the neighbors," Edna warned. Joe started to say something, but one look at his wife's determined expression made him change his mind. He stared first at his wife and then at Millie, who just looked at him with wide, innocent eyes. Finally, his voice deceptively quiet, Joe said, "I'll refrain from asking any questions right now. But as soon as Henry leaves, the four of us are going to have a discussion."

"Here comes Henry now," Trish piped up gratefully as the chief appeared from around the side of the house. She wasn't looking forward to the coming discussion at all. She knew Joe Radcliff well enough to know that he wouldn't be pleased to learn they had started secretly investigating potential suspects.

Poor Edna looked like she had just swallowed rotten tuna fish. The unspoken laws of matrimony demanded that she should have told Joe what she was doing, out of courtesy and respect, if nothing else. But Edna couldn't very well tell Joe that she knew if she had told him he would be upset. That sounded a little too juvenile, like the child who knew he would be punished for doing something wrong, but the temptation was just too great.

Oh, well, Trish thought to herself, maybe she and Millie could convince Joe that they had forced Edna to participate. *Yeah, right,* her inner voice whispered mockingly.

When Henry drew near, Millie asked hopefully, "Well?"

Henry sighed and shook his head. "Nobody is in the house now. Come on in and have a look around, and see if you notice anything missing or disturbed. I'll send our fingerprint expert over in the morning, so try not to touch anything." Millie was off in a dash, almost running toward her front door. Henry rolled his eyes and hurried after her.

"Should we go in too?" Edna asked with a worried look on her face as she watched Millie and Henry enter the house.

Joe shook his head. "Let's wait a while."

A few of the neighbors walked up to express their concern and offer any help before returning to their homes and locking up tight. One man Trish paid particular attention to as he spoke with Joe was Mr. Greenburg, the neighbor Millie believed moonlighted as a Peeping Tom. The image of this soft-spoken, thin, gangly old man spying on Millie was just too improbable to be true. However, as soon as Millie and Henry came back out of the house, Mr. Greenburg shuffled away in a hurry. Trish bit her lip to keep from grinning. Millie wasn't even carrying a rifle!

Millie's eyes narrowed as she walked up to her friends and glared at Mr. Greenburg's retreating back. "What did *he* want?" Trish noticed Millie was wearing her other slipper now.

"He came by to make sure you were okay," Joe said, unaware of Millie's past episode with her neighbor.

"I'll just bet!"

"Millie, never mind about that now," Edna gently admonished. "Was anything missing?"

Millie shrugged and shook her head, looking dumbfounded. "Not that I can tell—everything looks fine."

Henry placed his hands on his hips. "It might have been a kid thinking the house was vacant. School's almost out for the summer, you know, and the teenagers are staying out later. Maybe someone was just trying to cause some trouble, or maybe somebody needed money, got brave, and decided to try their luck in this neighborhood."

"That's a lot of maybes," Trish said doubtfully.

Henry frowned. "I'm just throwing out ideas at this point. Like I said, we'll take fingerprints tomorrow, but, I have to be honest with you, unless our culprit is in the database already, we won't know more than we do now."

"We appreciate all you're doing, Henry," Joe said tactfully. "I must say, I would have expected someone else on your force to have answered this call so early in the morning. Are you working twenty-four-hour days now?"

Henry grinned and shook his head. "Nah, Mac's mother-in-law is visiting from California, so I gave him the evening off. He begged me to work, but I figured he could score some brownie points with his wife if he was home." Both men chuckled at the lame joke.

Edna looked at Trish and rolled her eyes. "What is it about mothers-in-law that can make the strongest male cower?" That shut them up.

"Well, I'm glad you were here to handle this." Joe reached out to shake Henry's hand.

"No problem. I'll send an officer around in the morning, Millie. In the meantime, I don't think you should be alone in the house until that glass pane is replaced."

"I completely agree," Trish said firmly. She looked at Millie and spoke in a tone that brooked no argument. "You can spend the rest of the night with me."

Millie sighed. "That's probably a good idea. I doubt anybody would be stupid enough to come back tonight, though."

"Well, there's still no sense in taking chances. If you do discover anything is missing after you look around again, just give me a call. And don't have that pane replaced until after we take the fingerprints, okay?" After Joe assured Henry that he would take care of that himself, Henry waved good-bye and drove off.

Millie stifled a yawn. "I'm just going to grab a few things, and then we can go to your house, Trish. I'm exhausted."

Joe followed Millie into her house while Trish looked on suspiciously. That twinkle in Millie's eyes belied her claim of exhaustion. However, the woman *was* eighty years old, she chided herself, amazed once again at Millie's stamina. The events of the last few days would have worn down someone half her age. Then, suddenly feeling bone-weary herself, Trish grinned wryly. She was over half Millie's age, herself.

Joe and Millie came out of the house, Millie carrying a small vinyl bag. "Oh-oh," Edna whispered, "I wonder if Joe still wants to talk."

Trish had forgotten all about the "discussion" Joe wanted to have. "I hope not," Trish whispered back. "I don't think my mind is sharp enough right now to explain our actions."

Edna nodded. "We'll end up sounding like old busybodies instead of the experienced professionals we really are." Trish choked on a laugh as she whipped around to look at Edna. There was a definite glint in her eyes before she winked and turned to address Joe. "I think we've had enough excitement for one night . . . or morning. You get some rest, Millie, and we'll help you clean up the mess and look around again later today." Edna leaned over and gave Millie a hug. "Don't you worry about a thing. Come on, Joe. We need some sleep, too."

"But . . ."

"No buts, dear—everybody is tired." Edna slid her arm through Joe's and started walking toward their own house. "Call us when you get up," she said to Millie and Trish over her shoulder.

"That girl's good," Millie chuckled as they entered Trish's house.

"You can say that again. Do you want anything before we go to bed?"

"No, I'm fine. I'm not really even that tired. I just didn't want to talk to Joe tonight. He's an old worrywart."

Trish grinned. "I thought as much. Still, we need to try and get some sleep. Tomorrow's going to be a long day."

"You mean today," Millie said with a yawn, following Trish to the guest bedroom.

Trish woke feeling amazingly refreshed after the earlier sleepless night and then the events of Millie's break-in. She even tried to exercise some, but she was afraid the loud clanging of the metal weights would wake Millie. It was no big deal, anyway. There was always tomorrow. Besides, just thinking about doing it was an improvement.

Feeling thinner already, Trish sat sipping her coffee and reading the newspaper when Millie walked in. "Good morning." She looked up with a smile. "Did you get any sleep?"

"I tried to," Millie grumbled, making her way to the coffeepot still in her nightgown and slippers. "That dang contraption you got there makes so much noise it would wake the dead."

"That's a lie," Trish said sweetly, refusing to be drawn into an argument this early. "I only did it once." The curlers were gone from Millie's hair, and Trish noticed she had applied a light touch of makeup. She looked relaxed and rested, despite her grumpy attitude.

"Well, you did it once too many," Millie said as she sat down and took a sip of her coffee. "Actually, I slept pretty well. I didn't think I was tired, but once my head hit the pillow I was out."

Suddenly Trish caught a whiff of a strange odor, a faint chemical smell. "I'm glad you were able to rest." She looked around the kitchen trying to figure out where the smell was coming from. "The stress probably wore you out more than you thought. I wonder what time they'll come take fingerprints," she said, poking her head under the table and sniffing.

"Oh, it'll be any time now, I imagine." Millie watched silently as Trish got up and walked to the trash can in the corner and stuck her nose in it. Sighing deeply, she put her coffee cup down and crossed her arms over her chest defensively. "Oh, all right, it's me!" she snapped.

Trish stood up straight and looked at Millie with a puzzled expression. "What are you talking about?"

Millie's lips drew into a tight line as she glared accusingly at Trish. "Not too many people I know put bug spray in the bathroom cabinet next to the hair spray!"

Trish cocked her head and frowned. "What do you mean . . . ? Oh, no, Millie, you didn't!" Trish pinched her lips together, desperately trying to keep from laughing out loud. The indignant expression on Millie's face warned her there would be hell to pay if she did, but, try as she might, Trish couldn't stop the laughter from erupting. Clutching her stomach, she leaned against the counter with tears streaming down her face.

Millie sat in stony silence, a sure sign that she didn't see the humor in the situation. When Trish could finally breathe normally again, she asked, "Are you all right? You didn't get it in your eyes, did you?" The concern was sincere, but the grin plastered across her face negated some of the sentiment.

"Of course I'm all right! If I wasn't, I could have died here waiting for you to regain your composure. Nice to know you care so much."

Trish took a deep breath and wiped the tears from her face. "This is classic, Millie," she sighed. "I do believe this is a first, even for you. Didn't you read the labels on the cans? Raid and AquaNet are hardly the same product."

"I wasn't wearing my glasses," Millie sniffed.

"Well, you'll have to wash it out. I don't recall reading a warning label on the bug spray can about the danger of spraying your hair, but it can't be good for it." Biting her lip to keep from laughing again, she went to the bathroom and got the shampoo and conditioner. She helped Millie get situated at the kitchen sink before she had to back away. The pungent, sweet chemical smell from the bug spray was overwhelming. Shoot, she was laughing again, but she just couldn't help it.

"I really am sorry," she chuckled, watching Millie dunk her head under the water faucet.

Before Millie could reply, the doorbell rang. Thankful for the interruption, Trish went to answer it. Still grinning, she opened the door and ushered Edna and Joe inside. She was about to relate what had happened to Millie when she noticed their serious expressions. Immediately, she sensed something was wrong.

"It seems that Millie isn't the only one who has had an unexpected and unwelcome visitor recently," Joe said, placing his hands in his pockets.

Trish's hand flew to her heart. "Good heavens, don't tell me you were broken into also?"

Edna shook her head. "No, not us—it was Sam."

Trish's eyebrows drew together. "Sam had a break-in *again*?"

Edna nodded sadly. "I'm afraid so. Unfortunately, I don't think the police believe him."

Trish took a deep breath and motioned them into the kitchen. "You better come and sit down and start at the beginning. To be honest, I'm having trouble believing this!"

"Believing what?" Millie mumbled. She was standing on a step stool with her head buried in a sink full of lather.

Edna raised her eyebrows. "Don't ask," Trish whispered as she got a clean towel from the laundry room and placed it close to Millie's elbow. She poured Joe and Edna coffee as they sat at the table.

Millie soon joined them, the towel wrapped turban style around her head. "What's going on?"

"We were going to the grocery store this morning," Joe began, "when we saw Sam's car in his driveway. We walked over to say hello, but when he answered the door we could tell he had been crying. We thought it was the emotion of being in the house again, but someone had broken in to the safe in his spare bedroom, and it was empty. Everything in that safe has been stolen."

Chapter Nine

Joe stirred sugar into his coffee. "Sam was waiting for the police to get there. It seems he had some cash in there and some of his important papers, but the tragedy is that all of Susan's jewelry was in there." Joe shook his head. "It's gone. The man is just heartbroken."

"Yes," Edna nodded. "Mac must have been working this morning because he drove up in his patrol car soon after we got there, and Sam told him what had happened. I got the distinct impression Mac didn't quite believe him."

"The police are bound to be suspicious," Joe said charitably. "Sam is facing a murder charge. They probably believe he staged his own break-in to prove how easy it would be for someone to enter his house and kill Susan. Again, there was no evidence of forced entry—either into his house or his safe."

"Is Sam there now?" Trish asked.

"No, he said he only came by to water his plants and

get some more clothes. He left right after Mac did. Edna and I told him we'd come by Shelley's to see him later."

"The police are off their rockers!" Millie exclaimed loudly. "Didn't we tell Henry about the spare key?"

"I don't believe we did," Edna said thoughtfully. "We started to, but he interrupted us, if you remember."

"When did all this happen?" Joe asked.

"Uh . . . it was part of a conversation recently," Millie stalled. "I really don't remember when."

"Joe," Edna said hurriedly, "why don't you go get that key right now? Then, call Sam and let him know you have it, and call Henry also."

Resigned, Joe stood up with a deep sigh. "This is not the end of this conversation, ladies," he warned. "I want to know what's going on."

Edna waited until the front door closed. "We're going to have to tell Joe."

Millie nodded. "We don't want you lying to your husband, Edna, and I keep putting my foot right in my mouth. We'll tell him today."

Trish chewed her bottom lip nervously as she looked at her two friends. These two break-ins were related somehow, but not for the reason the police probably assumed they were. Sam didn't have anything to do with either of them, but Trish had to admit it did look suspicious. With Sam showing up the morning after Millie was broken into and discovering his own house had also been broken into, well . . . it was probably too much of a coincidence. There was also the fact that nothing had been taken from Millie's, but Sam had lost some valuable items.

A slight shiver ran down her spine. It may very well

be just a coincidence, or the act of an immature juvenile looking for some money, but Trish didn't believe it. She had a gut feeling that they were dealing with a very determined, very dangerous person who was out to destroy Sam Wiley.

The question was, what would this person do if he found out three meddling old ladies were just as determined to stop him?

Edna was curling Millie's hair with a curling iron, a technique, according to Millie, that was sure to burn off all her hair, when Trish looked out her window and spotted Larry Thompson, along with another officer, pull up in front of Millie's house. Edna hurriedly brushed out Millie's hair, spraying it lightly with hair spray this time before they all rushed out the door and across the street.

Larry smiled when he saw them. "I heard you had some excitement last night."

"You can say that again." Millie looked with obvious mistrust at what appeared to be a bulky gray tool box the other officer was carrying. "What's that?"

Larry chuckled. "Ladies, meet Lewis Conrad. He's with the San Antonio Police Department and does all our fingerprint work for us. He's the best in the business." Lewis smiled a friendly smile at them, but he seemed impatient to get down to work. Trish had the impression he was a no-nonsense kind of guy.

"Well, come on in, then," Millie said. "Would anybody like some coffee or tea?"

"Coffee sounds great," Larry smiled gratefully. "Lewis?"

"Nothing for me, thanks." Lewis set the case down

on the floor by the back door and knelt down to open it. "Anybody touch anything since the break-in?"

"No, we were very careful not to. In fact, this is the first time Millie has been inside her house since Chief Espinoza left last night, I mean early this morning. She stayed with Trish."

"I understand that you aren't the only one who's had an uninvited visitor recently," Larry said.

"That's right," Millie said. "And I'll bet you dollars-to-doughnuts that the two incidents are somehow related."

Larry picked up the small chicken-shaped salt shaker from the center of the table and lightly tapped it on the bottom from side to side. Finally, he took a deep breath and nodded slowly. "You may be right."

Trish's eyes widened. Finally—somebody believed them! But in the next instant, her hopes were crushed as Larry continued in a reluctant voice. "One guess is that you were broken into by a stranger. Sam Wiley heard about it and staged his own break-in to throw doubt on his murder charge. Or," he paused significantly, "Sam broke the glass in your door to make it appear you were broken into and then staged the break-in at his house."

"That's ridiculous!" Edna exclaimed. Millie's eyes narrowed but she didn't say anything. Trish wasn't surprised. After all, Millie had thought all along that this was the conclusion the police would come to.

Slowly, Millie stood to her full height—which, viewed from a distance, as Trish saw from over by the kitchen cabinets, was barely taller than the table. Leaning forward with eyes narrowed, in what she probably thought was a threatening stance, Millie placed both hands on the table. She looked like a small, purple, fire-breathing dragon. "Look here, buster, if you think I'm going to answer any questions or discuss this case with you while you have that attitude, then you can think again."

Quickly, Trish turned her back on the group at the table and pinched her arm hard to keep from laughing out loud. It didn't help that she'd seen the startled expression on Lewis's face as he knelt by the back door brushing black powder on everything. She'd just bet that within the hour Millie's name would be all over the SAPD's offices. Oh, what she wouldn't give for a video camera! Millie had truly missed her real calling in life. Yessir, Dirty Harry would have been proud!

When she had herself under control, Trish turned back around. Edna sat still, her eyes darting back and forth between Larry and Millie as though she was afraid they were going to draw guns or something. Larry was trying valiantly to hide his own laughter behind a cough. Millie stood there staring daggers at him, her expression unchanged.

Larry said gently, "Millie, it's not my attitude. I'm just telling you what some of the theories are. It's also possible that the same intruder broke into both your and Sam's houses, or that two entirely different people are responsible for each break-in. As a professional, you don't rule out any possibility, regardless of how unpleasant or unlikely the assumption may be."

Millie appeared slightly mollified. Standing straight, she crossed her arms over her chest and peered at Larry. "What does your gut tell you?"

Larry shook his head slowly. "I honestly don't know." When he saw Millie start to puff up again, he quickly added, "But I will tell you that I haven't closed my mind to anything yet, and I promise you that I will thoroughly check out every theory."

Millie regarded him silently for a minute. "All right, that's fair enough," she said, sitting down once again. "We have our work cut out for us, then. Trish, where's that coffee?"

"It's coming right up." Trish grinned. Another catastrophe had been narrowly avoided. Surprisingly, for all his youth, Larry seemed quite able to soothe Millie's ruffled feathers. Trish wondered if he had a troublesome relative in his life that gave him the experience to handle Millie's bizarre personality. Or, maybe it was just the nature of his job. Regardless, she appreciated the patience and respect he showed Millie.

"Okay, let's start with the theory that the same person broke into both houses. What's the connection?" Millie frowned at Edna. "Does anyone have any ideas?"

Edna chewed her bottom lip as she tried to think. "I can't think of any reason you and Sam would both be targets. You don't live right next door to each other. You don't even live on the same side of the street. Of course, you're both widowed now, but there are a lot of single people on our block."

"Trish," Millie said as she accepted her coffee and looked up, "what do you think?"

Trish sighed. Her gut was telling her that Millie was right, but she didn't have a clue as to why. "If someone has guessed we're trying to prove Sam did not kill Susan," she mused, "then they might be trying to scare us. But that still doesn't explain why Sam's house was broken into."

Larry frowned, deep in thought. "Millie, do you have a safe anywhere in this house?"

"Do I have a safe *here*? No, why do you ask?"

He shrugged his shoulders. "I'm just trying to come up with similarities. Sam's safe was broken into, you know."

Millie's eyes flew open. "That's it!" Before anybody could ask what "it" was, Millie jumped up from her chair and ran into the living room. Trish hurried to follow with Larry and Edna close behind. She wondered if the bug spray had short-circuited Millie's senses, after all.

Millie was standing in front of her antique roll-top desk, quickly opening and shutting the drawers and shuffling haphazardly through the papers and miscellaneous items on top. "Just what I thought," she said smugly as she turned to face them. "My address book is gone!"

Larry cocked an eyebrow. "Your address book is missing? What would anybody want with your address book?"

Millie crossed her arms over her chest and leaned back against the desk. "The combination to Sam's safe was in there."

Edna's hand flew to her mouth. "Oh, my goodness, that's right! Sam gave you the combination in case of an emergency!"

Trish held up her hand. "Slow down a minute and think. Who would know that? I only found out about it the other day when we were . . ." Trish's voice trailed off as she remembered when she had learned of it, the day they were snooping in Sam's house. "Millie, think carefully," she said gravely. "Did anybody else, besides Edna, know about that?"

Millie shook her head with a self-satisfied smile. "Nope."

Larry frowned at Millie. "You seem almost happy about this."

"I am. It means we're right about somebody trying to set Sam up."

Trish's thoughts swirled in her head. "It wasn't a ghost," she whispered, a chill racing up her spine.

"What do you mean, dear?" Edna said into the stunned silence.

Trish took a deep breath. "Remember when we were in Sam's house the day after he was arrested? I was too embarrassed to say anything, but I felt a strange, eerie sensation, as if we weren't alone." Trish knew her instincts had been right on target that day, and the reality was chilling. "Well, we weren't alone, but it wasn't Susan's ghost. Whoever is behind this mess, the murder, the theft, the devious plan to convict an innocent man, was also in Sam's house that day. Millie, he . . . or she . . . heard you tell me about the combination to Sam's safe and where you kept it."

It was a sobering thought, knowing they had all been in extreme danger that day. Trish only hoped that Larry would consider their theory more seriously now and work fast to discover who was behind the crimes, with or without Chief Espinoza's permission. Regardless, the stakes had just been raised in the mysterious circumstances involving Susan Wiley's death. Having been in Sam's house that day, the killer knew that all three of them were convinced that Sam did not kill his wife.

"Assuming you're right," Larry said, "can you remember exactly what you talked about that could have been overheard?"

Trish's memory was hazy. Had they mentioned they were going to start investigating on their own? She didn't think so, but what if she was wrong? If anything suddenly happened to Millie or Edna, or to herself, for that matter, would the police realize the events were connected? Maybe, she thought, since Larry was now aware of the incident at Sam's, but they couldn't count on it. There was still the problem of the evidence pointing to Sam, not an outsider.

"What do you mean *assuming* we're right? Of course we're right, Larry!" Millie exclaimed. "It all makes perfect sense. What are you going to do about it?"

"I'm going to keep investigating, that's what," he said. "And, I hope you're reconsidering sticking your noses into police business." Larry's tone was kind but there was an underlying firmness behind his words.

"I'd say there's a fat chance of that," Trish muttered. It was more important now than ever that they find out who was involved in the murder. The killer knew where they lived, their association with Sam, and their belief that Sam was innocent. Like it or not, they were up to their eyeballs in the investigation.

She listened while Larry asked Lewis to come take fingerprints off the desk also. "It's a long shot," he said as they walked back into the kitchen and sat down, "but it's worth a try."

"Did you find out anything about Mark Wilson?" Trish asked hopefully. Maybe there was something about Sam's former employee that would lead them in the right direction. A clue, any clue, would certainly be welcome news.

But Larry shook his head. "There's nothing so far, not even a parking ticket, but I'm still waiting for employment records and financial information. I promised I'd let you know if I find anything suspicious, and I will."

"But you do agree with us that Sam didn't kill Susan, don't you?" Millie asked. "I mean, it's obvious now that my address book has been stolen."

Larry smiled patiently. "I don't know if a judge and jury would consider that sufficient proof. I will agree with you, however, that it is an interesting turn of events."

Millie laughed delightedly. "You *do* believe us!"

"Just let me do my job, Millie." But the grin on Larry's face didn't take anything away from his stern warning.

Lewis walked into the kitchen just then carrying his case. "I'm all finished here. I'm sorry about the mess, but it's a necessary evil. You can just vacuum up the black powder and then wipe it down."

"You mean *I* have to clean it up?" Millie asked incredulously. "That's not fair!"

"I know, ma'am. That's just another outrage a criminal causes."

"We'll help you, Millie," Edna said hurriedly, anticipating Millie giving a lecture to the officer about his duty to protect and *serve*. Millie's lips were pressed firmly together in disapproval, but at least she didn't say anything more.

They all three walked with Larry and Lewis to the front door. "I'll keep in touch," Larry said. "In the meantime, get that glass pane repaired." Suddenly, he stopped and faced them. "You all need to keep your eyes open and stay alert. Call us immediately if you see anything suspicious. And . . . *do not do anything on your own. Do you understand?*"

Just then Edna spotted Joe leaving their house and walking toward Millie's. "We understand. Have a good day!" She waved good-bye while she and Millie backed up into the house. Trish understood immediately. It wouldn't do for Joe and Larry to get into a conversation before they had a chance to explain to Joe why they were on such friendly terms with the detective.

Larry raised both eyebrows, and Trish held her breath. Finally, with a small sigh, he turned and followed Lewis to his car. Larry had the engine running when Joe passed them, but, thankfully, Joe just nodded as he walked up the front sidewalk.

"Hello, Joe," Millie said as she opened the door wider. "Come on in and have some coffee. Did you get to talk to Sam?"

Joe planted a quick kiss on Edna's cheek as he followed them into the kitchen. "Yes, I did. And I told him that I have the house key. I came over to tell you that I called a glass company and they should be here within the hour to replace the pane in your door. Were those gentlemen here to take fingerprints?"

Edna nodded and sat at the table. "They sure left a mess, though. What did Sam have to say?"

Joe lowered his long frame into a chair. "Well, for starters, he told me about your visit to him the other morning." He thanked Millie for the coffee and then sat back, obviously waiting for explanations.

"Uh-oh," Millie muttered as she turned away to get the cream and sugar.

My thoughts exactly, Trish mused. She turned her eyes to Edna, wondering if she would want to start the explanation, setting the tone on how best to handle her husband. And, Edna, bless her soul, did just that . . . with complete honestly.

Edna proceeded to tell Joe, in a matter-of-fact, calm voice, about their early suspicions, what they had discovered so far, little as it may be, their discussions with law officials, and ending with Millie's stolen address book. Nobody interrupted her, not even Millie. And, to his credit, Joe sat listening attentively, not one trace of impatience or belittlement ever crossing his face.

Trish watched the exchange with envy. Edna held nothing back, not even the real fear the women had felt while in Sam's house that day. This was a conversation between a husband and wife who truly loved and respected each other, something Trish had never shared with her own husband, or *The Rat* as she had resorted to calling him ever since the divorce—which explained why she wasn't still married, she thought wryly.

When Edna finished, she took a sip of her coffee and then leaned her elbows on the table. "What do you think, dear?"

Joe crossed his arms over his chest and cocked his head. "I think you may be on to something."

Just then, Millie let out a hoop and a holler that would have made any sports enthusiast jealous. "I knew you'd believe us, Joe! Edna, you've got a good man there. Make sure you hold on to him." Trish hid a grin behind her hand. After forty-five years of marriage and two grown sons, she thought Edna was doing a pretty good job of *holding on* to her husband.

"What I was also going to say," Joe said with a pointed look at Millie, "is that you may be going about it all wrong."

Millie's face fell as she looked curiously at Joe. "How can you say that, after all we've uncovered?"

"You haven't actually uncovered anything," Joe said patiently. "What you've got so far is only a guess, albeit a reasonable guess," he said with a hand held up to forestall Millie's interruption, "but you don't have any real proof. Why didn't you come to me with any of this? You know I don't believe Sam is guilty, either."

Edna gave her husband a tender smile as she reached across the table to squeeze his hand. "I didn't want to worry you at this early stage, but when it started getting down to the nitty-gritty, I definitely would have included you."

"Well, I think it's getting down to the 'nitty-gritty' now, don't you? If Millie's address book was stolen by the same person that killed Susan Riley, then it's become downright dangerous. We need to turn this information over to the police and let them do their job, and then we need to call Sam's attorney."

"We already have," Millie said stubbornly. "Henry doesn't believe us, but that nice detective, Larry Thompson, might. Anyway, he's agreed to keep an open mind. Personally, I think he believes we're a little wacky."

Joe's eyes sparkled. "Now, why would he think that?"

"Joe, be serious!" Edna said, shaking her head. "We don't have enough evidence to back up our suspicion to go to the attorney, and we're going to need some cold, hard facts before we go to the police again. That's what we're trying to get. And, according to recent events, I'd say we're on the right track."

Joe sat quietly for a moment. "If it's any consolation, Sam is starting to believe you. There was real fire in his eyes when he talked about the possibility that someone is setting him up. It seems that having his safe broken into after what happened to Susan is just too much of a coincidence for him to swallow."

"Good," Trish said fervently. "The last time we saw him he showed almost no emotion. If he's getting angry, then it's a good sign. Maybe now he'll be able to think of something that can help." Trish certainly hoped so. She had a feeling they didn't have much time.

"I agree," Joe said with a nod. "But, from this point on, ladies, you need to let the police handle it. Look at what happened to Millie! I won't have my wife and close friends putting themselves in harm's way any longer."

An uncomfortable silence filled the air. Millie looked down at her clasped hands, Trish looked down into her coffee cup, and Edna looked at Joe. "We won't be putting ourselves in danger. You're going to help us. And we've got Larry to help, also. We're not going to sit idly by while months pass, waiting for Sam to be able to clear his name. He should be able to grieve for his wife without having this awful charge hanging over his head." Edna voice was deceptively soft, her expression firm.

"I don't want that, either."

"I know that, dear, and that's why you're going to help. I promise you that we will be extremely careful and include you in everything we do. We may not be able to discover anything at all to back up our theory, but we're going to at least try. And anything relevant will be turned over to the police. I give you my word."

Joe looked at his wife for several long seconds and then shook his head, his voice resigned when he spoke. "Okay, we'll give this a try, but only if you keep your promise to involve the authorities when the time comes. And, I want to know everything that's going on. There will be no more meetings with the chief, or the detective, or anybody else unless I know about it. Are we all agreed?"

"Agreed," the ladies replied in unison.

Just then the doorbell rang. Joe went to answer it and

returned with the repairman to fix Millie's door. While Joe watched over the glass replacement, the three women set about cleaning up all the black dust left by Lewis' fingerprint work. When they had finished and the repairman had left, Joe brought up the point that it wasn't a good idea for Millie to stay alone in the big house.

"Nonsense," Millie said blithely, "this is my home and nobody is going to chase me out of it! Anyway, the thief won't be back," she said with certainty. "He already got what he came for."

Joe raised his eyebrows. "Remember, your theory that Susan's killer broke in here to get Sam's combination is only that—a theory. What if he was here to steal more, but wasn't able to because you woke up? He could very well be back."

Millie just shrugged nonchalantly. "I have a gun."

Trish groaned as Joe's eyebrows rose further. "What?"

"Actually, it's a rifle, but it isn't loaded. Do you think I'm crazy?"

Trish hoped Joe wouldn't reply. The answer was definitely debatable.

Joe stood with his hands on his hips as he glowered at Millie. "No guns—is that understood? If you want my help . . . *no guns!*"

Millie stared at Joe, a battle of wills, but thankfully he didn't back down. Finally, Millie sighed. "Okay— but I would only use it to scare somebody. I wouldn't shoot them!"

"No guns."

"I said 'okay'!"

"And I don't want you staying alone right now. Either someone spends the night over here, or you go somewhere else. It's only temporary, Millie, and it doesn't mean you're being chased out of your home. It's called being practical."

Practical wasn't a word Trish would normally associate with Millie, but, nevertheless, sensing no help from her friends, she agreed, even though it was plainly under protest.

Chapter Ten

It took most of Monday morning for the women to convince Joe that they were more than capable of questioning Mark Wilson on their own. Joe had a pre-scheduled bowling game with some old friends he was only able to see occasionally. There was no point in his canceling just to watch over them when they would be surrounded by people in broad daylight, they argued. Finally, after another stern warning to be careful, Joe left for his appointment.

Not knowing exactly when Mark took his lunch break, they arrived around eleven o'clock and settled back to wait in the parking lot. Trish parked between two nondescript vans on the second row so they were well hidden—not that anybody would be expecting to see them, but, as they were all very aware, they had to be cautious in all their moves from here on out.

Suddenly, Millie shouted, "Duck!"

Without questioning Millie's outburst, Edna slid

down in the back seat while Trish dived sideways. "Ouch!" she yelled as her head collided with Millie's. "That hurt!"

"Oh, hush," Millie muttered. "Your head's harder than mine. I should be the one yelling!"

"Why are we ducking?" Edna whispered.

"Mark just came out the front door," Millie whispered back.

Trish struggled to sit up, rubbing the side of her head. "For goodness' sake, Millie! He can't see us from there, and we need to see where he's going."

"Oh, yeah, that's right," Millie said in a hushed voice. "I guess I just got a little panicked."

"And stop whispering!" Trish said between clenched teeth. "He certainly can't hear us."

"Okay!" Millie shouted, causing all of them to jump. "Any other orders?"

Edna startled giggling as she sat up straight. "I'd say we're a little tense, wouldn't you?"

Trish just shook her head and looked out her window. "Where did he go?"

"In that red pickup truck over there," Millie said, motioning with her head. Quickly, she exchanged her regular glasses for dark sunglasses, pulled down the sun visor in front of her, and fastened her seat belt. "Let's go."

Trish cocked both eyebrows and looked at her for a moment. She wouldn't be surprised if Millie also carried a decoder ring and a secret phone in the bottom of her red tennis shoe. Millie sighed impatiently. "Let's go!"

The pickup truck was pulling out of the parking lot. Trish slowly fell in behind, following at a safe distance.

They didn't have far to go. Mark Wilson turned into a nearby strip center and parked in front of a busy café advertising daily lunch specials on the front glass. "Joe and I have eaten here before," Edna said. "The food is really good, and they're famous for their apple pie."

Trish's stomach rumbled its own opinion. Guiltily, she thought about her twice-used exercise equipment at home, but then shoved the thought from her mind. She was working, for goodness' sake. She needed the energy. Besides, who in their right mind would pass up apple pie?

"I'm not in the mood for apple pie," Millie said thoughtfully as she pushed the sun visor up. "That meatloaf special on that poster in the window sounds good, though."

"Are we here to investigate the menu or Mark Wilson?" Trish asked irritably. "Okay, look, we need to remember the plan. We walk in, very casually, and find a table. Then we happen to notice Mark. If he's sitting alone, we ask him to join us and then bring up the subject of how his job is going since Sam sold his business and then Susan's death. Watch carefully for any strange expressions or a sudden change in his tone. Of course, if he's sitting with somebody, then we wait him out and confront him in the parking lot right before he leaves. Remember, we're going to act casual and unobtrusive. Has everybody got it?"

"Got it," Millie and Edna responded in unison. Millie pushed open the car door and scrambled out. "Let's go."

So much for subtlety, Trish thought with exasperation a few seconds later. Millie barreled through the door and headed straight for the table where Mark sat.

A waitress had just placed a glass of iced tea in front of him. "Hello, Mark! What a surprise to see you here. Do you mind if we join you?"

He didn't have time to answer. In the process of adding sugar to his iced tea, he watched Millie plop down across from him.

Edna shot him a quick, apologetic smile. "How nice to see you again, Mark."

Mark laid his spoon on the table, his eyes round with surprise. "Uh . . . yes, same here."

Trish tried to smooth over the awkward moment. He obviously didn't remember them. "Gosh, I guess the last time we saw you was at Susan Wiley's funeral. I know Sam appreciated your coming." She saw recognition register in Mark's mind and breathed a sigh of relief.

"Do you still keep in touch with him?" Millie asked sharply as she peered over the top of her menu. Thankfully the waitress appeared just then to take their order, so the quick kick Trish gave Millie under the table went unnoticed. As soon as they got back home Trish was going to make Millie write the word *subtle* one hundred times!

As soon as the waitress left, Edna started up the conversation with a friendly smile at Mark. "Are you still in the same line of work?"

Mark leaned back in his chair. The shell-shocked expression he'd been wearing on his face ever since they had bulldozed their way to his table seemed to be easing somewhat. "Yes, I am. As a matter of fact, I work for Bennie Johnson, the man who bought out Sam. Bennie's a nice guy. I'm basically doing the same thing I did for Sam."

"Oh? And what exactly is that?" Edna asked sincerely.

Mark began discussing his job function and the similarities and differences in the work he now did for Bennie all during the meal. Trish sipped her iced tea and breathed a sigh of relief. Edna had drawn Mark into easy and friendly conversation so that now when the pertinent questions came he probably wouldn't become suspicious—unless, of course, Millie opened her mouth again. But they were running out of time. Mark probably only had an hour for lunch, and the clock was running fast.

"Sam had a lot of loyal employees. I'll bet some weren't so thrilled when he decided to retire and sell his business." Trish had to fight to keep her mouth from dropping open. It was a perfect segue into the answers they were looking for . . . and from Millie, no less!

Mark gave a slight chuckle. "You can say that again. Most of us were happy for him, but there were a couple who were downright mad."

Trish's ears perked up. "Oh?"

"Yeah. Mary Chavez, Sam's bookkeeper, complained for days. When Sam found out that Bennie had his own bookkeeper, he tried to help Mary find another job. He even set up some interviews for her. But she still kept blaming Sam for ruining her life, as she put it, and didn't even try to get another job. Sam gave her a month's severance pay even though she stormed out of the office the day before he officially retired."

Edna shook her head. "Some people you just can't help no matter how much you may want to."

Mark agreed. "She wasn't even that good a bookkeeper. She called in sick quite a lot and was always behind on deadlines, but Sam kept working with her." Trish caught Millie's eye across the table. Mary Chavez's name was on the list Sam had given them.

"That's such a shame," Edna murmured. "You said there were a couple of people upset. Did anybody else feel the same way as Mary?" Edna asked the question nonchalantly as she took another bite of her pie. Millie also stayed silent as they watched Edna artfully draw information from Mark. He appeared genuinely happy with his position under Bennie's ownership, and if he held any hard feelings against Sam, he was hiding it extremely well.

He shrugged as he leaned back in his chair and dropped his napkin on his plate. "Most of us kept our jobs, those who wanted to, anyway. Old Tom Jones stayed on for a while, but he was really upset that Sam didn't sell the business to him—as if he had the money! Anyway, Bennie didn't much like him, so when Tom demanded more money, Bennie refused, and Tom up and quit."

Tom Jones—Trish was quite sure that name had also appeared on Sam's list. "What is he doing now?"

Mark shrugged. "I'm not sure. I heard he tried making it as a subcontractor for a while, but he was overcharging and underperforming. Word gets around in the construction business. If you take advantage of people, you're more or less black-balled. He's probably drawing unemployment and blaming the world for his problems."

Trish wanted to know more about Mary's and Tom's general attitudes and if there was anybody else who might be holding a grudge against Sam Wiley, but Mark signaled to the waitress for his check. "I have to go check on a crew. I really enjoyed seeing you ladies again. Tell Sam I said hello when you see him." Mark smiled, unfolded his tall frame from the chair, and nodded a redundant good-bye. Trish watched him leave, a thoughtful expression on her face.

"So, what did you think?" Millie asked around a mouthful of pie. "I don't think he's our man."

"Neither do I," Edna sighed. "Mark's a nice man and appears to have been a loyal employee. He doesn't seem to think too much of Mary Chavez or Tom Jones, though."

"I agree," Trish said. "I wish we could have talked to him longer. I'd like to know more details about any confrontations he might have witnessed between them and Sam."

"I would have asked him," Millie said sweetly, "but I was afraid I'd get kicked again."

Trish rolled her eyes. "You'd better start thinking before you just blurt out the first thing on your mind, or next time I'm wearing steel-toed boots."

"That's an attractive image," Millie muttered as she dropped her napkin onto her plate.

Joe hadn't returned from his bowling game when they got back to Trish's house. Edna reached him on his cell phone, and, as promised, filled him in on what they had found out. He agreed to go by to see Sam and find out if there had been any strange encounters with any of his former employees, especially Mary or Tom.

Trish was preparing coffee when the doorbell rang. "I'll get it," Millie said, placing her pen on the paper where she had just crossed Mark Wilson's name off the list and rising to answer the door.

"If it's a salesman, I'm not here!" Trish shouted after her.

But it wasn't a salesman. Henry Espinoza followed Millie into the kitchen. "Good afternoon," he said with a nod to Trish and Edna.

"Hello, Chief," Edna said with a welcome smile. "Sit down. We were just about to have some coffee. Would you like some?"

"Thank you, I'd love some. I was hoping you'd be over here, Millie," he said, lowering himself into one of the chairs at the table.

"Would you like cream and sugar?" Trish asked with a quick glance in his direction. Henry looked quite attractive in the dark green polo shirt and jeans, not quite so stern and . . . *official.*

"Just black. I came by to tell Millie that, unfortunately, the fingerprints didn't reveal anything."

"It doesn't surprise me," Millie said with a shrug. "I really didn't think we'd find out who did it that easily."

"It was a long shot," Henry agreed. "We'll schedule a patrol car to drive by at different times during the night shift for the next few days, to see if we spot anybody acting suspicious. That's about all we can do at this point. You never know—we may get lucky. According to Larry, the only thing you noticed missing was your address book, right?"

Millie nodded. "That's right. It's the one that had the combination to Sam's safe in it."

"Millie . . ."

"Don't worry, Henry. It would probably give me a heart attack if you took our theory seriously. You can thank us later."

Trish hurriedly changed the subject before Millie and Henry went another round. "Larry Thompson is such a nice young man. Does he have a family?"

"No, he's single. His parents still live in Houston where he was raised. He came to work for us about a year ago. He's a great guy and good at his job."

"We're counting on it," Millie muttered.

"What was that?"

"Nothing. Any new clues on who killed Susan Wiley?"

Henry looked at her wryly. "I was about to ask you the same thing."

Millie gave a good impression of being taken aback. "Why would you ask that?"

Henry raised his eyebrows. *Please, dear Lord,* Trish prayed silently, *don't let Millie mention Mark and what he had told them today.* Henry would just give them another lecture about all the evidence pointing to Sam.

"Our opinion hasn't changed," Edna said. "The truth will come out, hopefully sooner rather than later, but, regardless, we know Sam is not guilty."

Henry looked at them intently for a moment. Millie, blessedly, kept her mouth closed under the scrutiny, even though she looked guilty as sin. Finally, Henry sighed and drained his coffee. "Well, I just wanted to let you know about the fingerprints and to make sure you got your door repaired. You still need to be careful and stay aware of your surroundings. The thief probably won't be back, but you don't want to take anything for granted."

Trish stood also and walked toward the door. "Thank you, Henry. We'll all keep an eye out and let you know if we see anything out of the ordinary." She breathed a sigh of relief when he said good-bye and left. She knew Millie could only contain herself for so long.

When she went back into the kitchen, Edna and Millie were deep in discussion. "That's a good idea," Edna was saying.

"What is?" Trish asked as she sank down into the chair.

"We're going to find out where Mary Chavez and Tom Jones live while it's still daylight."

Trish raised one eyebrow. "Why do we want to know where they live?"

"Because," Millie said impatiently, "first, we find out where they live. Then we find out where they work, and then we find out if they hang out anywhere. If, by chance, either one of them is guilty, we sure aren't going to find any clues around here. We need to go to their turf."

Trish paused. *Their turf?* "Why don't we just ask Sam? He may know where they live."

"And let everybody know what we're up to? All we'll get is another lecture to just let the authorities handle it."

"But, Edna," Trish pointed out, "you promised to tell Joe everything."

"I know. And I'm going to. I'm going home right now and leave Joe a note."

Trish's lips twisted. "Why don't you just call him?"

"I don't want to interrupt him."

"Besides," Millie added, "he's probably with Sam right now."

Trish's lips twisted again. "Flimsy."

"Yeah, but we'll probably get away with it," Millie said with a saucy grin. "You get on your computer and do one of those search things to get their addresses. Edna, you run home and leave that note, and I need to go grab something. We'll meet back here."

Fifteen minutes later, armed with directions and Millie's binoculars—the all-important "something" Millie had grabbed from her house, for what purpose Trish and Edna couldn't fathom—the three women climbed into Trish's car and headed toward Mary Chavez' house. According to the information Trish had gathered, she was married and lived in the southern part of San Antonio in an older residential neighborhood. It shouldn't take more than twenty minutes to get there.

It took thirty-five. After two wrong turns navigating through unexpected road construction, they finally found the small red brick house. "Someone's home," Millie whispered as she slumped low in her seat. "See the car in the driveway?"

"Millie, sit up! And stop that whispering. You're making me nervous. Who do you think is going to overhear us?"

Millie ignored her. "Aren't you going to stop?"

"Oh, that wouldn't look suspicious at all, would it? No, I'm going to circle the block. Edna, when we pass the house again, try to memorize any of the car details so we'll know it if we spot it again. Then we'll cruise around the neighborhood a bit and see if we can find out where Mary does her grocery shopping and stuff like that. We've got to find a way to bump into her somehow so that we can strike up a conversation."

Edna nodded eagerly as she sat up straighter in the back seat and pulled a small pad and pen from her purse. "Okay, that's a good idea."

"What makes you think Mary is going grocery shopping today?" Millie asked.

Trish glanced over at her friend sardonically. "I don't. It could take several trips over here before we get a chance to talk to her. We'll have to come by at different times to get an idea of what her schedule is."

Millie nodded slowly. "That's a good plan," she said approvingly. "What are we going to say to her when the opportunity presents itself?"

"I've been giving that some thought. We are going to have to pretend that we've met her before when she was working for Sam."

"Oh, Trish, that's brilliant!" Edna exclaimed when Trish once again turned onto Mary's street. "That will work."

Millie seemed to mull the plan over in her mind. "Edna's right, Trish. It is a good idea. And it gives us the perfect opening to talk about Sam."

"Shh!" Edna ordered. "I need to concentrate."

Millie hunkered down in the front seat and Edna peered through the side window as if her life depended on it when Trish drove past Mary's house again. "I got it," Edna said with satisfaction. "It's a white Dodge Intrepid, late-model with a small American flag on the rear window."

"Good job," Millie cheered, winning her a pleased smile from Edna.

Trish grinned. Whether their efforts to find out if Mary Chavez was somehow involved in Susan's death led to anything or not, it still felt good to actually be doing something. They needed a break in this case. Then she groaned, realizing she was starting to think like one of the television cops Millie loved so much.

Chapter Eleven

It was on their third trip to Mary's house that they finally got lucky. Trish had just passed the house and was rolling to a stop at the end of the block. By chance, she glanced in her rearview mirror. "Oh-oh," she muttered.

Millie had started to sit back up in her seat, but at Trish's words she slid back down. "What's wrong?" For some reason, Millie thought it was important that she do her "observing" from the floor board. It wouldn't be so bad if she didn't demand constant updates on what was going on.

"That Dodge Intrepid just pulled out of the driveway and is heading this way."

"Oh, my goodness!" Edna exclaimed. "Hurry, get out of here! We can't be seen, or it will ruin our plan." Edna's head whipped forward and backward in time to her frantic words, as if she couldn't decide whether to look at the approaching car or her companions in the front seat.

Trish quickly turned right, her eyes darting to the rearview mirror. Had they aroused suspicion by circling the block or driving too slowly? But the car turned left, and Trish let out the air she had been holding. Millie eyed her speculatively. "You know, Mary might be going grocery shopping, after all. It would be a shame to miss this opportunity."

"I can't even see who is driving the car, Millie. It might not be Mary at all."

"There's only one way to find out. Hurry up around the block again and get behind that car."

Trish met Edna's eyes in the rearview mirror. After a few seconds, Edna took a deep breath and nodded. "She's right. Let's do it."

Trish made a quick turn, causing Millie's head to bounce off the side door. She couldn't help but grin. "I'm sorry. That wasn't intentional."

Millie just looked at her wryly. "Of course it wasn't."

"There it is," Edna said. "The car just made a left turn—hurry!"

"We don't want to get too close, Edna. There isn't much traffic—we shouldn't have too much trouble following."

"But," Millie reminded them, "we do need to see if it's a man or a woman driving."

"True," Trish said with a nod. "I'll get close enough to see, and then I'll back off again." When she made the left turn, she spotted the white car a couple of streets ahead of them. She sped up slightly to get closer to the car. "It's a woman," she said softly as she spotted the back of the driver with a ponytail and long, dangling earrings.

"Good," Millie said excitedly. "Follow her."

Edna sighed audibly. "Joe is going to kill me."

Trish always navigated fairly well on highways, able to keep her bearings and arrive safely—if sometimes late—at her destination. It was the side streets and numerous subdivisions that gave her trouble—like now.

She prayed they were not lost to the point of no return as, once again, she followed the white car onto a long, winding road that bordered another residential area. She had absolutely no idea where they were and, when questioned, discovered that neither of her passengers did, either.

Thankfully, there was enough traffic to allow Trish to remain unnoticed as she trailed from a discreet distance, but she was seriously wondering if Mary was just out for a joy ride. "She's turning again," Trish sighed as she saw the car's turning signal flash on.

"I'm starting to get dizzy," Millie muttered.

"You wouldn't feel dizzy if you sat up," Edna said patiently. "You're probably getting motion sickness."

"I never get . . . !"

"I can't follow this time," Trish interrupted hastily. "There aren't any cars between us anymore, and it looks like . . . yes, she's turning into a . . . what looks like a mobile home park. I'm going to have to pass the entrance and swing back around."

"Great, it's a mobile-home park. I hope we don't lose her," Millie grumbled.

"Well, I can't help it! She may have already spotted us following her, and she's turning just to make sure."

"There's a side street up ahead," Edna said. "Turn there and we'll wait a few seconds to see if she comes back out."

Trish kept her head straight forward and never even

glanced at the white car as she passed the entrance to the mobile home park. She did notice, though, from her peripheral view, that at least there weren't gates or fencing around the property. At the next street, she turned right and then pulled into the first driveway she saw, then quickly backed up and drove very slowly to the end of the street again.

"Do you see anything?" she asked, nosing her car forward.

"No," Edna said. "Not yet."

"Let me look." Millie grunted as she struggled to sit upright in the front seat. She leaned forward, resting her elbows on the dashboard, bringing the binoculars that had been hanging around her neck up to her eyes. Trish placed her chin in her hand, her elbow resting on the steering wheel. "It isn't that far away, Millie. I don't think your binoculars are going to help."

Millie said nothing as she turned the focus knob back and forth several times. Finally, she lowered the big, bulky binoculars and squinted toward the first row of mobile homes plainly visible a few hundred yards across the street. "Humph, you may be right," she agreed. "I don't see anything."

"It doesn't seem like there are any cars or people moving around," Edna observed.

It did appear as if the mobile home park was deserted. Of course, it was early in the afternoon. People could be at work or out running errands. From their vantage point, all that could be seen were a few rows of attractive mobile homes on either side of the main entrance. The homes had small front yards, some with low fencing, some outlined with landscape bushes and gardens. The park was large enough that they couldn't tell how far back the homes went. Regardless, there was no sign of the white car.

"What do you want to do?" Trish asked both Edna and Millie.

"Go on in!" Millie exclaimed.

"Let's wait a minute," Edna said at the same time.

Trish chewed the inside of her lip thoughtfully. If they had indeed been spotted, then going into the mobile home park would confirm Mary's suspicions, making it almost impossible to plan a surprise encounter in the future. If, however, Mary had no idea she had been followed, then even if she did see them enter the park she wouldn't think anything about it. Weighing the odds, it was pretty unlikely that their subterfuge had been noticed.

Trish squared her shoulders, took a deep breath, and pulled out into the street. "Edna, get down in your seat and hide yourself. Millie, you stay sitting up this time. We'll just make a quick drive-through and see if we can find Mary's car."

"Look out!" Millie shouted.

Trish slammed on the brakes, and not a minute too soon. A large delivery truck was fast approaching with its horn honking loudly. The driver glared at them as he sped past, his hand raised in the universal sign of extreme anger. Millie sank back in her seat, her hand clutching her chest. "You about gave me a heart attack!"

"Well, mine's not beating too steady right now, either."

"There are evidently some benefits to lying down in the back seat," Edna joked.

Trish took a steadying breath and wiped her hands on

her pant legs. Carefully, she looked both ways before once again pulling out. "I hope that wasn't an omen."

"Nonsense," Millie said, "that guy was going way too fast."

"Thanks for trying to make me feel better, but it was my fault, just the same. We could have been in a serious accident."

"Well, we weren't, so stop worrying about it. Let's just find Mary."

"Tell me what you see since I can't look, myself," Edna reminded them.

There was a large wooden sign with faded lettering at the entrance to the park welcoming them into Southwest Mobile Home Park and warning them to watch for children playing. Trish drove straight down the main road until it ended and then turned left onto another street, her eyes darting from side to side as she tried to find the white car. She noticed the further they went into the park the less attractive the homes were. Older mobile homes with sun-bleached paint and unkept yards sprinkled her view as she mindfully kept her speed at the posted speed limit. She wondered where the children were that she was supposed to keep an eye out for.

"Do you see anything?" Edna whispered from the back seat.

Trish shook her head. "I don't see a thing. It's almost spooky." Old cars, some obviously not in running condition, littered several gravel driveways, but, otherwise, there was no sign of life and no sign of Mary's car. Trish turned right at the end of the block onto another row of homes, these much the same as the other ones.

"There she is!" Millie suddenly exclaimed. "Hurry! Stop!"

Reflexively, Trish put her foot on the accelerator, causing the car to jump forward, then slammed on the brakes causing the tires to squeal and the car to rock. "Make up your mind, Millie!"

"Hey, what's going on?" Edna asked nervously.

"Not now, Edna! Just pull over here in front of this mobile home, Trish."

Trish did as Millie asked—not because she thought it was a good idea, but because they were going to draw attention to themselves if they didn't take *some* action. The white car was parked on the side of the road in front of a mobile home desperately in need of some repair work. Two windows were busted out and covered with plywood on the side facing them, and an old air conditioner window unit jutted out from a rear window.

As far as Trish could tell, the best thing about this situation was that, even though there were only four homes between them and the one Mary was parked in front of, Mary would be driving away from them when she left instead of driving right by them. Small favors, Trish muttered to herself as she placed the car in park, leaving the engine running. She rolled down her window, feeling the soft, warm breeze blowing gently in the afternoon sunlight. She could think of half a dozen things she would rather be doing than sitting in a run-down mobile-home park watching a vacant car.

"Uh oh," Millie said quietly.

"What's happening?" Edna asked.

"Not now, Edna! Trish, there's a man in this front yard and he's looking at us suspiciously."

Trish peered sideways, trying not to appear too obvious. Well, she had wondered where the people were who lived in the park. It was just their luck that the only one they found just happened to be sitting in a lawn chair by the front door of the mobile home they were stopped in front of. "Pretend like you're looking for something in the glove box," Trish said quickly through lips that didn't move. Right as Millie began an award-winning performance of someone totally engrossed in the contents of the glove box, Trish spotted movement up ahead. "There's Mary!" she exclaimed.

"Well, that's just terrific," Millie said sardonically.

Trish looked over at her in surprise, but she soon realized what Millie was upset about. The man from the front yard was walking toward them. Dressed in baggy jeans and a white T-shirt, the man appeared larger than he probably was . . . and he didn't appear to be too happy.

Millie slammed the glove box closed and rolled down her window. "Excuse me, sir. We're lost. Do you know where we are?"

Trish bit the inside of her lip to keep from groaning out loud as the man bent down. They didn't have time to engage the man in conversation—although how he would answer Millie's strange question she couldn't imagine—because Mary was about to get into her car. Suddenly, Trish saw Mary turn, place one hand on her hip, and raise her other hand palm-out. She was shouting something toward the mobile home she had just exited, obviously toward someone Trish couldn't see, and she seemed to be very angry.

"You're at my house," the man snarled. Trish jerked her attention to the not-so-friendly man, a little concerned about the tone of his voice. About to speed off, regardless of whether they drew attention to themselves or not, she saw the man's eyebrows suddenly shoot up as he glanced in the back seat.

"Hi," Edna said cheerfully, still sprawled in a horizontal position.

Up ahead, Trish saw Mary get in her car and slam the door. She turned quickly to look at the man. "Oh, silly me, I just realized where we are. Don't worry, Sally," she said with a glance over her shoulder, "we'll be at the hospital in no time."

"Sally?" Millie asked, turning to stare at her. "Who are you talking to?"

No doubt about it, Trish was going to strangle her. "Thank you for your time," she said quickly to the man as she put the car in gear and pulled away, noticing that Mary had just reached the end of the street.

"Oh! You didn't want to use her real name. That was good thinking," Millie said. "That man was sort of creepy, wasn't he?" Trish glanced in her rear view mirror and saw the man standing there, hands on hips, watching them. She couldn't agree with Millie more.

"Can I sit up now?" Edna asked impatiently.

"No!" Trish and Millie said in unison.

"At least tell me what's going on!"

"We're following Mary again," Millie said.

With a pointed look at Millie, Trish said, "I hope she goes back home. We really are lost, you know."

Millie just waved a hand in dismissal. "We can stop and ask directions if we need to. What we're doing is important."

"I hate to remind you girls, but what we're doing is exactly what Joe warned us not to do. If we're gone much longer I'm going to have a heck of a time smoothing his ruffled feathers."

Trish grimaced. "You're right, it is getting late. Let's follow for just a few more minutes. Maybe we'll get back on a street we recognize. I hope so, anyway. This atmosphere sure is depressing."

"Do you think this place is important to our investigation?" Millie asked.

"It's probably not," Trish admitted ruefully. "More than likely, Mary was just visiting a friend or relative. I don't think I could find it again, anyway."

"I know I couldn't," Edna said from the back seat. "I'm so turned around right now that I actually thought Millie's question to the man about where we were made sense!"

Trish started laughing, but Millie only shook her head.

Mary didn't go back home. They followed her for several miles until she finally pulled into the parking lot of a Jim's Restaurant. Trish entered through the second driveway and parked a few rows behind Mary's car, where they could see inside the restaurant through the large glass panes. "Edna, we'll leave in just a minute," she promised. "The main street there runs directly into Interstate 10, so we're not lost anymore. Let's just see who she's meeting."

But Mary wasn't meeting anyone. They watched as she disappeared for a moment behind a wall, then came back out wearing a different shirt with black slacks—a uniform. "Aha," Millie exclaimed, peering through her binoculars, again unnecessarily, "this is where she works!"

"Can I sit up now?" Edna asked.

"Oh, of course," Trish said. "Sorry."

Edna sat up and stretched. "Why is she working as a waitress when she's a bookkeeper?"

Trish shook her head. "I don't know. Maybe she's not a very good bookkeeper, like Mark said."

"What are we waiting for?" Millie asked. "Let's go in."

"Not now, Millie—I really don't have time. Joe's probably already home by now."

With one last look through the restaurant window, Trish put the car in reverse. "I think we've done enough spying for one day. Finding out where Mary works is a godsend."

Millie leaned back in her seat and yawned loudly. "I'm hungry. Why don't we pick up some chicken on the way home, and we'll call Joe over to tell him what we found out? That way you won't have to tell him by yourself," she said to Edna.

"Yeah, that's a good idea." Edna wasn't worried about Joe getting angry, because he would understand, but since she was hungry too, it would be a great way to kill two birds with one stone. Satisfied with the plan, she didn't feel guilty at all about justifying her reason not to have to relate the day's events by herself.

Forty-five minutes later, they were in Trish's kitchen spreading plates and silverware on the table when Joe walked in carrying a small cardboard box. Edna smiled at him as she carried napkins to the table. "Mmm, something smells awfully good in here," he said.

"We've been cooking all day," Millie chuckled.

"And you even went to the trouble of packing it in colorful containers. What's the special occasion?"

"Just knowing we have a handsome man to share our meal with does the trick," Millie quipped.

Edna walked over and gave him a quick kiss on the cheek. "Hi, honey. You sure got here fast. What are you carrying?"

"I'll tell you in a minute." Joe placed the box on the countertop and sat down. "Who wants to start telling me about what you ladies did today?"

"Oh, no, let's not do that yet," Trish said, walking over with a pitcher of iced tea. "Let's eat first. I'm starved."

"I am too," Edna said, passing around the box of chicken. "Besides, we want to know how it went with Sam."

During the meal, Joe told them about his visit. "I'll have to say he looks better than the last time we saw him. I hate to say this, but I think the robbery may have sparked some life back in him. He's angry, not about the money, but about losing Susan's jewelry."

Trish sighed. "The sad thing is that I doubt if the police will ever recover anything that was stolen."

"They won't even look if they think Sam staged the whole thing," Millie pointed out.

"Did he give you any information on Mary Chavez or Tom Jones?" Trish asked.

Nodding, Joe chewed and then swallowed. "Yes, but it was like pulling teeth. Sam doesn't like to say anything negative about people."

Millie snorted inelegantly. "You can say that again. When we first suspected Susan was murdered, Sam about chewed our heads off. He wouldn't help us at all until we threatened not to give him any peace until he did."

Joe chuckled. "Torture works every time. I did find out a few interesting things. First of all, Sam believes Mary lied on her application about being a full-charge bookkeeper. She had a lot of trouble staying up with the work load. He decided to do on-the-job training with her, and she did show some improvement. But when the other company wanted to use their own bookkeeper,

Sam said it was as though Mary went through a sudden personality change. She was really angry and became downright mean. He hasn't heard from her since. He doesn't know what she's doing now."

Trish remembered the show of temper Mary had displayed outside the mobile home earlier. She didn't know the woman, but it appeared that she used anger quite often to make her feelings known. God help the customer who complained about the food or service at the restaurant where she now worked.

Edna stood and began clearing the table. "What did you learn about Tom?"

"Tom Jones." Joe nodded and took a sip of his coffee. "Tom worked for Sam for a number of years. He supervised jobs, ran crews. Around the last year or so, before Sam retired, Tom hinted around that he was having some financial problems, so Sam gave him some work on the side, things Tom could do on his own. Tom wanted to buy the company when he found out Sam was selling, but Sam knew Tom wasn't experienced enough to run a whole operation. Well, Tom wasn't real happy about it, and it pretty much destroyed their relationship. It turns out the new guy didn't like him, either. Tom didn't last long. Sam doesn't know what he's doing now."

Trish sat back and crossed her arms. The two former employees might not be murderers, but they were still the only two leads at the moment. If Tom Jones and Mary Chavez could be eliminated from the list of suspects, then the next step would be customers Sam had before he sold his business. Sam would surely give them trouble over that line of thinking.

"So, what did my favorite sleuths find out today?" Joe asked, his eyes twinkling. He was either really getting into this detective stuff, or he was ready to pounce on them for interfering needlessly. *Better tread carefully,* Trish thought as she glanced at Edna.

Of course, Millie had never understood the meaning of *tread carefully.* "We found out where Mary Chavez lives and where she works."

Joe's eyes narrowed slightly. "I knew you were going to try to find out where she lives. How did you also find out where she works?"

Edna started to respond, but Millie beat her to it. "We got lucky when we found her house because she was just leaving. We thought of a way to approach her, so we followed her." Millie had a self-satisfied expression on her face, obviously proud of their accomplishment, but Joe didn't look impressed. Fortunately, Millie left out the part about the mobile home.

"She made a stop first at a mobile home park, but we don't know who she was visiting. After that we followed her to the place she works. She's a waitress at a restaurant." Trish groaned silently and sent an apologetic look to Edna for *The Mouth.*

Joe took a deep breath and asked, "Are you sure she didn't see you following her?"

"Not a chance," Millie blurted smugly. "Edna and I took turns ducking down low in our seats. Even if Mary had spotted us, she wouldn't have seen three women at the same time."

Trish could tell Joe was trying to hide a grin. That was a good sign. He might think their methods were amateurish, which, when hearing Millie tell it, certainly sounded that way, but at least he wasn't mad.

"I see I made a very wise decision today," Joe sighed.

"What is that, dear?" Edna asked, obviously relieved also.

Joe reached over and grabbed the box he had brought in. Opening it, he pulled out a small object and handed it to Edna.

"What's this?" she asked.

"It's a cell phone. I'm sure the only reason you didn't let me know the extent of what you were doing today was because you didn't have a way to get in touch with me. That won't be a problem any longer."

Edna kept her smile in place and swallowed. "How thoughtful you are, dear."

Chapter Twelve

"Take a left here." Trish sat with Millie in the back-seat of Joe and Edna's Expedition. It had taken over an hour the night before to convince Joe that talking to Mary Chavez was necessary in their investigation, but finally he had agreed on two conditions: one, that he come along, and, two, that he drive. He had heard enough horror stories over the years not to trust any of them to drive while they were excited.

"Let's go over the plan one more time," Edna said from the front seat. "Millie, please listen carefully."

"Hey, did you forget that I came up with the plan in the first place?"

"No, dear, and it's a good plan. But you do seem to have a habit of straying off-script. This might be our only chance to find out what we can about Mary. We don't want to blow it."

Millie sighed deeply. "Oh, all right, go over it one

more time if it will make you happy. I feel like I'm in grade school."

"Sometimes you behave like you're in grade school."

Trish groaned to herself. They didn't have time for this. "First of all, we find out what section Mary is working in. Then, we go in and order dinner. While Mary is taking the order, Edna tells her that she looks familiar. We engage her in conversation and come to realize we had seen her at Sam's office a few years ago. We ask her if she heard Susan had passed away. Everybody needs to watch her reaction carefully. If she gets curious as to what we're doing in the area, we mention that we've been visiting a friend.

"During the whole meal, we keep asking friendly questions and try to find out as much as we can about her life now. Remember, we don't want to appear too curious or suspicious in any way, just friendly. Has everybody got it?"

"Got it," Edna and Millie replied in unison.

"Is that it up ahead?" Joe asked.

"Yes," all three of them replied, and excitement began to fill the air.

Joe parked the car and waited a few minutes for the women to spot Mary through the large windows. Soon they were entering the restaurant, for all appearances just a group of friends out for dinner. There was a sign at the hostess station asking that patrons wait to be seated. When a young, pretty teenager approached them and asked what there preference was, Millie pointed toward the back and said they'd like to be seated in that area.

"The smoking section it is. Follow me, please." Smiling, the young girl missed the look of dismay cross

Edna's face. Edna had quit smoking several years ago after developing an allergy to cigarette smoke.

Once they were seated, Joe leaned over and whispered, "Edna, if you want, you and I can go grab a hamburger and sit in the parking lot until Millie and Trish get to ask their questions."

Edna sighed. "No, that's not necessary, but thank you, dear. We won't be here long, and actually, it's not too bad in here." She squeezed his hand and smiled. "I'll be fine."

"If you change your mind, you just let me know, okay? We can always think of some excuse to leave."

Trish picked up a menu from the center of the table and surreptitiously looked around. There were booths along the walls with tables placed comfortably in the middle. Wide glass panes completely adorned two of the walls, giving the area an open feel. Twilight was fast approaching, and from her vantage point she could see soft, muted lights from traffic along the highway and from houses in the nearby neighborhood.

Friendly conversation flowed steadily from the other patrons of the restaurant, some of whom were obviously regular customers. Glancing at the menu, she was surprised at the wide variety of entrees they had to offer. She could get used to this questioning stuff if they continued to hold their meetings in restaurants.

Suddenly Edna coughed, buried her face in her menu, and lightly kicked Trish under the table. Trish glanced from her to Millie, who nodded imperceptibly. Mary must be coming toward them. Joe picked up his own menu and leaned toward Edna as he asked if she knew what she wanted. Satisfied that they truly represented just a group of friends out for an evening, Trish drew a calming breath and looked down at her menu. They had all agreed that she would begin the subtle questioning, and she only hoped she didn't pull a *Millie* and jump the gun out of nervousness.

"Are you ready to order?" Even though she had been expecting Mary to approach from behind her, Trish jumped slightly at the friendly voice. She glanced up quickly and smiled. "I think so. Millie, why don't you start?"

Mary Chavez was younger than Trish expected, probably in her early thirties. She had a great smile with dark, flashing eyes and long, silky hair once again pulled back from her face. She was also very good at her job, making helpful suggestions while Millie placed her order. It wasn't quite the impression of an inefficient, angry bookkeeper that Trish had envisioned.

"Thank you, dear," Millie said when she finished placing her order, handing Mary the menu with a smile. Suddenly, Millie's smile faltered and the color drained from her face. She was staring at Mary as if she had just seen a ghost. Nobody else seemed to notice Millie's strange behavior as Mary began to take Edna's order. Concerned, Trish leaned forward and caught Millie's eye. Millie swallowed and shook her head slightly, but before Trish could determine what was wrong, it was her turn.

She ordered the shrimp special and closed her menu, noticing Millie's hand shake slightly as she reached for her iced tea. With no idea what was wrong, Trish had no option but to play out their plan, but she was worried. Millie's behavior was completely out of character.

As soon as Joe completed his order, Trish leaned forward with what she hoped appeared to be an uncertain smile and said to Mary, "You look so familiar . . . ah!" Startled, Trish glanced around trying to figure out which one of her friends had just kicked her painfully. Since both Edna and Joe were looking at her as if she had lost her mind, it had to have been Millie. Trish sighed. Who else was there?

Millie was staring at her with eyes wide and lips pinched. Shoot, Millie was going to blow this if she didn't stop acting so strange. What was wrong with her? With everyone else they had talked to, Millie had been strong and gung-ho, even aggressive. Now she was acting as if she was scared to death.

Trish sent Millie a silent warning with narrowed eyes before she turned back to Mary, forcing her smile back into place. "Have we met before?"

"Oh no," Millie exclaimed loudly, "I'm so sorry!" Millie's glass lay on its side, tea spreading quickly over and down the table.

"Don't worry about it, dear. Everyone has an accident now and then," Edna said soothingly as she quickly reached for a handful of napkins from the dispenser on the table and tried to blot up the mess.

"I'll go get a rag and a fresh glass of tea," Mary said sweetly. "This happens all the time."

As soon as Mary left, Millie leaned over and swatted Trish on the shoulder. "Can't you take a hint?" she hissed.

Trish's mouth dropped open as she rubbed her shoulder. "What are you talking about?"

"I'm talking about the fact that Mary Chavez is wearing earrings that closely resemble a pair that I know Susan had!"

"What?" Edna asked incredulously. "Are you sure?"

"I'm as sure as I can be. The last thing we need to do is bring up Sam's name right now."

Joe lowered his chin and cleared his throat. Mary was back at the table. "Here we go," she said, placing another glass of tea in front of Millie. "I'll have this cleaned up in no time." As Mary wiped the table, Trish looked at the earrings she wore. Small, elegant diamonds encircled a single pearl in the beautiful studs. They were a little dressy for the uniform Mary was wearing, Trish thought to herself, but that didn't mean they didn't belong to her. Trish sat back and looked at Edna, noticing with dismay that everyone at the table was staring at Mary's ears.

"Um," she said quickly, trying to think of something to distract Mary before she looked up and noticed she was the center of attention. "Could we have an order of cheese sticks also?"

"Of course," Mary said as she straightened. "I'll get those for you right now."

As soon as Mary was out of earshot, Millie leaned forward. "Well," she whispered, "what do you think?"

Edna's voice trembled. "I've seen those earrings on Susan before." Joe leaned over and placed a hand over hers. "Honey, don't jump to conclusions. More than likely Mary just has a similar pair."

Millie shook her head slowly. "I can't swear to it, but I think those are the ones Sam had made especially for Susan for Christmas last year."

Trish looked over her shoulder to make sure Mary wasn't near. "The only way we'll know for sure is to get Sam to look at them."

"And how do you propose we do that—yank them out of Mary's ears and take them over to Sam?"

Trish really hated it when Millie resorted to sarcasm. "Of course that's not what I meant!" she replied irritably. "Sam will have to come here."

Joe looked over Trish's shoulder and cleared his throat. "Oh, look," he said loudly, "it's coming just in time. I'm starving."

Mary walked up to the table and placed the hot cheese sticks with four plates in the middle of the table. "Enjoy the cheese sticks," she said with a smile. "Your meals will be ready soon. Can I get you anything else right now?"

"These look beautiful," Millie said dramatically.

They looked beautiful? Trish was hungry, and she did enjoy good food, but she couldn't ever remember referring to something she ate as beautiful! Edna was looking at Millie curiously, and it was all Trish could do not to grin. But that temptation was quickly replaced by stunned surprise as Millie said admiringly, "They're almost as lovely as your earrings, dear."

For a moment nobody moved at the table except Millie, who nonchalantly reached for a cheese stick. Mary, thank God, seemed unaware of the tension. "Thank you. You don't want to know what I had to do to get them, though," she said with a laugh. "Let me know if you need anything." Still grinning, Mary turned to wait on another table.

Small shivers crept up Trish's spine. She looked around the table. Millie's eyes looked like they were about to pop out of her head. Edna's mouth was hanging wide open. Joe's lips were pinched in a tight line.

It took a few minutes, but soon life returned to the table. "Oh, my goodness," Edna whispered, "was that a confession?"

"I don't think that's very likely," Millie said wryly. "But it is rather telling, don't you think?"

Trish opened her mouth but nothing came out. Taking a sip of tea, she cleared her throat and tried again. "I'm not sure. We may be reading too much into this. I will agree, though, that it was a very strange remark."

"Here comes our dinner," Joe said softly. "Everyone try to act normal."

If Mary noticed that everybody at the table was sitting stiff and silent with plastic smiles on their faces, she didn't let on. She served the meal quickly and efficiently, bringing all the anticipated condiments without having to be asked. She looked at the remaining cheese sticks. "Would you like me to box those up for you?"

Edna looked up sharply, her eyes wide. "Please do that," she said in an uncharacteristically high-pitched voice.

Mary's eyebrows rose a fraction, but she made no comment as she reached for the uneaten appetizer. "I'll be right back."

Trish looked down at her plate. The shrimp platter, which had sounded so good just a short while ago, now held no appeal whatsoever. Evidently, she wasn't the only one who had lost her appetite, either. Scratch that. Surprisingly, Millie seemed to have lost her earlier fear. She was digging into her grilled chicken dinner as though she hadn't eaten in a week.

Trish glanced at Edna, who shook her head slightly and pushed her plate back. "I'm not very hungry," Edna remarked.

Joe sighed. "I hate to admit it, but neither am I. We'll get these boxed up to go and eat later when we've calmed down."

"You have to eat," Millie said between bites. "We need to keep our strength up. Finally, we have a tangible clue."

"We don't have anything except more suspicion," Trish said quietly. "And you know how Henry feels about our suspicions. He's not going to listen to us. We need to get Sam to verify that the earrings belonged to Susan."

"Trish is right," Joe said. "I wish there was another way, though. It may not be as easy as we think. We don't know how often Mary wears those earrings, and we don't know how she's going to react when she sees Sam. Or, for that matter, we don't know how Sam is going to react if he believes those earrings are Susan's. Remember, he's a very hurt, angry man."

"I still say that's a good thing," Millie said, finally pushing her plate away. Nobody else had touched their food. "He *should* be angry. Look at everything the murderer has taken from him."

It was a somber group that left the restaurant a few minutes later. Mary had packed up their untouched food, clearly puzzled as to why only one of them had eaten, especially since they had all proclaimed that they were starving when they'd sat down.

So focused on their agenda, Joe and the ladies hadn't noticed the woman sitting alone at a nearby table. She had been watching them for quite a while and had even shamelessly eavesdropped on their conversation. She had been amused by their obvious tactics initially, but there wasn't anything funny about them noticing the earrings.

What a sweet twist of fate, the woman had thought, that she had been in the restaurant when those four had come in. This visit had turned out to be very informative. Very informative, indeed, she had grinned as she had watched Mary walk away after refreshing her iced tea, the earrings sparkling in the light.

Millie was right, Edna thought as they walked over to Trish's early the next morning. They did need to check out every possibility on what could have occurred the morning Susan was killed, but after finding Mary Chavez last night, it was hard to focus on anybody else. However, as Millie had pointed out a few minutes before, it could be that Mary Chavez was only involved in the theft of Sam's safe. Admittedly it wasn't a likely scenario, but it had to be considered.

Well, there wasn't much they could do right now on that front, anyway. Joe was on his way over to Sam's house to talk to him about the earrings and the part they wanted him to play to verify if, in fact, they were Susan's or not. Once that was established, they could then discuss what to do.

Until then, there was still the lead on Tom Jones to check out. "A good detective never leaves a stone unturned," Millie said.

Trish rolled her eyes. "We're not detectives, much less *good* detectives."

"How can you say that after what we found out last night?" Edna asked.

"We may not have found out anything."

"That's exactly why we need to keep investigating," Millie said pointedly. "Come on, Trish, get the directions to Tom Jones' place and let's get going. It's not going to take that long. We're just going to drive by his house and get a feel for the area. That's all."

Trish had just applied the brakes at the stop sign when Edna noticed Larry Thompson turning onto their street. She waved gaily as he slowed and pulled his car up alongside them. "Don't say anything about Mary Chavez," Millie warned suddenly.

Trish rolled down her window and smiled. "Hello."

"Good morning, ladies," he said, his drop-dead gorgeous smile warm and friendly. "Where are you heading off to?"

"The grocery store."

"The dry cleaners."

"The bank."

Larry's eyebrows rose as any normal person's would at their fumbling response. Trish silently groaned as she forced a laugh. "Actually, we're going to all of the above."

"Ah, I see," he said, shaking his head, his brown eyes dancing. "What you really mean to say is that you're following up on a clue you don't want me to know about." He waved away their automatic denial with a smile. "I was just going to stop by and let you know I haven't forgotten you. Nothing suspicious has turned up on Mark Wilson, so I thought you may have someone else in mind you wanted me to check out."

Millie sat quietly in the backseat, but Trish could almost feel her tense up. "No, um . . . not right offhand. We don't have the list of names with us, anyway. Perhaps you could come back by in a couple of days." Maybe by then Sam would be able to verify if the earrings were Susan's or not and they could talk to Larry about Mary Chavez.

Before he could say anything, a car pulled up behind him. He looked in his rearview mirror and sighed. "Perfect timing," he muttered. "Okay, just please be careful . . . while you run your errands." Grinning, he waved and pulled off.

Trish took a deep breath and pressed the gas pedal. "I'm not sure he believed us," she said wryly.

"It doesn't matter," Millie said. "The next time we see him we'll be able to tell him what we've been doing."

"If all goes well, we will," Edna said, a stark reminder that all they were doing at this point was guessing.

"It will. My gut tells me that we're on the right track," Millie said confidently.

Trish wished her own gut was as sure as Millie's.

Chapter Thirteen

"**I** think we're almost there," Edna said, looking at the directions. "Take a right here on Roosevelt Street and it should be just a couple of miles further." Edna laid the directions on her lap and then cocked her head, her brows lowered in puzzlement.

"What's wrong?" Millie asked, leaning forward to look at Edna.

"Don't tell me we're lost!" Trish exclaimed.

"No, it's not that. For some reason, this looks familiar."

"Maybe in your younger days you used to run the streets around here," Millie suggested with a sly grin.

Edna frowned. "That's not likely." So far, all they had seen on Roosevelt Street were bars and fast-food places. Trish chuckled. Try as she might, the image of Edna running in to grab a quick hamburger between barhopping was impossible to conjure up, regardless of how young she may have been.

Finally, neighborhoods starting sprouting up on both

sides of the street. They passed a small undeveloped stretch of land when Edna said, "It should be right up here on the right."

Millie leaned forward in her seat and peered through the front window. "Oh, no, it can't be!" she whispered at the same time Trish pulled over on the shoulder of the street and slammed on the brakes.

"*Oh, no,* is right," Trish replied.

Trish was just a few yards from the address that should be Tom Jones'. And that address sported a large sign at the entrance that read Southwest Mobile Home Park. There was silence in the car as all three women pondered this latest development. Trish turned the car around and headed back home. No wonder Roosevelt Street had sounded familiar. They had just traveled a different route to get to it this time. Evidently, Mary Chavez knew a shortcut.

Sam was more than eager to do his part in trying to determine if the earrings that Mary Chavez wore were indeed his wife's. He was so eager, in fact, that Joe had to coach him several times on how to act calm and natural both before, and after, his encounter with Mary. If she grew suspicious, then she would get rid of the evidence before any of them could blink, thereby destroying any chance they would have of going to the police. "He said-she said" wouldn't go over too well with Henry—not since he already believed Sam was only trying to cover up a crime.

They all agreed not to tell Sam about Mary's visit to Tom yet. He had enough on his plate right now without adding fuel to the fire. If he got angry before his meeting with Mary, he could very well spill the beans.

Sam strode casually into the restaurant while Joe and the women waited outside in Joe's SUV. They were parked around back where there were no windows for them to see what was going on inside, but, more importantly, nobody from inside the restaurant could see them, either. Was Sam talking to Mary right now?

Trish found it hard to believe that their sweet waitress of the night before could be capable of murder. Still, more and more women were committing violent crimes. Passion, jealousy, money . . . all these motives could possibly make a woman snap. But what could have been Mary's motive? She doubted Mary was in love with Sam, so that ruled out passion and jealousy. Killing Susan for financial gain didn't make sense because there had been no theft until long after the murder.

Trish sighed and leaned her head back on the car seat. Why try to rationalize a crime that only someone completely insane would justify? It was impossible. On second thought . . . Trish had just turned to Millie with a teasing smile when she caught sight of Sam coming around the corner of the building. That was fast! He was walking briskly, his lips in a tight line. Trish's heartbeat sped up. Had he discovered whether the earrings were Susan's or not?

Sam climbed in and shut the door. "Let's get out of here."

Joe looked at him curiously. "Is everything all right?"

"Everything's fine," he said through gritted teeth, "just highly embarrassing. Mary wasn't wearing any earrings. I wanted so badly to question her about them." Sam's hands were clenched in tight fists where they lay on his lap. "When she saw me, she did everything she could to avoid me, but I guess she couldn't find anyone else available to wait on me. When she finally came over, she was overtly rude, making several snide remarks that anybody who was within the length of a football field could hear. Stuff like 'waitressing wasn't her first career choice, and was I able to make sure everybody else got fired, too?' " Sam shook his head. "To think I used to feel sorry for her."

Trish's heart sank. She looked at Edna and Millie who, by the expressions on their faces, felt the same way she did. What a wasted endeavor this had been. The earrings were such a strong clue, and they had pinned their hopes that a positive ID of them would guide the next step in their investigation. How were they going to get Sam to see them now? He couldn't very well march into the restaurant night after night in the hopes that one evening Mary would be wearing them.

"I'm sorry you had to go through that, Sam," Edna said soothingly. "I didn't get the impression that Mary could be that vindictive."

"Appearances can be deceiving, especially when you're trying to earn a tip," Millie said wryly. "What concerns me now is how are we going to prove those earrings are Susan's?"

"Maybe we should go ahead and tell Henry what we suspect," Edna suggested.

Sam chuckled bitterly. "I'm sure that would do a lot of good."

"We'll think of something," Millie piped in. "Don't you worry. I've got a hunch we're on the right track, and with or without the help of the police, we're going to prove it."

Trish bit her lip. *There Millie goes again, promising results that are not at all certain.* What they had was a lot of nothing, and that included not a shred of evidence that would back up even one of their theories.

"Sam, what kind of relationship did Mary Chavez and Tom Jones have?" she asked as Joe pulled out of the parking lot. There wasn't any point in keeping information from him any longer.

Sam looked over his shoulder with raised eyebrows, obviously surprised at the question. "Relationship? Mary and Tom? They didn't have a relationship. They were both married."

"I didn't mean a personal relationship," Trish said. "How did they get along at work?"

"They barely did," Sam scoffed. "They couldn't stand each other. Mary was always complaining about Tom's reports, and Tom was always saying that Mary picked on him to hide the fact she wasn't doing her job."

"Maybe they were hiding an attraction they felt for each other," Millie offered, nodding knowingly. "It's not unheard of for some people to use anger as a flirting method."

"That's not possible," Sam said, shaking his head. "You would have to have seen them together. No, there wasn't anything personal going on between Tom and Mary, and they had very little to do with each other at work. Regardless, what does Tom have to do with any of this, anyway?"

Edna proceeded to tell Sam what they'd witnessed when they had followed Mary that day. His brows furrowed as he listened to her. "Well, it does seem strange that they would have anything to do with each other. I can't imagine what it means, though. I seem to recall hearing that Tom got a divorce not too long ago, but I can't say for sure. And, as far as I know, Mary is still married." He sighed and rubbed his hand across his eyes. "I can't see how any of this could be tied to Susan's death. The earrings bother me, but we don't know if they are Susan's or not. And, for the life of me, I can't imagine Mary or Tom going to such lengths to hurt me."

Trish heard the frustration in his voice and she could well sympathize. He was facing a murder charge, and it seemed as if they were getting nowhere. They dropped Sam off at his sister's house, promising to get together with him in the next day or so when they had another plan.

Joe drove home in silence. When he pulled up in front of Trish's house, Edna climbed out also, telling him she would be home soon. This was a time for brainstorming, and Joe had a frustrating way of inserting common sense into these kinds of sessions.

Trish immediately started a fresh pot of coffee, regardless of the time, and they sat at the table waiting for it to finish brewing. "I'm tired of pussy-footing around," Millie said. "We're going to have to *make* something happen."

"Like what?" Edna asked warily.

"I don't know what. I just know that we need to do something . . . *anything!*"

Trish sighed. "I hate to admit it, but I agree." She paused for a second. "The one thing we do know is that Mary has some connection to Tom Jones. What we don't know is what that connection is. So that's where we need to start. We need to find out some basic information about Tom, where he works, what his schedule is, things like that. Maybe an idea will come to us."

Millie nodded determinedly. "Okay, at least we have a plan. Edna, you bring something for us to snack on, I'll bring the binoculars, and Trish, you bring drinks. We'll meet here at ten in the morning."

Trish looked at Edna with raised eyebrows. Should they stand up and salute?

The next day was a bright, beautiful day with soft clouds hanging in the sky and the comforting smell of spring wafting through the open windows. They had parked on one of the side streets across and down from Tom Jones' trailer. They could have been visiting any one of several trailers from their strategic vantage point, but it was unlikely anybody would notice. The place was like a ghost town.

"Did you ever call Joe?" Millie asked Edna as she lowered the binoculars. They had been watching Tom's trailer for over an hour now. The same older-model red pickup they had seen the other day was in the driveway, but there had been no movement around the trailer at all.

"You know I haven't," Edna said impatiently—and with a little guilt. "I've been with you all morning. I'm going to wait a little while before I tell him where I am. That way he won't worry—he won't know how long we were actually here."

"So much for your handy-dandy cell phone," Millie muttered under her breath.

"I heard that!"

"I don't know about you guys, but I'm getting hungry," Trish said. They were all getting bored, but the last thing she wanted was for Millie and Edna to get into one of their squabbles. Her patience would only stretch so far and she didn't want to be distracted from her thoughts. There had to be another way to approach Mary again without appearing too obvious. She was also having second thoughts about their decision not to tell the police their suspicions regarding Sam's former book-keeper. Maybe she could at least convince her friends that they should talk to Larry Thompson. He didn't seem to think they were all off their rockers like the chief did.

"We're not stupid, Trish. We know what you're doing," Edna said with a sniff.

Startled, Trish looked over her shoulder. Was Edna a mind reader now? Then she realized that Edna must be referring about her attempt to keep the peace with the mention of food. "Then why couldn't you have stopped arguing on your own?" she snapped, and then she sighed deeply and leaned her head against the headrest. "Sorry, I'm just frustrated. I can't help but feel we're wasting our time."

Millie reached over and patted her on the knee. "Don't worry about it. We're all a little short-tempered right now. I think you're right, we need something to eat. At least it will give us something to do."

"Right," Edna said cheerfully, "we'll all feel better after we eat." Lifting up the wicker basket she had placed on the back floorboard, she proceeded to pass out napkins and bottled water. Next, she handed Millie and Trish blue plastic-covered bowls with plastic forks.

"What's this?" Millie asked, warily prying open one edge of the lid.

"It's salad."

Trish turned to look at Edna. "You brought salad—for a stake-out?"

"Of course," she said primly. "Just because we're

working doesn't mean we can't eat healthy food. I already put my special dressing on it."

"And you call *me* crazy?" Millie exclaimed. "I was expecting finger food, you know, sandwiches, crackers and cheese, cookies . . . even doughnuts—not salad!"

"Well, next time you can bring the food," Edna said sarcastically. "In the meantime, eat or shut up."

Millie stared at her for a minute, then plopped back in her seat and jammed her fork into the greens. "Out of all the possible stake-out-worthy foods I could've had, I'm stuck eating this wimpy salad," she muttered in disgust.

Refraining from saying anything out loud, Trish sighed and opened her own bowl, promising herself a fat, juicy hamburger later on. She had just taken her first bite when a movement caught her attention. Looking up quickly, she saw Tom Jones come out of his mobile home and head toward his truck. He was wearing an open, dark flannel shirt over a while T-shirt and well-worn jeans. A blue baseball cap partly hid his facial features, but Trish got the distinct impression he wasn't a happy man right now.

Hurriedly, she swallowed and replaced the lid on her bowl. "There he is! He's getting ready to leave."

"Bingo!" Millie mumbled excitedly. Shoving one more bite into her already-full mouth, she sat up straight and began to close her lunch.

Edna was doing the same in the backseat and directing them to give her the bowls. "Finally, some action!" she exclaimed.

Trish pulled on her seat belt and waited until Tom had reached the end of the block before she pulled out to follow him. The excitement in the car was almost palpable. Millie had pulled the binoculars up to her eyes, even though Tom was only a few yards in front of them, and a quick glance in the rearview mirror showed Edna sitting forward, a gleeful smile on her face and her eyes wide open.

Nobody was quite sure where they expected Tom to go, but not one of them thought they would end up on Mary's street. "We've already established that Tom and Mary are seeing each other," Millie said, the disappointment clear in her voice.

Edna sighed audibly. "If all we're going to do is follow Mary and Tom back and forth to each other's house, we're never going to be able to help Sam."

Trish circled the block and drove by Mary's house one more time. Tom must have already gone inside. "There's not much else we can do today, regardless," she said crossly, pointing the car toward home. "In the last few days, we've established that Tom and Mary have kept up their acquaintance since leaving Sam, and that it's possible Mary has the same pair of earrings that Susan had, none of which proves that Tom or Mary was anywhere near Sam's house the day Susan was murdered."

"I still say the earrings Mary was wearing that night belong to Susan," Millie said.

"But we can't prove it," Edna said dejectedly.

Millie cocked her head to one side. "What if we point-blank ask her?"

Trish looked at her as if she had lost her mind. "And what do you think that would accomplish? You think she's just going to admit that she took them after she killed Susan?"

"No, but we could watch her reaction. If we get suspicious, we go to the police and tell them to check it out."

"She would get rid of them before that happened," Trish pointed out. "And that's assuming we could even get Henry to go over there. The odds aren't too good on that happening."

"You're right," Millie said wryly. "I'd rather try my luck in Vegas."

They fell silent the rest of the way home, each trying to think of a way to jump-start their investigation again. They had been so sure that, with a little snooping around, they would be able to come up with realistic suspects that would force the police to reconsider Sam as their primary target in the murder charge.

More than likely, it was just pure coincidence that Tom and Mary, the two people who were angry at Sam for selling his business, were still seeing each other. The problem was Trish didn't believe in coincidences. And there was that tiny fact that Mary had been wearing earrings that were identical to the ones stolen recently from Sam's house. There was a connection there, Trish was sure of it. But how were they to prove it?

She pulled into her driveway and stopped the car. "Look, I know none of us is comfortable going to the police. But what if we talked to Larry? He seems open-minded to new possibilities, and I'm pretty sure we can trust him. I don't think he's said anything to Henry about checking out Mark for us."

"No, I don't think so, either. We would have heard about it, I'm sure," Edna agreed. "You might have an idea. What do you think, Millie?"

Millie frowned and crossed her arms. "I thought we

were going to try and solve this ourselves. Are you both giving up so soon? Goodness, the first sign of frustration and you just want to throw in the towel."

"Don't get so dramatic," Trish said, rolling her eyes. "Face it, we need some help. We don't have to tell Larry everything."

Millie looked sideways at her and then finally shrugged. "Okay," she said, letting out a deep breath in resignation, "let's talk to Larry about the earrings. We can always say we ran across Mary by accident and recognized the earrings, and that we're concerned because of the theft at Sam's."

"But we don't want to say anything, at this point, about Tom and that we know he and Mary are in touch with each other," Edna inserted quickly. "Otherwise, he'll know we've been following them."

Trish nodded. "I agree."

Millie opened the car door. "I'll call Larry and tell him to come over to your house tomorrow morning, Trish. Edna and I will come over early. We'll decide what to do next after we hear what Larry has to say." She stepped out and then leaned back in. "Oh, and Edna, thanks so much for the *salad.* Next time, I'll bring lunch." With that she slammed the car door and marched across the street.

"What does she mean *next time?*" Trish asked with raised eyebrows.

"I've got a sneaky hunch she won't be bringing salad," Edna said with a cocky grin.

Later that night, Trish found herself walking aimlessly from room to room. She was restless, unable to relax, and didn't have a clue as to why. She pulled the front curtains aside and glanced over at Millie's house—for the third time in the last hour.

Ever since Millie's house had been broken into, Trish had fallen into a pattern of checking on her friend several times a night—not that she would ever tell Millie. No, hard-headed as ever, Millie had insisted on staying in her own house after that first night she had spent with Trish. No bully was going to alter her lifestyle, she had declared adamantly when both Trish and Edna had tried to convince her that she shouldn't be alone just yet.

Trish didn't think it was just a bored "bully" that had broken into Millie's house. Whoever had gotten inside had something to do with Susan's murder. She was sure of it. How else could the disappearance of Millie's address book be explained, the one that had the combination to Sam's safe?

Millie's independence was one of the things Trish most admired about her friend, but right now that trait was a major pain in the neck. All she could do was try to keep an eye out for her from a distance and hope she would notice if anything strange was going on.

Right now everything appeared normal. The night was quiet, the soft, muted porch lights on most of the houses casting a peaceful glow over the neighborhood. Majestic oaks allowed the branches that reached heavenward to sway gently with the evening breeze, offering a glimpse of the bright stars.

Trish imagined her neighbors sleeping soundly, believing they were safe in their beds in this old, established neighborhood. It was all so sad, she thought tiredly as she walked slowly toward the kitchen. They weren't safe. A murderer was on the loose, and it was very possible an innocent man was going to be convicted of the crime.

And a murderer would still be on the loose.

She sighed and let the curtains fall back into place.

Chapter Fourteen

Larry showed up earlier than expected the next morning. "Good morning," Trish said, wiping her hands on a towel. "Come on in. I just put cinnamon rolls in the oven, and I've got fresh coffee. The girls should be here soon."

"We need to have meetings more often," Larry said with a teasing smile as he rubbed his stomach.

If I were a few years younger, we'd be meeting much more often, Trish thought with a rueful sigh.

Once the coffee was served and the pleasantries exchanged, Larry leaned back in his chair. "So, what did you want to see me about?"

"I feel guilty talking about anything before Millie and Edna get here. You may not have noticed, but Millie can be a little . . . difficult."

Larry chuckled. "No, I hadn't noticed."

"Yes, she hides that aspect of her personality well," Trish grinned. "Believe me, she has already seen your car parked out front and will be charging over here before you know it. And if you and I were already discussing the case"—she shuddered at the mere thought, causing Larry to laugh out loud—"Millie would never let me forget it. Seriously though, I do believe we've got some interesting news for you."

Just then the buzzer on the oven went off. "Let me ask you something, Larry," Trish said over her shoulder as she went to pull out the pan of cinnamon rolls. "Do you honestly believe, with complete certainty, that Sam killed his wife?"

The question clearly took him aback. "I'm a detective," he finally said. "It doesn't matter much what I believe. It's all about what the facts prove."

Trish looked at him for a moment. "Evasiveness doesn't suit you, but I think you answered my question. I can't say I'm not disappointed."

Larry sighed and leaned forward, placing his elbows on his knees. "Please don't read more into what I said than what I meant. I promised to shoot straight with you, and I will. You have to understand my position, though. Nothing has come up so far that will clear Sam."

Trish bit her tongue. Now would be a great time to bring up the subject of Mary Chavez, but it wouldn't be fair to Millie and Edna. Where were they, anyway?

As if on cue, the front door opened and closed with a slam. "Hello? Trish? We're here," Millie's voice rang out. "Is that Larry's car out front?"

"You know good and well that Larry's here," Trish yelled, her nose stuck in the refrigerator, looking for the sweet, gooey icing for the cinnamon rolls.

Millie practically bounced into the kitchen, looking quickly from Larry to Trish.

"I haven't told him anything, Millie, so you can relax."

"I don't know what you're talking about. Hello, Larry, how are you?" Millie headed straight for the coffee pot while Edna greeted Larry and sat down.

"It smells heavenly, Trish," Edna said, accepting the coffee Millie brought over.

"This reminds me of my mother," Larry said. "Every Saturday morning she would bake cinnamon rolls or coffee cake and the whole family would gather around. We'd fight over the ones that had the most icing on them."

This reminds him of his mother, does it? Trish thought, pursing her lips. Well, everybody loves cinnamon rolls, but she couldn't help but wish she had made something else—like strawberry crepes or a fancy quiche.

"I'm anxious to hear why you wanted to meet with me this morning," Larry said. "Have you found out anything that will help your friend?"

"You bet we did," Millie said. "We know who killed Susan Wiley."

Trish almost dropped the tray she was carrying to the table. "Millie!"

"I can't believe you just said that," Edna admonished, her eyebrows raised all the way to her hairline. "That's not true."

"Well, it might be," Millie said defensively. "It depends on whether Super Sleuth here really cares about finding out the truth or not."

Larry took the slight dig with his usual charm and patience. "Tell me what you've got, and I'll see what I can do," he said, casually reaching for a cinnamon roll.

He looked puzzled and slightly disappointed when he didn't find the icing, but after a moment he chose the butter and spread it liberally over his roll.

Trish felt a pang of remorse which lasted only a second. It was time for new memories. She ignored the strange look Millie gave her and, purely out of stubbornness, reached for the sour cream.

"You need to investigate Mary Chavez." Millie reached for her own cinnamon roll but declined both the butter and the sour cream.

That was a good decision, Trish thought, trying to swallow her own roll without grimacing.

"And why is that?" Larry asked, wiping his hands on a napkin. He didn't reach for another.

Edna quickly filled him in on what they knew about Mary Chavez and carefully explained their concern about the earrings. Thankfully, Millie kept her mouth shut about Tom, even though her lips twitched several times as though she desperately wanted to interrupt.

When Edna finished speaking, Larry deliberately let his glance fall on each of them. "I thought we agreed you would pass any information on to me and stay out of any actual snooping."

"How would we know whether we had any information to pass on if we hadn't checked Mary out first?" Millie exclaimed indignantly.

"What you have is nothing," Larry replied, his tone revealing exasperation. "You have nothing to tie this Mary Chavez to Susan's death, and just because she has earrings similar to ones owned by the late Mrs. Wiley doesn't mean she killed her!"

"But you didn't hear her," Millie said, her eyes narrowing as she leaned forward. "She said we would never believe what she had to go through to get those earrings. And her voice was sly and sneaky when she said it."

"Oh, Millie, stop it," Trish demanded. "You're exaggerating something awful. Her voice was friendly, as if she was sharing an inside joke. We were all just shocked at the sight of the earrings and probably read more into her statement than we should have."

"Humph," Millie snorted, crossed her arms over her chest and sat back in her chair while she glared at Trish, "whose side are you on, anyway?"

Trish glared right back. "I'm on the side of the truth, and we're not going to get to it if you keep embellishing."

Larry raised his hand. "Ladies, please," he said with a deep sigh. "Look, you know I understand your concern. But I've told you before how dangerous this can be. This isn't a game. If you really believe a murderer is on the loose, why would you intentionally put yourselves in a risky situation?"

"Because a friend of ours has been charged with murder and we know he's innocent," Edna said softly.

"You think he'll check out Mary?" Millie asked around a mouthful of cinnamon roll. The icing had come out as soon as Larry had left, and they were just finishing off the plate.

Trish shrugged. "I don't know. Maybe he'll casually look into her, but I doubt he thinks there's anything to our suspicion."

"We have to get something more concrete," Edna sighed. "Does anybody have any ideas?"

"Well, it's a sure bet we can't go back to the restaurant," Millie said. She thought for a moment, tapping her fingers on the table. "Edna, you got a real good look at those earrings when Sam gave them to Susan, didn't you?"

"Yes, I certainly did." She smiled sorrowfully. "Susan was so proud of them. She showed them to me that very afternoon."

"Okay, then you're the one who is going to have to verify if Mary has Susan's earrings or if they are just similar. I don't like it, and I'm not sure you can pull it off, but we don't have a choice."

Edna's jaw dropped.

"And just how is she going to do that?" Trish asked with raised eyebrows.

"She'll do it by going to her house."

"Oh, of course. How silly of me to have even asked."

Millie just sat there with a pleased smile, and Trish didn't like that twinkle shining in her eyes one bit, and she really wished Edna would close her mouth.

"Do you think she's there yet?" Millie asked, unwrapping her hotdog.

"I don't know," Trish said nervously and glanced at her watch. "She probably is." They were sitting at a concrete picnic table outside the neighborhood corner store. It was a place that construction workers often sat to eat their lunches, but Millie and Trish were alone right now. Edna had dropped them off a few minutes before and should now be at Mary's house.

Trish was not comfortable with this at all. "How can you eat at a time like this?" she asked irritably.

Millie shrugged and took a huge bite. "I'm hungry. Besides, if anything goes wrong, I'll need the energy."

"No you won't, because if anything goes wrong I'm going to skin you alive."

Millie shrugged again. "Nothing is going to go wrong. It's a foolproof plan."

Trish took a deep breath, leaned over, and snatched a potato chip from the open bag in front of Millie. She didn't have the heart to bring up the subject of Murphy's Law.

Edna straightened her shoulders and steadied her nerves. How Millie had talked her into this, she would never understand. She rang the doorbell, plastered a smile on her face, and reminded herself that she was doing this for Sam. That seemed to help—some.

Mary lived in a house that could use a little tender loving care. The front door was in need of a fresh coat of paint along with the iron columns spaced along the wide front porch where a couple of potted plants cried out for water, their wilting leaves falling to the ground. To the left of the door, a large window faced the street, curtains drawn, the screen torn at the bottom. Everything was neat enough, and the house was really quite charming, but the minor repairs left undone gave the feeling that neglect was a common thing there.

Maybe Mary and her husband were renters, in which case the repairs were not their responsibility. Or, more likely, if they had fallen on tough times, then a lack of funds could delay the work from being done. But, really, how much did a gallon of paint cost, anyway?

Edna transferred the bag she was carrying to her other hand and reached up to ring the bell again. At that moment, she heard a chain sliding and the front door opened. Edna only jumped slightly, then quickly fixed her smile in place.

Mary stood in the doorway, an impatient look on her face. "Yes?"

"Hello," Edna said, in what she hoped was a chipper, friendly tone. "My name is Ed . . . , um, Edwina Granger. I'm your new Avon representative in the neighborhood." Mary's hair was pulled back into a pony tail again, and unfortunately she wasn't wearing any jewelry.

Mary shook her head. "I'm sorry. I'm late—"

"Oh, please," Edna said quickly, placing her hand on the door, "I promise this will only take a minute. You see, I'm new at this and I'm afraid I haven't been very successful. At my age, it's difficult. Who wants to buy miracle wrinkle cream from someone who's all wrinkly? Actually, I've just started using the products, and I believe I'll look ten years younger in a month or so. But my husband left me for a younger woman, and I desperately need this job. I really want to practice my presentation, and I guarantee you it won't take long. You don't even have to buy a thing. Please?" Edna stopped and took a deep breath, having just delivered the fastest speech in her life. Hopefully it had sounded pitiful enough. Just in case, she offered a weak little smile.

It must have worked. Mary sighed, but she was grinning as she opened the door wider. "How can I refuse? Come on in, but I must warn you that I only have a few minutes."

"Thank you," Edna gushed. Thank goodness Millie's daughter had actually sold Avon a little over a year before and had been able to furnish enough samples, as well as a genuine sales bag, to make Edna's story appear true. The only problem was the catalog. There hadn't been enough time to get an up-to-date one, so they'd had to settle for an old one. If Mary happened to notice, then Edna's newness on the job would provide a believable blunder.

Mary gestured to an easy chair. "Have a seat." She sat opposite Edna on the sofa. "I haven't used Avon in a while, but I do like their products. I won't be able to buy anything, but you can run your presentation by me and then leave me your number so I can order later if I want to."

"This is very kind of you. I'm not much of a sales-person, even though the products basically sell them-selves, so I appreciate your giving me the opportunity to practice." Edna pulled out some of the samples, arrang-ing them on the oval coffee table. "You have a lovely home." *Lovely* wasn't quite an apt description. Although clean, the furnishings were almost threadbare, and the walls were a yellowing color of off-white. The tan carpet would soon need to be replaced, along with the curtains, but the most disconcerting thing was the lack of person-ality in the room. No pictures, knickknacks or plants broke the austerity in the surroundings.

"Thank you. I'm sorry, I'd offer you coffee or tea, but I honestly don't have much time. I'll be late for work."

"Don't give it another thought, dear. What do you do for a living?"

"Well, right now I work as a waitress, but I've got ap-plications out for office work."

"Wait . . ." Edna stopped fumbling in the bag and looked up with feigned surprise. "That's where I've seen you before. You work at Jim's Restaurants, don't you?"

Mary cocked her head. "Yes, I do. Do I know you?"

"No, but you served me and a couple of friends re-cently. We were very impressed with your service,"

Edna said truthfully. "It takes a special talent to do what you do, coordination, patience, putting on a smile when you'd rather slap somebody. I certainly couldn't do it."

Surprisingly, Mary blushed slightly. "Thank you. It's not hard, really. I'm just doing it until I can find something better."

"So, you like office work?" Edna had emptied the bag of samples some time ago, but she was managing to make herself look busy. It was important to keep Mary talking, and there wasn't a lot of time.

"I love it. I lost my last job because the accountant was convicted of embezzling. I was the one who discovered the problem and told my boss, but it was too late. The losses were so great that the company couldn't stay afloat. Of course, I got a glowing recommendation, I had been there for fifteen years, but it's not easy finding another position at the same rank and rate of pay I was at."

Edna shook her head sympathetically. It was a true sentiment, actually; she felt the poor woman was delusional. If, in her mind, her skills were as great as she thought they were, it would be very difficult for anybody to teach her anything or give constructive criticism. There was also the possibility that Mary Chavez was a pathological liar.

Mary glanced at her watch. *Uhh,* thought Edna, *I'd better hurry this along.* "You know, Mary, there's another reason I remember you. In our latest catalog, there is a necklace and bracelet set that I think matches those gorgeous earrings you were wearing when I met you. I believe my friends and I even commented on them that night. I know you said you weren't interested in buying anything right now, but I absolutely adore jewelry. I was thinking of buying the necklace if I could find earrings to match. Where did you get yours?"

Mary frowned and reached for her bare ear lobe. "Oh, I know which ones you're talking about," she said, her expression clearing. "I didn't buy them. They were a gift—well, a payment, sort of. I did some work for a guy who promised to pay me, but when I finished he said he didn't have any money. I threatened him, and he gave me the earrings to shut me up." A shiver ran up Edna's spine at the cold look on Mary's face. She was smiling, but there was no humor in her expression at all. "I'm going to sell them eventually, probably for more than he owed me."

It was all Edna could do to act natural and continue speaking. "Good for you. Would you mind terribly if I look at them again? I might be in the market to buy them when you're ready to sell."

Mary hesitated. "Well . . . sure. In fact, I think I'll wear them today. It reminds me of the jerk and how I'm going to get even with him someday," she confessed with a grin. "I'll go get them, but I'm afraid I'm going to have to get going. Maybe you could come back some other time."

"Oh, of course—I'm sorry I've kept you so long. I'll start picking up this stuff." Mary left the room, and Edna quickly cleared the coffee table by sweeping everything into the Avon bag with her arm. She then sat quietly and forced her breathing to remain natural. In a few seconds, she would know whether Susan's missing earrings were in the possession of Mary Chavez. She didn't even want to think about what *job* Mary had done to have received them as payment. That statement could be analyzed later with her friends.

Mary walked back in the room with her purse slung over one shoulder and her keys in her hand. She held out her other hand to Edna. "Here they are. I'll be right back. I have to lock the back door," she said, dropping the glittering studs into Edna's hand.

Edna felt the room spin around her as she stared at the earrings, the brilliant diamonds twinkling. Her eyes began to burn, and her hands started shaking. She wanted nothing more than to make a mad dash for the door, into the protection of her car, and rush to the police station where she could hand over the earrings. She couldn't leave them with Mary! They didn't belong to her; she had no right to them. Sam had lovingly given them to his wife, the wife who had been murdered for no apparent reason.

Edna felt her heart squeeze tight, the pain and anger ready to lash out as she tried to control her emotions. Common sense eventually prevailed as she realized that leaving with the earrings would destroy all evidence tying them to Mary. She clutched the earrings tightly, said a silent prayer promising Susan the earrings would soon be returned to Sam, and then laid them gently on the coffee table.

"They're pretty, aren't they?" Mary's tone was breezy and friendly.

Edna gripped the bag in her hands tightly and fixed a smile on her face as she turned. "Yes, they're pretty. Thank you for letting me see them. I'll be off now." Edna's voice was husky and she could have kicked herself.

Mary looked at her quizzically. "Are you all right?" she asked as she scooped up the earrings and walked Edna to the door.

"Yes, yes, I'm okay," Edna said, clearing her throat. "I suffer from allergies. Well, I'll see you in a couple of weeks when the new catalog comes out."

"Okay," Mary said as she turned and locked the front door. "I'm sorry you didn't really get to practice . . ."

But Edna wasn't listening. She rushed to her car and fumbled with the keys. Her heart was pounding; she couldn't wait to get away from there. She happened to look up as she was placing the bag in the back seat and saw a black Camaro pull into the driveway. A woman stepped out, tall and slender with hair so blond it had to be a bottle job. The woman cast a quick look at Edna, and then seemed to do a double-take as she glanced over at her again.

Edna ignored her as she got in her car. Just before she pulled away, she noticed that Mary appeared rooted to the spot, and that her lips were drawn into a tight, angry line as she watched the blond-haired woman approach. Mary was probably upset at the amount of unexpected company this morning which was going to cause her to be very late for work.

Chapter Fifteen

Millie had just sat back down at the picnic table with a bag of popcorn when Edna pulled up. "It's about time," she yelled when Edna got out of the car. "Do you realize how long you've kept us waiting?"

"Shut up, Millie, and get in the car," Edna said, her voice barely audible. "Trish, you're going to have to drive." Edna walked around the car and got back in on the passenger side.

Millie was about to make a sharp retort when Trish shook her head and placed a hand on her arm. "Let's go," she said. Edna looked pale and drawn, barely able to stand. Something had happened. Quickly, they discarded their trash and got into the car.

"Did it work?" Millie asked eagerly.

"Your plan worked perfectly," Edna said, her voice still void of emotion, her hands clasped tightly in her lap. "We need to get out of here. Mary is on her way to work and she may pass this way."

Trish pulled away from the little store, her eye catching Millie's in the mirror. By unspoken consent, they remained silent, waiting for Edna to begin talking. And when she finally started, the story came out in a rush. Trish was shaken at the end, but she was relieved to notice that Edna appeared herself again.

There were tears in Millie's eyes and a stubborn set to her mouth. "Let's go tell Henry right now."

"Wait a minute," Trish said. "I think we should tell Larry first. He'll tell us what to do, and if Henry needs to be told now, then he can tell him."

"All right, Edna, give me your cell phone. I'm going to see if he can meet us now."

Edna reached in her purse. "Call Joe for me too. Tell him to meet us at Trish's house."

The story was related once again, this time with Edna's voice and composure back in place. Joe looked ready to explode, but he had too much dignity to tear into his wife in public. Trish didn't envy Edna's predicament, though. Tonight would not be fun at the Radcliffs' house.

"Now will you go arrest that woman?" Millie asked Larry pointedly.

"I can't just go arrest her," he said, placing his elbows on the table. "I will, however, go talk to her." He hesitated for a moment. "I hate to bring this up, but have any of you considered that the man she did a *job* for could have been Sam?"

"That's ridiculous!"

"How can you even think that?"

"You son . . ."

"Millie," Joe said sternly, "there's no need for that."

Millie snorted inelegantly. "We're doing everything

we can to do your job for you, Larry, and everything we uncover, you turn it around to try and prove Sam's guilt. I, for one, am sick and tired of it."

Larry rubbed his hand over his eyes. "We've been through this a million times, Millie. An investigator has to look at all the possibilities. I didn't say the man Mary Chavez was talking about *was* Sam. I merely asked if you had considered it. I can't afford to be blind-sided by the facts, and, in the end, I don't think you would want to be, either."

"Just keep your opinions to yourself then. You're in deep jeopardy of ruining our friendship."

Larry sighed. "I'll talk to Mary this week."

The next couple of days passed uneventfully. Trish had been able to get caught up on her bookkeeping and had even managed some deep cleaning on her house. Edna had worked on soothing Joe's feelings, and she and Joe had spent yesterday with their sons. Millie's grandchildren had come over and she'd grilled hamburgers. At least, Trish hoped it had been the grill shooting up all that smoke from Millie's backyard.

As peaceful as the days had been, it didn't ease any of their nerves. The phone lines burned up between them, hoping one or the other of them had heard something from Larry, or any news that would bring Sam's tragedy to an end. They were that sure that Mary Chavez had been involved in Susan's murder, and all that remained to officially close the case was her confession.

Millie was especially anxious for someone else to be charged with the crime—she couldn't wait to rub Henry's nose in it, or so she said.

It was on the third day that news finally came. Trish

was feeling so good about all she had accomplished that she decided to give her torture machine another try. She quickly changed into her exercise outfit—surely she wouldn't be interrupted this time—and poured a sports bottle full of water. Then she went and gently perched on the leather bench. Patting the cold, steel frame, she murmured softly in a sweet voice, "Now, we're going to be friends, aren't we? I promise not to overdo it this time and you promise not to kill me. Is that a deal?" She figured she may as well try a little psychology on the brainless contraption; her open antagonism toward the blasted thing sure hadn't gotten her anywhere.

She leaned back, locked her arms across the shoulder braces, and took a deep breath. Pressing forward with her arms, she felt the pull immediately, but it was manageable. She heard the click of the weights as they rose up while she pressed. Thrilled, Trish grinned and counted, "One . . ."

Then the unbelievable happened. The doorbell rang.

She released the shoulder braces and the weights fell with a loud clang. Frustrated beyond measure, Trish contemplated ignoring whoever was at the door. She didn't need superhuman powers to know it had to be either Millie or Edna. But if what they had to say was important, she would never forgive herself. That didn't mean she had to like it, though.

Marching angrily to the door, she swung it open. "Can't I get a minute's peace around here?" She shouted before she realized it wasn't one of her friends, after all. Larry Thompson stood on her front porch, staring at her as if she had lost her mind.

Trish winced and covered her mouth with her hand. "Oh, Larry, I'm so sorry. I thought you were Millie.

Come on in." She ushered him in, still apologizing, her face a bright red.

"You and Millie are that good of friends, are you?"

Trish chuckled as she sat across from him. "Actually, we are. She would have come back with a sharp retort and then marched on in. So, what can I do for you?"

Instantly, Larry sobered. He took a deep breath and leaned forward, placing his elbows on the table. "I was hoping I could get all three of you together, and Joe too."

Trish's eyebrows raised but she didn't say anything. This didn't sound like it was going to be good news. "Millie's daughter is still over at her house. Do you want me to call her?"

Larry thought for a moment and then shook his head. "No, you can fill her in later. What about Edna and Joe?"

"I'll call them," she said, reaching for the phone. After a few minutes she hung up and shook her head. "They're not home. Larry, is something wrong?"

Larry raked his fingers through his hair. Trish was getting worried. Something must be terribly wrong. "There's been . . . um, a development."

Oh no, she prayed silently, her heart sinking to her toes, *please don't let him say they've found more evidence against Sam.*

"Would you like something to drink?" Trish was stalling. She didn't want to hear whatever it was Larry had to say. It wasn't good, of that she was certain.

"No, I'm fine. Look, there's no easy way to say this. I went over to Mary Chavez house. I was going to question her, to threaten her with a search warrant if she couldn't explain the earrings." His gaze held hers firmly. "She's dead, Trish."

It took several seconds for Larry's words to register.

"What did you say?" she asked, her voice sounding weak even to her own ears.

"I'm afraid it's true. It looks like a suicide."

Trish jumped up from her chair and started pacing. "That's ridiculous!" Her mind was racing. Mary was dead? No, it didn't make sense. Edna hadn't said a word about Mary's being depressed or full of despair. And as sensitive as Edna was, she would surely have noticed. They had all seen her just a few nights ago, too. Mary had been friendly and smiling with them, and then when Sam had seen her she'd evidently still had enough passion to be angry about losing her job. Angry people didn't commit suicide, did they? No, the ones who killed themselves were people who decided they couldn't go on, were listless, felt hopeless . . . Trish leaned against the kitchen counter and buried her face in her hands. Here she was trying to rationalize a totally irrational behavior.

"When did Mary die?"

"I don't know for certain. The medical examiner will give us a pretty accurate time. A neighbor told me that her husband is a truck driver. We're trying to track him down now."

"Who is 'we'?"

"I was out of my jurisdiction. I called the San Antonio Police Department, and then I called Chief Espinoza. He wants to see all of you as soon as possible. He has a few questions." Larry's voice was flat and matter-of-fact.

"What did you tell Henry?"

"I told him the truth—or most of it. I only told him about you seeing Mary wearing the earrings."

Trish nodded, grateful he had left out the details of their snooping. "Why do you think it was a suicide?"

"There's a bullet hole in her head and a gun in her hand."

Trish glanced out her front window again and then resumed pacing. Was Michelle ever going to leave? Trish wanted desperately to tell Millie what had happened to Mary, but she wasn't about to march over there and blurt it out in front of Millie's daughter. She didn't even know how much Michelle knew about her mother's escapades. To add to her frustration, Edna still wasn't home, either. She had hit the redial button on her phone enough times to cause blisters to erupt.

Trish plopped down on the sofa where she had a clear view of Millie's house. She was half afraid that Henry would drive up wanting to talk to them. She had told Larry they would all go over to the station early tomorrow, but that might not satisfy Henry. He was going to want to know what their interest in Mary had been, why they believed she had a pair of Susan's earrings, and, for good measure, he'd probably yell at them some.

Movement across the street caught her attention. Michelle was giving Millie a hug on the front porch—finally! She waited until Michelle had driven off before she practically flew out her front door and started across the street. At the curb, she saw Edna and Joe turn onto the street and she waited until they pulled up alongside her.

"Hi," Edna called out as she rolled down her window. "Want to come over for some coffee?"

"Can you come with me for just a minute?"

Edna's eyebrows rose. "Where?"

"To Millie's. It's important." Joe looked at Trish a

moment, and then he nodded and backed up his car into Millie's driveway.

As soon as Millie let them in, Trish said, "I've got some horrible news."

"What is it?" Edna's eyes rounded as she looked at Trish with concern.

She proceeded to tell them what Larry had said. "I told him that we'd come by tomorrow to talk to Henry," she concluded. "They don't know exactly when it happened. The medical examiner is working on it. I guess they'll talk to her fellow employees at the restaurant to find out the last time she was at work. You may have been the last person to see her alive, Edna."

"Well, not the last person. Didn't I tell you? When I was leaving, a woman drove up," Edna said, and she briefly described the woman. "I don't think Mary was too happy to see her."

"I wonder who she was," Trish mused. "It might be helpful in establishing a time line. We'll tell Henry about her tomorrow."

Joe spoke for the first time. "I'll go with you. Sam's attorney may be interested in this latest development. Besides, if Henry decides to lock you three up, you'll need someone there to post bail."

"That's very funny, dear," Edna said, but she wasn't smiling.

Joe was the designated driver the next morning as they headed toward the police station. "When we finish here, I'll drop you ladies off and go see Sam. He needs to be told what has happened."

"That's good. I'll be over at Trish's if you need me for anything."

"Just remember," Millie said earnestly from the backseat, "we only answer Henry's questions with a 'yes' or a 'no.' Don't offer any information, and don't tell him everything we know."

Trish sighed in exasperation. "For goodness' sake, Millie, the whole reason we're going to see Henry is to discuss what we know about Mary. We'll have to tell him everything."

"No, we don't," she cried. "Henry hasn't offered to help us one bit, and now he wants us to give him all our evidence so he can take the credit. I say, no way!"

Joe coughed and quickly looked out the side window to hide his smile. *What evidence could these three think they had?*

Larry was waiting outside when they drove up, and he escorted them into a spacious room with a large oval table and comfortable chairs. A sideboard held coffee cups, sugar, and creamer. They provided all the comforts of home, Trish thought nervously as she sat down. The only one who looked perfectly at ease was Joe as he pulled out a chair for Edna, but then Joe always looked perfectly at ease.

When Larry left them to get coffee for everybody, Millie started circling the room, looking under the table, the chairs, and behind the wall pictures.

"What in the world are you doing?" Trish hissed.

"I'm looking for bugs. This is nothing but a fancy interrogation room. Stay on your toes, girls."

"Millie, please stop acting like we're guilty of something, and sit down," Edna said. "Henry is not our enemy."

"I'm not, unless you lie to me." Henry appeared suddenly in the doorway and closed the door behind him.

Millie sat down with a huff. "There's no need to lie when you don't even pick up on the truth."

Trish cringed. Millie was too far away to strangle, but Joe could slap her if he would just lean a little to the left. But Joe just sat there, his pursed lips the only sign he was not pleased with Millie's remark.

Henry seemed to take it all in stride as he said hello to everybody and sat down. He carried a notebook and pen and jotted something down, probably the address of the prison he would be sending them to if Millie didn't keep her mouth shut.

Larry came in, then, with a large thermos of coffee. "Please, everyone, just help yourself. I have to make a few phone calls, but I'll see you before you leave."

Joe raised his eyebrows at Edna, but she shook her head. "Nothing for me, thank you, I'm fine."

Millie pushed herself from the table and sauntered over to the sideboard. Trish closed her eyes for a moment and sighed. She could tell by Millie's demeanor that she was getting ready to say something they were all going to regret. She wasn't wrong. "Okay, Henry," Millie said as she poured a cup of coffee, "let's cut to the chase.

"I'm sure Larry has filled you in, and you know what we know. Whoever murdered Susan also murdered Mary Chavez. So why don't you drop the charges against Sam and go after the real killer?" Then she turned suddenly, in what she probably thought was a dramatic gesture, and leaned against the sideboard, narrowing her eyes at Henry over the rim of her cup.

Henry leaned back in his chair, tapping the end of his pen against the notebook. "Gee, Millie, why didn't I think of that?" he said sardonically, rolling his eyes. "Now, sit down, please."

Millie glared at Henry, but did as she was asked.

"Larry has already filled me in on most of the details, but I'd like to get the story directly from you. Please talk one at a time—Millie, you go last—and tell me about Mary Chavez. Don't leave out any details, regardless of how insignificant you think something is. Trish, you start."

Trish cleared her throat. *This was just terrific.* "Well, you already know we were going to try to find out who could have had a motive in setting up Sam for the murder of his wife. We decided to start with ex-employees. We got word that, when Sam sold his business, the new owner was bringing in his own bookkeeper, the position Mary had held while working for Sam. We also learned that she was not very good at her job and was extremely upset when she was let go. Actually, there were two employees who were downright angry, Mary and a man named Tom Jones. We haven't talked to him." At least that much was true. Henry didn't need to know that they knew where Tom lived, though.

She cleared her throat again before continuing, wishing she had gotten some coffee. "We found out where Mary was currently working, and we decided to pretend that we recognized her to gauge her reaction when we mentioned Sam. We never got that far, though, because Millie thought she recognized the earrings Mary was wearing as the same ones stolen from Sam's safe."

Henry was listening intently, jotting down copious notes off and on. "Go on."

"Well, we needed proof before we came to you . . ."

"So you were going to eventually tell me all this, huh?"

"Of course we were!"

"Of course you were," Henry sighed. "Go on."

"We developed a plan for Edna, who would be able to identify the earrings better than anyone, to get up close to Mary."

"And how was she going to do that?"

"She was going to pretend to be selling Avon." Henry cocked his eyebrows but didn't say anything. "And it worked. Edna was able to see the earrings close up, and they were definitely Susan's."

Henry looked over at Edna. "How can you be so sure?"

Edna straightened in her chair. "Sam had the earrings made special for Susan, but the telling sign was the clasp on the studs. Susan always had a problem with the clasps coming off her pierced earrings, so Sam had large, clear plastic ones made. That actually isn't so unusual, but Sam had them made extra-large, to make it easier for Susan to grip them. I know for a fact that the earrings Mary Chavez showed me that day belonged to Susan." When Edna finished, her voice was shaking, but her eyes were clear and determined.

"Did you tell Mary that you knew she had Mrs. Wiley's earrings?"

"Of course I didn't. All I could think of was getting out of there."

Henry sat quiet for a moment, nodding his head. "So that's the last any of you had anything to do with Mary? You didn't talk to her or follow her to work again?"

"No, but there was a woman who drove up just as I was leaving that day."

"Oh . . . Can you tell me about her?"

"I was so upset I didn't pay her much attention, but she was driving a black sports car. Mary must have known her because she seemed upset. I know she was running late for work."

Henry seemed interested in information about the other woman and made Edna describe her as best she could. It would be difficult to track her down with only Edna's vague description, though. They would have to rely on the coroner's report for a time of death.

"You forgot something, Edna," Millie said.

"What did I forget?"

"Mary told us the night we first met her at the restaurant that we wouldn't believe what she had to go through to get the earrings. Then, when Edna was talking to her, she said she had done a *job* for a man who paid her with the earrings," Millie said smugly. "Now are you going to drop the charges, Chief?"

"You're kidding, right?" Henry asked incredulity.

"I most certainly am not!"

"I'm trying to find out if the two cases are related. If they are, then I will have jurisdiction. If not, then the San Antonio Police Department will have the lead on Mary's case. Suicide or not, they'll investigate." Then he looked at each of them. "Regardless, I have to determine if it's possible that the man Mary mentioned could be Sam."

Chapter Sixteen

"What was it you said about Henry not being our enemy, Edna?" Millie was still fuming from their visit with Henry.

Edna sighed. "He's not, Millie. I believe he honestly thinks he's just doing his job."

Joe had dropped them off at Trish's a short while ago so he could go talk to Sam. He wasn't going to tell him everything that Chief Espinoza had said, though. Trish had been quiet during the drive, lost in her own thoughts, while Millie had sputtered and raged and Edna had sat miserably, almost in tears at the thought that they could have just made things worse for Sam. Joe had remained silent as well, but the telltale sign of red splotches across his cheeks revealed his anger.

Now, sitting at the dining table, Trish sipped her coffee. Something wasn't right. Henry wasn't just being obstinate, she was sure of it. No, there was a reason he was so doggedly convinced that Sam had murdered his wife and then later staged the break-in. It was a sure bet, also, that he wasn't going to tell them what that reason was.

And then there were the questions surrounding Mary's suicide. It was all just a little too coincidental to be a random act, but what was the connection? There had to be one, other than the scenario Henry had suggested. And it was highly doubtful now that he would share the information he received from the coroner after the names Millie had called him before storming out of his office earlier. Now they might never know why Mary had taken her own life, but the reason could be important in proving Sam's innocence. Of course, there was the chance, a really good chance, that whatever the reason was, it could slice both ways: Sam could end up looking even guiltier than before.

"I wonder if Larry will tell us what the official findings are concerning Mary's suicide," Trish said out loud. "I don't think we'll be hearing anything more from Henry." Her pointed look at Millie went unnoticed.

"That poor girl," Edna said. "I still can't believe it. Why in the world would Mary commit suicide?"

"She didn't." All eyes turned to Millie as she stood abruptly and started pacing the kitchen floor. "Did you ever tell Larry about seeing Mary at Tom's, Trish?"

"No, and I feel guilty as all get-out. I was so shocked when he told me about Mary that I couldn't even think straight."

"I think it's a good thing that you didn't."

"Why?" Edna asked. "We're going to have to tell him sometime."

"We're not without something that will tie Tom to both Susan's and Mary's murders."

"Millie, you have no proof whatsoever that Tom Jones is involved in either death! You can't just go around accusing somebody like that. And what makes you so sure that Mary didn't kill herself?"

"Think, Edna! Mary was a fighter. Just look at her reaction to Sam! We know her anger at him was unjustified but *she* didn't think so. If she was despondent, she wouldn't have wasted her energy being so publicly rude to him. If Mary was in on Susan's murder, then she may have threatened Tom and he decided to get rid of her. Or maybe she found out about it and then threatened him. Either way, Tom is definitely responsible for both women's deaths. I'd bet my house on it."

"Oh, I don't know . . ."

"Wait a minute," Trish said. "As much as it surprises me to say this, Millie may have a point."

"Gee, thanks," Millie said, rolling her eyes. "Of course I have a point! It's the only thing that makes sense."

"I don't know if murder ever makes sense, but if there is some common link between these incidents, it must be through Tom."

"How are we going to get anybody to listen to us, though? We're not exactly overwhelmed with support right now," Edna pointed out.

Millie stopped pacing. "We're going to have to find the proof ourselves."

Trish and Edna looked at each other and then at Millie. "What did you say?" they asked in unison.

"First, we need to find out what kind of relationship Tom and Mary had, and we need something to prove that connection. I think that would be very interesting information for the police to have. And I mean the San Antonio Police. Forget Henry—he's too stubborn."

Trish almost laughed. *Henry's too stubborn?*

Millie caught Trish's look but chose to ignore it. "It might make them suspicious since Mary was married. At the very least, they would probably question Tom. Who knows? He may get nervous and let something slip."

After a moment, Trish nodded. "You may be on to something, Millie. But how do you propose we go about proving it?"

She wished she hadn't asked.

"I don't like this at all. If Joe finds out, he is going to kill me."

"Do you think if you say that one more time we'll take you more seriously?" Millie hissed. "We told you to stay at home and we'd take care of this part."

"I couldn't let you do this by yourselves! What if something goes wrong and you need help?" Edna replied indignantly.

"Then hush up about it! You're making me nervous."

Trish wished they would both hush. This was one of the most hare-brained plans Millie had ever come up with. That she and Edna had gone along with it didn't say much for their brains, either. But they were desperate for answers, and if they didn't gather some proof then someone was going to get away with two murders. Still, the plan was dangerous . . . and downright stupid.

Once again, they were sitting in Trish's car watching Tom Jones' mobile home. Only this time they weren't waiting for him to leave so they could follow him; instead, they were hoping he would leave so that they could get inside. They each had a flashlight and were dressed in dark clothes to blend in with the approaching nightfall. Millie also wore a fanny-pack loaded with a screwdriver, a chisel, and two pairs of Playtex gloves. Trish wasn't about to ask Millie which television shows she regularly watched. She didn't want to know.

The mobile home park was even spookier at night, and felt unnaturally quiet for an early Saturday evening. Nobody was outside tending gardens or visiting with neighbors, walking dogs or sitting on porches—the usual things you would see in a neighborhood on a calm, clear evening. Some lights were visible in a few mobile homes, but more of them were completely dark. Trish shivered in spite of the warm night. This was not a place she would choose to live.

From their vantage point, they could see two shaded lights in Tom's windows, one in the main part of the trailer and one toward the rear, probably a bathroom. The same old pickup sat in the driveway, so they were fairly certain he was at home.

They hadn't discussed just how long they would wait to see if Tom would leave. Trish was ready to go five minutes after they had parked, but she hadn't said anything to her friends. Still, she figured they couldn't wait too long because Joe assumed Edna was just out for a short time with her friends.

Trish hated lying, especially to such a good man, but Edna had been adamant. She had intentionally left her cell phone at home and would explain that this had been a last-minute idea. And then she promised she would tell Joe everything once she got home. Her argument was that they couldn't afford Joe's common sense right now; they had a murderer to catch. Trish could kick herself. How could she have thought that crazy argument had made sense?

Suddenly, there was movement at Tom's trailer. The

door opened, splaying a hazy beam of light out onto the yard. Instinctively, the three women ducked. "This may be it," Millie whispered.

"Part of me hopes so, and part of me hopes he's just taking out the trash or something," Edna replied. "Maybe we should go back home and talk about this some more."

"Stop being such a coward, Edna," Millie chided. "We already talked this to death. It's time for action!"

"I think he's coming out," Trish whispered, peering over the top of the steering wheel.

Edna moaned and sank down further in the back seat. "I think I'm going to be sick."

"You're such a wimp," Millie muttered.

Trish threw Millie a sidelong glance. "Take it easy on her, Millie. You and I don't have anyone to answer to. Even if we live through this episode, it's still possible Edna will be killed if Joe finds out about it. Have some mercy, for goodness' sake."

"Oh, that's right," Millie grinned. "Sorry, Edna. By the way, what are your favorite flowers?"

"You two are so funny," Edna said indignantly. "I'm seriously thinking of disowning you both when this is over. If it wasn't for Sam, I'd do it now."

Trish caught Millie's eye and winked. Edna was much better off being irritated than crippled with fear.

"What's happening now?" Millie asked.

"Nothing, yet. Wait a minute . . . I think he's coming out!" The light shifted slightly in front of Tom's trailer as the front door opened. Tom Jones stepped out, then turned to lock the door.

"I think he's leaving," Trish breathed, her heartbeat picking up time considerably.

"Edna, you remember to get in the driver's seat and

stay in the car, regardless of whatever happens. If we need to get out of here in a hurry, you're going to be the getaway driver."

"I remember the plan, Millie," Edna snapped. "Just hurry up and get it over with."

Tom Jones sauntered over to his truck. Suddenly, headlights appeared through their back window. "Get down," Trish said. "Get down!"

A moment later they heard a car slowing as it passed by them, and then all was quiet again. "Did we miss Tom? Did he leave?" Millie asked.

Trish raised herself up enough to see over the dashboard. "No, he hasn't left yet . . . Oh, shoot!"

"What is it?" Millie and Edna asked simultaneously.

"The car that just went by stopped at Tom's. He's walking over to it."

"Well, he wasn't expecting anyone or he wouldn't be leaving. Probably it's somebody just asking directions," Millie said.

"Maybe. He's leaning down now at the driver's window."

After a long silence, Edna whispered, "What's he doing now?"

"He's still leaning down at the driver's window." Trish felt like a commentator at a sports event relaying play-by-play action. "Now he's . . . Wait. He's jabbing his finger at the driver. He looks angry."

"Remind me never to ask him for directions," Millie grumbled.

"Now he's laughing," Trish said, her voice puzzled. "This guy is strange."

"He could have a mental problem," Edna said. "Everyone we've talked to has said that Tom has a bad temper."

"And you came to that conclusion because Trish said he was *laughing?*"

"It could explain the mood swings, you old bat." Edna was clearly miffed.

"Hush! The driver is getting out of the car. No . . . Oh my goodness, Tom is kicking the driver's door! Edna may be right, Millie."

The dark shadows made it impossible to see Tom's face clearly. Trish wished they were closer, so that they could hear what was being said, but her instincts told her they had better get out of there. If one of the neighbors called the police, there was a chance they would be discovered watching Tom. He must not be worried about the police, though. He appeared to be yelling, his arms flailing wildly as he continued to kick at the car. If this wasn't evidence of some kind of emotional breakdown, she didn't know what was.

"I think we need to leave," she said quietly. "I'm afraid to start the car right now, though. He'll hear it and know someone has seen him."

"No, we need to stay," Millie said. "What if he ends up killing the driver? We could be witnesses. We could catch him red-handed!"

Edna sat up slowly. "Would you please stop talking about murder?" Then she leaned forward, peered through the window and gasped. "That's the car that was at Mary's!"

Millie sat up. "What are you talking about?"

"That car, the day I went to see Mary—that's the same car that drove up when I was leaving!"

Millie and Trish looked at each other and then at Edna. "Are you sure?" Trish asked.

"I'm positive," Edna said, her eyes wide as she raised

a trembling hand to her mouth. "It's the same black Camaro. Is a woman driving it?"

Trish shook her head. "I don't know. I haven't seen the driver."

Millie looked at Trish. "Why would that same car be at Tom's?"

Slowly, all three women shifted their gaze to look out the window. Why, indeed?

Suddenly, the reverse lights came on and the car started backing up. Then, with a squeal of tires, the car shot forward down the street. Trish nervously tapped her fingernails on the dashboard. "Well, that's just great. What do we do now?"

Millie bit her bottom lip. "Follow the car—hurry!"

"What about Tom?" Edna exclaimed.

"We know where Tom lives, so we can come back. But we need to find out who the driver of that car is. This may be our only chance. Put the pedal to the metal, Trish!"

Without thinking, something that was becoming a habit when she was with Millie, Trish turned the key in the ignition. Tom was standing in the same place with his hands on his hips, staring after the car, but at the sound of Trish's car starting, he glanced over at them. There was no choice, so they sped right past him.

"He saw us!" Edna shouted.

"He saw a car, Edna. He didn't see us," Trish said, more to reassure herself than Edna. She prayed she was right. When they turned the corner, they were just in time to see the black car exiting the mobile home park.

"It's turning right, Trish—hurry!"

"I'm going as fast as I can!" Trish snapped. "You can drive if you think you can do any better."

"Pull over, then!"

"Oh, please, no," Edna begged.

"It was a rhetorical statement, Millie. You aren't driving."

"We'll probably lose the car, then," Millie huffed. "We may as well go for coffee somewhere."

Trish gritted her teeth. One of these days . . .

When they reached the exit, Trish turned right, the taillights of the Camaro barely visible up ahead. She *put the pedal to the metal* and hoped the police weren't in this area at the moment. By now, night had completely fallen. Bright, colorful lights from the neighborhood stores lining both sides of the street were a distraction, but Trish was able to keep herself focused on the car in front of them, and she was fast gaining on it.

"Millie, look in the glove compartment and pull out that pad. I want to get close enough to get the numbers off the car tag and then we'll fall back."

"All right, that's a good idea." Eagerly, Millie did as she was asked and sat poised over the notepad like a secretary awaiting dictation.

Trish sped up even more, her hands locked on the steering wheel in a death grip.

"We're getting dirty looks from some of the people in the cars we're passing," Edna said.

"What do we care?" Millie asked. "We'll never see them again, anyway."

"We won't unless we hit one of them," Edna said wryly, sinking down low in the seat. *That's exactly what I'm worried about,* Trish thought and concentrated on the traffic. When she was close enough to the car to read the numbers, she called them out to Millie and then fell several car lengths behind. Only then did she take a deep breath and relax. They might live through this, after all.

It was impossible to see who was driving the car, but if it was the woman Edna had seen at Mary's, what could it mean? Could she be a mutual friend of both Mary and Tom? That was probably the answer, but then why had there been all the anger at Tom's house? If the woman had been there to relay the news about Mary's death, surely Tom wouldn't have reacted that way. This might very well be a wild goose chase with a perfectly innocent explanation, but, somehow, Trish didn't think so.

She was brought out of her musings when the car ahead suddenly turned left.

"Don't lose it!" Millie exclaimed.

"I'm not going to, but don't yell like that again. You'll cause me to have a wreck!"

Trish slowed and followed, noticing with dismay that there were no other cars between her and the black Camaro. A few yards up, the car turned again, and again Trish followed. The next turn brought them back to the main street. Puzzled, Trish wondered where they were going. Then, as soon as there was a break in traffic, the black car made a U-turn in the middle of the road—and Trish understood.

They had been spotted.

Trish paced the floor in her kitchen. She had dropped Edna and Millie off a little while before, and she was trying to unwind after the unsettling events of the evening, but a sense of impending doom loomed over her, and she couldn't shake it. She spotted her exercise machine out of the corner of her eye and resolutely turned her back on it without a qualm. Exercise was definitely out of the question.

Common sense told her it was perfectly understandable she would feel spooked right now. Tom Jones had seen them, or at least their car, and the driver of the black Camaro had seen them too. If either of these people had killed Susan Wiley, would they hesitate to kill again? And just where did Mary Chavez fit into all this? The questions swirled in Trish's mind, but they were no closer to finding an answer than when they had decided to prove Sam's innocence themselves.

She walked to the living room and peered outside. Everything appeared normal. Millie didn't have the sense to be frightened, and Edna felt secure with Joe. Trish hadn't voiced her fears aloud, of course, but she felt responsible for the safety of all of them.

She gave a deep sigh, checked all the locks on the doors, and went to bed. She wouldn't be getting much sleep tonight.

She was wrong. As soon as her head hit the pillow, she was out. It was sometime later that she was awakened by the ringing of the phone. Instantly awake, she grabbed the phone, her heart in her throat. "Hello?"

"I told you! I was right—I told you so!" Millie's singsong voice rang out with glee.

Trish rubbed her eyes. "What are you talking about? What time is it, anyway?"

"It's morning, and I'm talking about Mary Chavez. I just saw a small blurb on the news. Mary didn't kill herself. She was murdered!"

Chapter Seventeen

"This is serious, Trish." Millie was on her second cup of coffee and had repeated the same sentence for the third time now.

Finally! Trish wasn't sure that jumping for joy would be appropriate, but, nevertheless, she was thrilled Millie finally understood what a serious situation this was. Playing detective definitely had some bright spots, and she felt that some of their clues would be instrumental in closing out the case, but now it was time to let the real pros take over. It would even be nice to let Millie be the one to call Chief Espinoza, to tell him everything they knew, and then maybe they could all go do something that old women normally did.

"Tom Jones must realize we're on his trail, but he probably doesn't know exactly how much we actually suspect. We've got to be very careful. We can't afford to make any mistakes that could make him go underground."

Millie got up from the table to get yet another cup of coffee. "We still don't have any hard evidence."

Trish blinked, visions of shopping and dining out fleeing from her mind. "Are you crazy?"

"Well, that depends on who you ask." Millie smiled impishly. "Now, I called Michelle early this morning and gave her the tag numbers from the car. Since she works for an insurance company, she'll be able to tell us who the car is registered to. I told her to call me over here." She sat back down and looked at her watch. "Edna will be here soon. Get me some paper and a pen, will you?" Practically licking her chops, Millie rubbed her hands together. "We're getting close, I can feel it!"

"Stop it, Millie!" Trish demanded, her eyes almost popping out of her head. "Stop it right now, or I'm going to have you committed. Do you realize what you're saying? There have been two murders—two! This is out of our hands now. We're done . . . finished . . . kaput . . . the end! Do you understand?" Trish's voice had risen and her hands were clenched tightly on the table. She *had* to make Millie stop this now, and, if it came right down to it, she'd physically sit on top of her to keep the old coot safe.

"I understand that you're quitting right when we're about to solve Susan's murder." Millie's voice had risen a few octaves too. "And here I thought Edna was the wimp," she added, sticking her nose in the air.

"Why, you—"

"What's going on in here?" Edna asked from the doorway, a worried frown on her face. "I knocked, but nobody heard me. I can't imagine why, with all the yelling going on. Anyone care to fill me in?"

"Millie's crazy."

"Trish is a wimp."

Edna held up a hand, a smile pulling at her lips. "Slow down, please. I've known you both a long time now. Trish is definitely not a wimp, and Millie, there *are* times that you're not crazy. What's this all about?"

Millie huffed and sat with her arms crossed while Trish explained to Edna what had caused the disagreement.

"Well," Edna began, and then sat down, clearing her throat, "well, I guess I can understand both your opinions."

"What do you mean?" Trish asked incredulously. Millie looked over at her with a smug expression and smiled.

"Well," Edna hesitated. She swallowed, her gaze focused on her fingers twisting nervously on the table, and then swallowed again. "It's just that Joe and I talked to Sam last night on the telephone—just about things in general, you know, and to see how he was doing. He just sounded so . . . dejected. It broke my heart," Edna took a deep breath and looked up. "I think the enormity of everything that has happened is really sinking in, and he's feeling helpless and alone. I'm worried he may fall into a state of depression that he can't pull himself out of."

The room was silent for a while. "That's the main reason we need to let the police do their job," Trish said, but her tone lacked conviction, even to herself.

"No, that's the main reason we need to speed things up and solve this ourselves," Millie said in a quiet, firm voice. She held up a hand when Trish started to interrupt. "Look, despite what everyone thinks, I'm not crazy and I'm not stupid. Sure, there's a chance that justice will ultimately prevail and the real killer will be discovered, but how long is that going to take? Since the police believe Sam is guilty, they're not seriously looking at anybody else. So, what happens to Sam in the meantime? This is a good, decent man we're talking about, one who just lost the love of his life." Millie's voice was slightly shaking now. "But if we do anything further, we have to do it together or not at all. I vote we continue our investigation, find out who the monster is who could have done this, and free Sam to go through the grieving process and then move on with his life."

Edna reached over and squeezed Millie's hand. "Count me in," she said quietly. Then they both looked at Trish.

She swallowed past the lump in her throat and gave a weak smile. "What? You're acting like I have a choice in the matter."

Millie grinned and then got up to give Trish a big hug. "That's my girl! And, by the way, I never thought you were a wimp. I just wanted to get under your skin."

Just then the phone rang. "That's probably Michelle," Millie said and hurried to answer it.

Of course, Trish thought to herself, shaking her head wryly, *I never get any phone calls here at my own home.* But Millie was right; it was her daughter. She wrote something down on the pad by the phone, her eyes wide in apparent wonder at something Michelle was saying. Trish quickly explained to Edna why Michelle was calling. They could only hear one side of the conversation, but by Millie's comments—"Are you positive? . . . That's fantastic! . . . Do you have an address?"—the information Michelle was relaying was obviously important.

A minute later, Millie hung up the phone and sat back down. Excitement was almost exploding from her very pores. "You're not going to believe this! Guess who the car is registered to."

"Who?" Trish and Edna replied in unison.

"It's registered to . . . Clarissa Jones!"

For a moment, Trish and Edna both had blank expressions on their face. Then a chill started to spread down Trish's back. "Tom Jones' wife."

"Well, she's his ex-wife, to be exact," Millie said, a satisfied smile on her face. "I've got her address too."

"What was Tom Jones' wife doing at Mary's?" Edna asked.

"I don't know, but we're going to find out," Millie said and rose from her chair. "I'm going to go lock up my house and change shoes. I'll be back in a minute." She was gone before anyone could say anything more.

"I guess that means we're going somewhere," Edna said, her lips twitching in amusement.

Trish let out a sigh and nodded. "Well, at least one statement Millie made is true."

"What's that?"

"She's not stupid."

"It doesn't look like anybody's home," Trish said, slowly driving by the tan stucco townhouse. Amazingly, they had found Clarissa Jones' house without any trouble. They were either getting better at directions or they were just plain lucky. No, they were definitely getting better, Trish thought smugly as she pulled up a few houses away and parked. "Now what do we do?"

"We wait."

"And how long do you propose we wait, Millie?" Trish asked, keeping the impatience from her voice with effort. She knew they were all tense, wanting to find solid answers, and she wasn't in the mood for another squabble. "It's mid-morning. Clarissa could be working, or out shopping. It's broad daylight, and I'm not particularly comfortable sitting out here where everybody and their dog can see us."

"Trish has a point, Millie. We don't want to be too obvious. Now that we know where the house is, we can come back anytime."

With one last look at the house, Millie sighed loudly and turned around. "Okay, let's go. We've got to do something, though."

Trish knew she was going to regret her next comment, but since they had all agreed they were going to finish this to the end, they might as well get aggressive—or really, really stupid—in their tactics. "We need to go back to Tom's."

Millie thought for a moment. She turned slowly then, and looked at Trish with raised eyebrows. "That's a great idea, if I do say so, myself."

"I don't think we should go now, though," Trish said. "It'd be the same problem with the daylight."

"Why do we need to go back to Tom's?" Edna asked. "We know that Clarissa went to Mary's house, but we're still just guessing about Tom's involvement."

"I'd bet my bottom dollar that Clarissa and Tom are in this together," Millie said, her face set in tight lines. "Probably like Bonnie and Clyde, they think they can get away with anything. But they're wrong. They've got us on their tail, and we're going to prove they're guilty."

And I'll bet they're just shaking in their boots, Trish thought.

Trish peered over the dashboard and saw Tom get into his truck. When his taillights disappeared around the corner she looked at her companions seriously. "Are you both absolutely positive that you want to do this?" The day had dragged by as they had waited impatiently for the darkness of night to fall. Then, with nerves stretched to the snapping point, they had driven to Tom's, parked a few houses away from his trailer, and waited for some kind of movement.

"I'm sure," Millie said emphatically.

After a moment Edna nodded. "I'm sure."

Trish took a deep breath. "Okay, I'm going to pull the car a little closer. Millie, we've got to act fast. For all we know, Tom may have just gone to the store for a gallon of milk or something. Edna, you stay in the car and if you see Tom coming back, you honk the horn twice and then drive to the entrance of the mobile-home park and wait."

"Okay, I've got it," Edna said.

Millie reached over and patted Edna's hand. "Don't worry. Remember, if anything goes wrong, we'll meet you at the entrance. Don't wait more than ten minutes, though. If we don't show up, you drive up the road to that Laundromat we passed on the main street and call Joe immediately."

Edna sighed deeply. "I know, I know. Just please be careful, and please, please hurry."

Trish looked at Millie. "Are you ready?"

"Let's roll!" Millie replied, tightening the dark scarf she wore over her hair. Trish normally would have laughed at Millie's bravado, but right now she was too frightened to do more than roll her eyes. What they were going to do was dangerous and illegal. It was also necessary.

Trish pulled the car up in front of the trailer right next to Tom's. Without a word, she and Millie got out of the car, and Edna got into the front seat. The sky was dark with slowly moving clouds covering the moon. There wasn't a street light or a porch light to help guide the way as Trish and Millie walked hand in hand toward Tom's trailer. Millie wasn't quite as unaffected by their adventure as she pretended, Trish thought with sympathy as she felt the slight tremor in Millie's hand.

The lights were still on inside Tom's trailer, and for the first time Trish wondered if someone else might live there. She whispered her thoughts aloud to Millie who only shrugged and said, "There's only one way to find out." Walking up to the door, she pounded on it hard.

Trish gasped and jumped three feet in the air. What was Millie thinking? What in the world would they say if somebody came to the door? She really wished Millie would start thinking things through before she acted so impulsively.

After a few seconds, Millie casually sauntered away from the door and started peering in the windows. "Nobody's here," she whispered loudly as she opened her fanny pack and pulled out the bright yellow gloves. "Put these on," she said, throwing a pair to Trish. Next she pulled out a screwdriver and started feeling around the window frames. "Maybe one of these windows is open and we can crawl through."

Trish wasn't crazy about crawling through a window. With their luck, one of them would get stuck just as Tom came home. If only he had been careless enough to leave a door open. Just for the heck of it, she reached for the front door knob. To her utter surprise, it turned easily. "Millie, the front door is open," she whispered loudly.

"Now that's what I call luck!" Millie said, scrambling back to the door.

"Maybe it's not so lucky. It could mean Tom won't be gone for long."

"You've got a point. We'd better hurry." Millie pushed the door open and walked right in. Trish forced herself not to look over her shoulder as she followed. Hopefully, if anybody was looking, they wouldn't draw any unnecessary attention. Oh yeah, there was a fat chance of that, she thought, considering the bright, colorful gloves.

They were immediately assaulted by the stench of stale tobacco and greasy food. They were in the main living area of the trailer. Against the far wall was a beige leather sofa, an end table, and an old, beat-up coffee table. Closer to the door was a recliner and another end table facing a television. A lamp without a shade stood on the table, and there was clutter everywhere, old newspapers on the sofa and the floor, overflowing ashtrays on the coffee table and end table. Trish noticed there were paper bags of just about every known fast food joint thrown carelessly around the room.

There was no personality in the room, no pictures, no memorable knickknacks, nothing but trash. Trish shuddered. Who could live in such filth? She knew Millie had brought the gloves to protect against fingerprints, but she was thinking they might very well protect against disease, as well. Bless Millie and her thoughtfulness.

Trying not to breathe too deeply, she saw that Millie was carefully looking through the mess around the sofa with one hand while the other one covered her mouth and nose. Trish sighed and looked around. They weren't sure what they were looking for, just anything suspicious, anything that would explain the situation between Tom and his ex-wife, anything they could use to start putting together all the different pieces.

Stepping over a pile of newspapers, Trish started flipping through a pile of unopened mail on the end table by the recliner. It looked like a lot of notices from bill collectors. Well, you would hardly think that someone with plenty of money would live like this. She replaced the mail on the table and looked around. Millie could probably cover this room by herself, so the smartest thing to do would be to split up.

One peek in the small bathroom made her quickly come to the conclusion that nothing would be hidden there. And, if it was, it could stay hidden. Fighting a wave of nausea, she moved on down the hall. The next room was made only slightly more bearable by the open window. A light breeze ruffled the faded curtains, a welcome reminder to Trish that fresh air was only a few steps away.

Evidently, this room served as both the master bedroom and the dirty-clothes hamper. Disgusted, she walked gingerly through the mess, but she was fast becoming dejected. Even if anything was here, it was going to be impossible to find it. A bulldozer would be the only efficient answer.

She took a deep breath and held it as she bent down to look under the bed. At that same instant, Millie came running into the room. "Trish!"

Startled, Trish raised up, banging her head painfully on the bed frame. "Ow!"

"Hush! I think I heard Edna honk the horn a few min-utes ago, and I just saw headlights from the window!"

Trish's jaw dropped. "What do you mean . . . *'a few minutes ago'*?"

"Give or take a minute or two. We need to get out of here," Millie whispered and closed the door.

"Why didn't you call out to me?" Trish was looking around wildly, trying to find some means of escape. This was not good, not good at all.

"I was busy! Now stop complaining, and let's find a way out of here. We can't go out the front door," she said unnecessarily.

Trish looked over at the open window and grimaced. So much for luck. "Okay, our only chance is the window. Millie, pull that old card table chair over here—hurry!" Trish went to the window and opened the drapes fully. Just as she had hoped, the screen was old and not secured by any security measures. She pushed hard and it flopped onto the open ground. "Okay, I'm going first so I can help you on the other side. I'm warning you, though," she said, pulling herself up and over the ledge, "if you find any reason to stall, I'm leaving your butt here. This is no time for games or heroics."

Just then, they heard the front door open. Millie was jumping nervously from one foot to the other. "Just hurry, for goodness' sake!"

Trish landed on the ground with a thud. It was further down than she had anticipated, but it was still manage-able. Millie's head poked through the opening. "No," she whispered loudly, "Come out legs-first! I can't catch you if you take a dive head-first."

"Oh." Millie's head ducked back in and then one leg jutted out. Soon, she was sitting on the ledge. "Are you ready?" It was a pointless question, because Millie jumped at the same instant she uttered it. It wasn't quite what Trish had in mind. She hadn't planned on actually catching her friend; she'd intended to help her crawl down. Instead, all she managed to do was break Millie's fall with her body as they both tumbled to the ground, arms and legs akimbo.

"Are you okay?' Trish asked breathlessly. The thought of Millie breaking an arm, or a leg, or worse, had Trish worried.

"I'm fine. Now, get off me so we can get out of here!"

Trish's eyes widened, and she held a finger to her lips. She thought she had just heard Tom's bedroom door open. Gesturing frantically with her hand, she motioned for Millie to follow her. They scrambled over to the next door neighbor's trailer and ducked behind it a second before a stream of obscenities flew out Tom's open window. Trish saw Millie purse her lips in disapproval, and she prayed fervently that Millie wasn't about to march over there and give Tom a piece of her mind. The mud sticking to her hair just might give them away.

But then the cursing stopped, followed by only low muttering, and then the sound of his voice died out altogether. Her relief was short-lived as it suddenly dawned on Trish that Tom might be coming outside to replace his screen. Grabbing Millie's hand, they made a mad dash through the mobile-home park—well, as mad a dash as two older women could make—ducking between trailers and keeping an eye out for anyone following them. It seemed that all they left behind, though, was a wave of barking dogs.

What seemed like an eternity later, they saw Edna sitting in the car at the entrance of the mobile home park, just as she had been instructed to do. "Let's go," Trish said breathlessly as she practically pushed Millie into the car and then fell in after her.

Edna looked at them in shock. "What . . ."

"We'll tell you in a minute. Just get out of here!"

Edna snapped her mouth closed and put the car in gear. When they were a few miles away, Trish took a deep breath of relief and settled down in her seat. That was when she heard the giggling coming from the tiny woman beside her—actual giggling! In disbelief, she turned to Millie. Maybe she had gone into shock or something. Should she slap her, or throw cold water on her? What were you supposed to do when someone went into shock?

"Either someone tells me what happened back there, or I'm going to stop this car in the middle of the road," Edna snapped. "You both look like you just went mud wrestling."

Trish looked at both herself and Millie, and then she just couldn't help it. She started giggling too, and then outright laughing. It wasn't fair to Edna, she knew, but when you looked at the situation she and Millie had just been in from a distance, it really was quite funny.

"The main thing, Edna," she said between chuckles, "is that it was a complete waste of time."

"Actually, that's not necessarily the case," Millie said, sitting up and reaching into her fanny pack. She opened her hand for all to see. One of Mary's earrings, previously stolen from Sam after Susan's murder, lay nestled in her open palm.

Chapter Eighteen

Edna kept glancing over her shoulder at the earring in Millie's hand, her eyes wide and her mouth open in a silent gasp. Trish could excuse the first time the car swerved, maybe even the second time, but when it happened a third time, she figured they weren't going to do anybody any good dead. "For goodness' sake, Edna, pull over now! You're going to get us all killed."

"Oh . . . oh, yes, okay." Taking the directive literally, Edna crossed two lanes of traffic and pulled into a convenience store.

Trish sent up a silent prayer of thanks and then turned to Millie. "Where did you find that?"

"It was in Tom's den. That's why I almost didn't hear Edna honking. I was looking for the other one."

"That directly ties Tom to Mary's murder, doesn't it?" Edna asked.

"I would think so. But does it tie him to Susan's murder?" Trish shuddered, thinking how close they had come to being discovered by Tom in his own house.

"That's not the only thing I found," Millie boasted. She dropped the earring into Trish's hand and reached back into her fanny pack. "This is strange, though. I'm not sure what it means."

"What is it?" Trish asked, slightly in awe at what Millie had accomplished that night.

Millie unfolded a crumpled piece of yellow notebook paper. "It's some kind of list. It was tossed in a corner with some other trash." She peered at the writing. "Turn on the light, Edna."

"Don't tell me you found a list Tom made detailing the steps to murder?"

"Very funny, Trish," Millie said absently, and then she began to read. *"Wife! . . . Children! . . . House! . . . Job! . . . Reputation!* These are all written in large letters with exclamation points beside them and underlined. Then, at the bottom of the page, he's written the word *'REVENGE!!!!'* in all capital letters with four exclamation points, and then, in small handwriting, he's written *'problems are meant to be solved.'* This is pretty strange, huh?"

"It's very strange," Edna agreed.

Trish tried to put her racing thoughts in order. "Maybe it's actually not that strange."

When Edna and Millie looked at her, she tried to explain. "What if the top part of the list refers to things he's lost? He could blame Sam for all of that. So to get back at him, he kills Susan."

Millie nodded slowly. "We always thought someone was trying to frame Sam."

Edna tilted her head. "So, you think the word 're-venge' refers to Susan?"

Trish shook her head. "It could, but I doubt it. What if it refers to Mary?"

Millie snapped her fingers. "Of course, that's what it's got to mean! Mary knew that Tom had killed Susan, so she must have been blackmailing him to get the earrings!"

Edna frowned. "It still doesn't explain why Tom's ex-wife was at Mary's house."

"It was pure jealousy," Millie said. "Clarissa Jones thought Tom bought the earrings for his new girlfriend. She went over there to confront Mary, to warn her to stay away from her man."

Trish shuddered. "I can't see any woman wanting to claim Tom Jones as *her man,* but there's no accounting for taste." Then, a thought occurred to her. "What if Clarissa knows he killed Mary?"

"How would she know that?" Edna asked.

Trish leaned her head back, thinking of different scenarios. "I don't know, but it could explain why she was at Tom's house that day arguing with him."

Millie put her treasures back in her fanny pack and zipped it shut. "There's only one way to find out."

"What's that?" Trish and Edna asked in unison.

"We need to talk to Clarissa Jones."

"We absolutely do not!" Edna exclaimed. "We have to tell Henry."

Millie snorted. "Yeah, right, so he can tell us to go jump in a lake?"

Trish sighed and twisted her neck from side to side to ease the sudden tension. "So far, we can't prove anything. Millie's right, Edna. We need to find out what

Clarissa knows. And, more importantly, we need to find a way to get that one earring and the list back into Tom's home."

Millie jerked upright. "Wait a minute. I never said anything about going back to Tom's."

Trish turned her head to look at her. "Sorry, we don't have a choice. We got that evidence illegally. It will be worthless unless the police find it themselves."

"You're right," Millie agreed soberly. "But this time I'm wearing a haz-mat suit."

Trish laughed. "Get one for me too. Have you ever seen such a mess as Tom's house?"

Millie grimaced. "Never—I'll be surprised if we don't come down with some awful disease. By the way, how are you going to explain all this to Joe, Edna?"

"I don't want to talk about it," Edna said primly, and then put the car in gear. "And, Millie, you'd better keep your trap shut until I do." Millie grinned wickedly, but thankfully *kept her trap shut!*

The next morning dawned bright and clear, with a soft, warm breeze fluttering the air. It was unimaginable that she and her friends were investigating a cruel act of murder on such a beautiful day, Trish thought, vowing to never again take for granted the simple beauty the world had to offer, or a selfless act of kindness from a fellow human being. There was pure evil walking about, and all that separated it from good was one instance, one wrong decision made lightly without any regard to the people hurt and the lives forever changed.

Trish set her lips in a tight line. Maybe today they could help right that wrong, and hopefully set a good man free so he could begin to pick up the pieces of his life and once again be able to appreciate the sweet goodness in his world. It would take time—Sam had been through too much—but she had no doubt he would recover, if he was given the chance, that is.

What they were doing today was probably the stupidest thing they had done so far in trying to help Sam. Clarissa Jones' part in all of this was an unknown factor. She could be nothing more than a jealous lover betrayed, or she could very well be a partner-in-crime. She could also be very dangerous. Either way, the women knew she had information that could clear Sam.

Trish found herself second-guessing their decision not to tell anybody where they were going this morning. It had seemed perfectly logical when they were laying out their plan that their mission should remain secret. Part of it was because it would be too hard to explain how they had garnered the information they had so far without someone blowing a gasket, and another part was, regrettably, pure pride. Having uncovered so much on their own, they wanted to see this through to the end, to solve the crime and tell Sam the nightmare was over. And, as Millie had stated emphatically, it would be nice to rub Henry's nose in it too.

With effort, Trish pushed her doubts aside. It was too late to change anything now. Besides, Edna had her cell phone in case anything went wrong, and all they were going to do was question Clarissa, not accuse her of anything. Everything would be fine as long as they were careful and kept their wits about them. She glanced sideways at Millie, who was sitting beside her in the front seat of the car. Unfortunately, her friend usually had trouble keeping her wits about her. Hopefully, today wouldn't be one of those times.

Millie was pouting. She kept glancing every so often at Clarissa's house and letting out huge sighs, frustrated that Trish and Edna had both vetoed her idea of banging on the woman's door at six-thirty in the morning. "I still say it's not too early." Millie had been at Trish's house promptly at five-thirty A.M., and seemed surprised, and more than a little put-out, that Trish was not already dressed and ready to go.

Trish looked at her watch. "Let's wait another fifteen minutes," she said with forced patience. She was just as anxious as Millie was to confront Clarissa, but common decency demanded they at least wait until eight o'clock.

"Now, remember, Millie," Edna said, "we let Trish start the conversation with Clarissa. We're just the back-up. If we all start talking at once, she's liable to tune us out." Edna looked tired, with bags under her eyes and her complexion a little pale. But receiving a phone call at six in the morning from a wild woman exploding with energy would tend to do that to anyone.

Millie sighed loudly and slumped in the seat. "I know, I know. But, believe me, I'm going to keep an eye on her expression. If I think she's lying, or covering up something, then I'll give you a signal, Trish."

"You don't think I'll be able to tell if she's lying?"

"It never hurts to have two pair of eyes on something."

Trish grinned. "So, what's the signal going to be?"

Millie thought for a moment. "I'll roll my eyes."

"Now, that's what I call subtle."

Millie shrugged and looked at her watch, then suddenly sat upright. "Come on, it's time!" She was out of the car before either Trish or Edna could blink.

Edna sighed and got out of the car, smoothing her

blouse. "Actually, I'm surprised we kept her in the car as long as we did."

"I heard that!"

With Millie leading the way, they crossed the street and approached Clarissa Jones' house. The curtains were drawn and the front porch light was still on. Millie marched up to the door and rang the doorbell.

"Thanks for giving me some time to compose myself," Trish whispered angrily.

"You're welcome."

"What if she's not at home?" Edna kept looking over her shoulder, whether to scope out a path to escape or to see if anybody was watching, Trish wasn't sure.

Millie pressed the doorbell again. "You asked that before, Edna," she said in a voice praying for patience. "Her car is probably in the garage. We've been here for over an hour, and we know she hasn't left."

"Of course, we don't know if she ever came home," Trish pointed out, just as they heard the front door rattle.

Millie threw a sly smile over her shoulder and then stepped back behind Trish. "I told you so."

The front door opened and a tall woman dressed in a long, blue bathrobe, her tousled blond hair showing dark roots badly in need of a touch-up, stood glaring at them. Trish guessed by the frown on her face that she wasn't too happy to have visitors, but there had been an instant, just before the frown had fully settled in place, where Trish had noticed a spurt of surprised recognition cross her face. Did she remember Edna from the other morning at Mary's? If so, she must think they were there to sell Avon. That would definitely explain the irritation.

"Can I help you?" The voice wasn't too friendly, either. Deep and husky, and full of impatience, she sounded as though she deeply regretted answering the door.

"Are you Clarissa Jones?" Trish asked.

The woman's dark, brown eyes narrowed slightly. "Who wants to know?"

"Can we come in, dear?" Edna's smile was friendly and understanding. "We would really like to talk to you."

But Clarissa started to close the door. "I don't think so. I'm late for an appointment."

"It's about Tom," Trish said quickly and stuck her foot in the doorway. That was not too smart for someone planning to start a vigorous exercise program. She could only pray that Clarissa would have enough compassion not to slam the door shut. "It's important."

"I believe it's in your best interest to hear us out," Millie piped in.

Clarissa looked at them for a minute. "Oh, all right," she said with an exaggerated sigh, "come on in." Opening the door wider, she stepped back. "But why you think I want to hear anything about Tom is beyond me." It wasn't the warmest of invitations, but Trish would take it.

They walked into a small tiled foyer. Stairs leading to the second story were in front of them, with a living room to the right and a dining room to the left. It was rather dark with the curtains drawn, but the house appeared clean and airy with a minimum of furniture and knickknacks.

Clarissa closed the door and gestured toward a beige sofa against the far wall of the living room. "Have a seat. I'd offer you coffee, but like I said, I don't have much time."

Trish and Edna sat down, perched on the edge of the

overstuffed sofa. Millie, however, made the mistake of sitting all the way back. She was struggling to sit in an upright position when Clarissa chose the armchair across from them and said, "Okay, so what's so important? And, you can start by telling me who you are."

Trish could feel Edna's and Millie's eyes on her. Clearing her throat, she clasped her hands in her lap to keep them from shaking as she looked Clarissa straight in the eye. It was so important that they get as much information from Clarissa as possible, yet this strategy could very well backfire. Clarissa could clam up and throw them out, and in the worst case imaginable, she could tell Tom why they had come to see her. Trish took a breath and said, "You were seen at Mary Chavez' house the day she was murdered."

Clarissa leaned back and casually crossed her legs, but not before Trish noticed the sudden death grip she had on the arm rest. "Who?"

Trish's gaze held steady. "You know who," she said quietly, but firmly. "And now I believe you know why we're here."

There was perfect quiet in the room. Millie had finally surfaced from the cushioned seat of questionable comfort, apparently none the worse for wear. "We know that Tom killed Mary, and we also know that he killed a very good friend of ours, Susan Wiley. Now, we believe you could be in extreme danger yourself, but we can't help you unless you tell us everything you know." Millie paused for effect, her gaze never faltering from Clarissa's. "And, by the way, we don't have a lot of time ourselves, either, so start spilling your guts."

Trish held her breath. She could tell by Millie's voice and attitude that she was trying to come off as *gang-*

tough. Unfortunately, it didn't come off as such. She wanted badly to stomp on Millie's foot unobtrusively to hush her up, but Millie's feet didn't quite reach the floor, and if she shoved her in the side, Clarissa would see the action and know they were bluffing.

"We're trying to help you, dear," Edna said in the ensuing silence. Her voice was gentle and soothing. "We know you were at Mary's, and then you were seen at Tom's mobile home."

The reaction they got was not what was expected. Instead of questioning them on how they knew these facts, or how they came to suspect Tom, or, for that matter, how they had found her, Clarissa seemed to almost smile before she suddenly leaned forward and buried her face in her hands. Crumbling into tears, she sobbed, "I've been so frightened. You don't know Tom. You don't know what he's capable of."

Edna quickly got up and went to comfort Clarissa, patting her softly on the back. "There, there, you aren't alone anymore. You have nothing to be afraid of any longer."

Millie looked over at Trish, her surprised expression matching Trish's thoughts. Clarissa hadn't denied anything!

Millie fought to keep the glee from her voice. "Tell us what you know, Clarissa," she said. "We have friends on the police force who can help you."

After a moment, Clarissa sat up and rubbed her eyes with the palms of her hands. When she started to speak, her voice was soft, almost as if she was afraid Tom would overhear. "I don't know where to start."

"The beginning would work for us," Millie said helpfully.

Clarissa nodded. "I didn't know Susan Wiley had been murdered, not at first, anyway. I was out of town and didn't hear anything about it until a few weeks later. I'm sorry to say I immediately suspected my ex-husband."

Millie quietly reached over and grasped Trish's arm. Was this it? Were they finally going to get the proof they needed to clear Sam? Had it all really boiled down to one man's jealous rage against another? Trish fought the urge to hurl specific questions at Clarissa, knowing it was important the woman tell her story in her own way, but there was nothing wrong in guiding her.

"Why did you suspect Tom? What did he have against Susan Wiley?"

Clarissa gave a bitter laugh. "He didn't have anything against Susan. But Sam, he hated. Tom blamed Sam for everything wrong in his life. That's why we got a divorce, you know. His hatred of Sam became a living, breathing thing. It consumed him. Well, I'd finally had enough. I told Tom to get over it, to be a man and get on with his life. He . . . he hit me," she said, lowering her eyes.

Trish fought to keep her expression neutral. They finally had it—the confirmation they needed to show that Susan's murder had only been a by-product of an attack against Sam. How could anybody hate that much? And then she answered her own question: only someone who was mentally and dangerously unbalanced. "So that's when you left him?"

Clarissa drew a deep, shaky breath and nodded. "Yes. Tom was angry and he put the blame of our divorce on Sam Wiley, also. Actually, I hadn't seen Tom in quite a while, but after I heard about Susan, I went over to his place to confront him. I knew if he was guilty I would have to go to the police with my information."

Millie tried, and failed, to hide her disgust. "Why didn't you? An innocent man has been charged with Susan's murder, and all along you've known who really did it."

A sudden chill ran up Trish's spine. It was almost as if the air stopped moving and a cold energy enveloped them as Clarissa's gaze flew up to meet Millie's. Her stare lacked any emotion or essence; it lacked . . . *humanity.* But the moment passed as quickly as it had started, and Trish began to doubt her own perception. After all, Clarissa was dealing with her own guilt and her own fears, and having someone openly accuse her of cowardice couldn't help the situation.

Trish placed an arm around Millie and felt the angry trembling in her shoulders. She felt the same, knowing what poor Sam had been through, but that fact wasn't going to help them right this minute. They still needed evidence from Clarissa, and alienating her would be a mistake.

"Millie, nobody knows what they would do in this situation," she said soothingly. "What's important is that we're getting to the bottom of this, and it will soon be over."

A moment passed. "I'm sorry, Clarissa. Of course, Trish is right. I had no right to jump on you. You were very brave even attempting to find out if Tom was guilty. Please go on with your story." Millie's voice was conciliatory, but Trish was aware that her trembling hadn't stopped, and anyone who knew Millie would know that the apology was as fake as Clarissa's long fingernails. It evidently calmed Clarissa, though.

"That's okay." She smiled weakly. "I'm sure I'd react the same way. The thing is, when I went to Tom's, he didn't deny it. He was even bragging about it. He said something about how he could start moving forward now, and that we could get back together. But he said something else that scared me to death." Clarissa drew in a ragged breath. "Apparently someone else knew about it . . . this Mary Chavez. He didn't say how she knew, only that she was blackmailing him. He showed me a letter. He had it in his bedroom in the night stand. He was yelling and waving the letter in the air like a madman. He said he had given her some expensive earrings to shut her up, but it wasn't enough." Clarissa shuddered and then looked at them. "He told me not to worry about it, though. He would take care of it."

"Oh, my goodness" Edna gasped, "*that's* why he killed her."

"I went to Mary's to try and warn her," Clarissa said, her voice breaking. "I know you were there," she said with a glance at Edna. "I didn't think you looked like the typical Avon lady, but nothing was registering at the time. I had to warn Mary!" Clarissa's eyes fell. "Unfortunately, she didn't believe me. She said I was just jealous, that she and Tom were going to get married as soon as she could get a divorce. If only that were true," Clarissa said through her tears, "then maybe Mary would be alive today."

Trish let out a breath she didn't know she was holding. So much of this they had already suspected. However, it still didn't explain why Clarissa didn't go to the police.

"Clarissa, why didn't you go to the police when Tom confessed to killing Susan?" Edna asked gently, reading Trish's mind.

"I was afraid," she said fiercely, as though angry with

herself. "My mother is still alive. She lives a few miles from here, and Tom knows I would do anything to protect her. That's why he threatened to hurt her if I said anything. He said this would all blow over, that we could have a normal, happy life again. God, he made me sick!" she said vehemently, balling her hands into fists. "But I believed his threats. And, then, when I heard that Mary Chavez had been killed, I knew for a fact that he was crazy, that he would do anything to justify his actions and protect himself. I couldn't take that chance with my mother's life. I'm in the process of getting her out of town for a couple of weeks. She has a sister in Dallas. Once I knew she was safe, I planned on going to the police." Clarissa sat back in the chair, visibly drained, but with a calm expression.

Trish leaned forward. "Clarissa, you said Tom showed you a letter from Mary he kept in his night stand. Do you think he still has it?"

Clarissa shrugged. "I can't be positive, but I'd bet that he does. He doesn't throw anything out."

Trish almost admitted knowing the same thing, but held back at the last minute and prayed fervently that Millie wouldn't volunteer information about Tom's living habits, either.

"Okay, here's what we're going to do. You have to tell everything you know to the police. They can protect your mother until Tom is in jail, and you won't have to worry about her. You stay here and keep your doors locked. We'll bring the police to you, or we'll take you to the station, but it probably won't be until tomorrow. There are a few loose ends we need to tie up to make sure Tom doesn't wriggle himself out of this."

"Yes, we have to—" Millie began.

"Come on, Millie," Trish interrupted, gripping her hand tightly and standing. "Clarissa, thank you very much for trusting us. This is all going to be over soon. Will you do as I asked and stay here until we get back to you?"

Clarissa stood and clasped her hands in front of her. "Of course I will. I can call in sick today. But, please keep me informed, won't you? My phone number is in the book."

"We will, dear," Edna said, squeezing her shoulder. "Don't you worry about a thing."

"I can't tell you what a relief it will be not to have to worry anymore about what that man might do," Clarissa said tremulously.

Chapter Nineteen

"Uh-oh, look who's here," Trish said as she pulled into her driveway.

"It's Larry!" Edna exclaimed. "That's perfect timing."

Millie turned to look at her. "This is horrible timing! Remember, we can't say anything until we put the stuff back in Tom's house."

"Smile, ladies," Trish said as she forced a pleasant smile on her face. "He's getting out of his car." Plastic smiles covered their faces as they got out of the car.

"Good morning," he called cheerfully.

"Good morning, yourself," Trish said.

"Where have you been?" Millie asked, dropping her smile. "Are you still trying to plant evidence on an innocent man?"

"Hello, Larry. What are you doing here?" Edna asked, a worried expression crossing her face before she remembered to replace it with the required smile.

Larry stopped and burst out laughing. "You three

never fail to surprise me. If I was a gambling man, I'd bet you have definitely been up to something, and that you're not going to tell me what it is."

Trish grinned. "Keep your dollars," she advised. "Come on in. We were just getting ready to make some coffee."

Larry held the door open for them. "Where have you ladies been so early this morning?"

"Look, Larry, you don't tell us your secrets, and we're not going to tell you ours," Millie said as she marched past him. "There's nothing wrong with a little bit of professional competition. Rest assured, though, that we've been working to clear Sam, which is probably more than you've been doing."

Trish stumbled over her own foot as she entered the kitchen. How much bail would Millie require to get out of jail for insulting an officer? And, more importantly, would it be wise to even try to get her out?

But Larry surprised them. "Oh, I wouldn't say that," he said casually as he sat down.

All three women stood still and stared at him. "What did you say?"

"Oh, no," he said, shaking his head, "I have to stay quiet about it—professional competition, you know."

Millie narrowed her eyes and gave him a fierce look as she sat down across from him. "That old ploy won't work with us, Larry. You're not going to get us to reveal anything. We don't play that squid prose quad game."

"Wh–? Oh you mean 'quid pro quo.' No, I wouldn't dream of it. I know that, as . . . *professionals,* it would be against your code of ethics to reveal information. I just came by to see how you all were doing."

"Well, we're good," Millie said with a nod. "We're fine. How are you?"

Larry gratefully took a sip of coffee from the cup Trish placed in front of him. "Oh, I'm fine, just fine. Are you enjoying this beautiful weather we're having?"

Millie took a sip of her own coffee. "I am, very much. Are you?"

"Yes, I am. As a matter of fact—"

"Oh, stop it, both of you," Trish laughed. "This is ridiculous!"

Edna was looking back and forth at Millie and Larry as though they had lost their minds.

Millie grinned impishly at Larry. "We've established that we're both stubborn. Now, are you honestly still looking into Sam's case—other than as a suspect, I mean."

Larry reached over and squeezed her hand. *"Hon-estly,* Millie, I can't talk about it. But I can tell you that some interesting information has come up, and that we're looking into it."

Millie jumped up from her chair and gave a whoop for joy. "I've known all along you were an ace detective!" She planted a kiss right on Larry's mouth. "If I were ten years younger, I'd marry you!"

"That's more like forty," Trish mumbled under her breath, but she felt the smile grow on her face as she, too, realized they were nearing the end of this nightmare.

They weren't that thrilled fifteen minutes later when Joe came over, though. His arrival coincided with Larry's departure, and it was obvious he wasn't going to put up with any nonsense. Sensing that Joe was at the end of his patience with them, they went through two pots of coffee explaining and apologizing, not necessarily in that order. Trying to tell him that they had not wanted to worry him was a flimsy excuse, even to their own ears. He knew immediately that it was more like they hadn't wanted him to stop their private investigation.

To say Joe was furious would have been a huge understatement. Even Millie was cowed into silence as they all sat there, ashamed and regretful at how they had taken Joe's kind nature for granted. But, as he so rightfully pointed out, there would be time for further recriminations later. Right now they had to concentrate on replacing the evidence they had gotten from Tom's and, once and for all, notifying the police. But, Joe informed them in no uncertain terms, he would be the one to go back to Tom's.

Dusk was just starting to settle when Joe dropped off Edna at Trish's. Millie was already there, pacing back and forth with nervous energy. The next couple of hours were going to be pure misery as they waited for news from Joe. Edna, as expected, was extremely worried, but she presented a calm front, sure in her belief that Joe could handle anything.

"Millie, please sit down," Trish requested. "You're driving me crazy."

"I can't help it," Millie snapped. "I don't see why we can't drive over to Tom's real quick and see what's going on."

"No!" Trish and Edna shouted in unison.

"Well, we need to play cards or something. We can't just sit here twiddling our thumbs, and you two aren't any good at waiting patiently. You're going to make me batty."

"That's a good idea, Millie," Edna hastily agreed before Trish could strangle their friend. "Trish, do you have any cards?"

Just then, thunder rumbled in the distance. "Where did that come from?" Trish asked.

"Didn't you listen to the forecast today? Strong thunderstorms possibly, today and tomorrow." Millie got up from the table. "We'd better get some candles and make a fresh pot of coffee in case the power goes out."

Trish looked at Edna and saw the fresh worry cross her face. "Honey, don't worry about Joe. I'm sure he'll be back before the storm hits, if it even does."

Edna nodded and forced her lips into a tight smile as she stood. "Of course, you're right. Where do you keep your candles?"

With a full pot of coffee, and candles and matches placed nearby, the women settled down to play cards. The thundering roar of the approaching storm was closer now, with intermittent flashes of lightning, but they tried not to pay too much attention to it. Millie was beating them both three games to one, and since she was such a gracious winner, they were determined to kick her butt. Unfortunately, it wouldn't be this hand, though.

"Ha!" Millie gloated.

"Oh, for heavens sake," Trish said, stretching in her seat, "I need a break." She got up to pour coffee for everyone while Edna shuffled the cards and Millie went to the bathroom. It was while she was in the process of lighting one of the candles that they heard the front door open.

"Thank goodness," Edna exclaimed and jumped out of her chair, "Joe's here!" She hadn't made it two steps, though, before she stopped, staring in shock. "Clarissa?"

Trish whirled around, the match still in her hand. For a moment, she was too startled to say anything. Clarissa entered the kitchen wearing jeans and an oversized dark sweatshirt with pockets. Her hair was pulled up under a dark blue scarf and she was smiling as though she had been invited to the party. But her eyes were frightening. They were cold and unnaturally bright, almost feverish.

"Hi, ladies. Surprised to see me?"

"What are you doing here, Clarissa?" Trish asked as she blew out the match. *And how did you find out where I live?* she wanted to add. Her mind was racing, knowing that something was terribly wrong.

Clarissa giggled. "I was in the neighborhood and thought I'd stop and say hello to my new best friends."

"What's wrong, dear? Has something happened to your mother?" Edna had taken a step toward her, but Clarissa jumped and jammed her hand into her pocket.

"Stop right there! Don't come any closer."

Edna stopped but held her arms out. "Clarissa, we can help you," she said gently. "Tell us what has happened."

Trish hadn't moved. She watched the interaction between Edna and Clarissa, wondering if there was any way she could defuse the situation. Obviously, Clarissa had a gun in her pocket, and, obviously, she meant to use it. And, then, all too late, Trish realized her mistakes. Clarissa wasn't an innocent victim of Tom's delusional mind. Exactly what part she had played in this whole sordid business was unclear, but that she was as dangerous and unbalanced as her ex-husband was certain.

Trish wanted to somehow warn Edna, who was oblivious to what was really going on. And Millie—sweet mercy, she was just down the hall! If she came blustering her way in here, as was her custom, this scene could escalate into a red zone before anyone could take a breath. Trish knew that she had to do something, but what?

Edna was still trying to get through to Clarissa, believing that Tom had done something horrible to Clarissa or her mother and that the poor woman must be in shock. "This is going to end tonight," Edna said soothingly. "We're going to the police and Tom will be locked up forever. He won't be able to hurt you anymore."

"You stupid woman!" Clarissa screamed, and poor Edna reacted as though she had been slapped.

Cold fury enveloped Trish, but she had to stay calm. She was responsible for the safety of two of the most important people in her life, and nobody was going to hurt them if she still had a breath left in her body. Edna stood a few feet from Clarissa, directly in front of her. Trish was behind them and slightly to the left of the table. Without moving her head, she looked slowly around at her nearest environment for some sort of weapon.

"That's right," Clarissa sneered, "you are all so stupid. I've known since the night at the restaurant where Mary worked what you were up to. How do you think I found out about the earrings? Yes," she chuckled at Edna's unbelieving stare, "you were all talking about Mary wearing Susan Wiley's earrings. That was a godsend, and I've been meaning to thank you."

"You killed Mary Chavez," Edna whispered.

"Duh!" Clarissa mimicked, holding her arms out. "So one of you has a brain, after all."

"And did you also kill Susan?" Edna asked, her voice breaking.

Clarissa dropped her arms and looked to the heavens. "I take that back. Of course I didn't kill Susan, you idiot! Tom killed Susan. I already told you that."

"You told us a lot of things, Clarissa," Trish said suddenly. She wasn't sure how much more abuse Edna could take before falling apart. *Please, Edna,* she prayed silently, *step back. Start moving away from Clarissa.* "You told us things like how you were so afraid of Tom and what he might do to your mother. So, while you're insulting our intelligence for believing you, why don't you go ahead and fill us in on the rest of the story—the *real* story this time?"

The look Clarissa shot her was pure evil. There was madness shining through her eyes, as though she'd just realized that someone else was there. "Oh, I will," she said, her smile an ugly sneer. "I'll enjoy rubbing your faces in the fact that you've been so wrong about everything. But first, where's the old bat?"

For a moment, Trish almost giggled. Millie would be furious at being called an "old bat." Then, realizing her own fear was on the verge of taking over, she fought to gain control over her emotions. Their very lives were in extreme danger, and giving in to the fear was not going to save any of them. She had to stay calm. "If you mean Millie, she's not here. She left a short while ago to change clothes—something about wanting to look her best when the police get here."

"She may be all dolled up," Clarissa cackled, "but it won't be for the police."

"Why are you here in the first place?" Trish suddenly wanted to know. "Could it be that Tom is really innocent of everything you accused him of, and you knew we would find that out?"

Clarissa laughed. "That's just another example of your incredible stupidity. No, actually I'm here because Tom *didn't* die."

Trish frowned. "What are you talking about?"

"Oh, did I forget to mention that fact?" she asked sarcastically. "You see, Tom tried to commit suicide tonight. Or, at least that's how it's going to look. But somehow the shot didn't finish him off. I waited a while to see if he was about to kick the bucket, but someone knocked on the door. So, you see, that's why I still have the gun. I didn't have time to wipe it clean and place it in Tom's hand."

Edna drew in a ragged breath. She realized what Trish had just realized herself. That knock on the door had come from Joe. But Clarissa didn't know that, and Trish wanted to make sure that fact remained. "I'll bet you jumped out a back window."

Clarissa grinned. "For once, you got something right. By now the neighbor has probably called the police and an ambulance—if Tom's still alive, that is. It will be all over the news in the morning. So, now you can understand why I'm here."

Trish sighed as if bored, and noticed with relief that Edna had actually taken a couple of steps back. The main thing was that Joe was safe. Clarissa thought it had been a neighbor at Tom's door. "Are you going to tell us the true story or not, Clarissa?"

The lights suddenly flickered as thunder boomed loudly and the rain started to pour. *Not now,* Trish begged silently. Clarissa could panic, and Edna still wasn't far enough away from her for Trish to help.

Clarissa's eyes darted between Trish and Edna as she slowly reached in her pocket and pulled out a small handgun. Edna gasped and took several steps back. *Good girl,* Trish encouraged silently, her heart pounding in her chest, but she kept her expression flat.

"Well?" she asked again, hoping to get Clarissa talking.

Clarissa grinned. "Are you sure you want to hear how stupid you all were before you die?"

"Oh, definitely," Trish said as she nodded, "and then that way, when I'm reincarnated, I won't make the same mistakes."

"Aren't you the funny one?" Clarissa snarled. "But I think I will tell you, just the same." She planted her feet slightly apart and crossed her arms over her chest, the gun still nestled in her right hand. "You see, Tom really did kill Susan Wiley—and, for all the reasons I told you," she said with a wink. "It looked like he was going to get away with it, too. Well, I couldn't have that. Tom hated Sam for ruining his life, and I hated Tom for ruining mine. I needed something to plant in Tom's house that would tie him to Susan's murder. This may shock you," she said with a wicked grin, "but I was in Sam's house when you three tried your silly re-enactment of the murder."

Trish remembered the strange feeling she'd had that day that they were not alone in the house. "Then, you were the one who broke into Millie's house, weren't you?"

"Give the girl a star!" Clarissa said. "Yes, you three actually told me where the combination to Sam's safe was kept. Well, I stole the old lady's address book, broke into Sam's, and got the earrings. It was truly brilliant, wasn't it?"

"Yeah, it was brilliant," Trish said dryly. "Go on." Where was Millie? There was no way she was still in the bathroom, and Trish could only hope she had seen what was happening and escaped across the street to call the police.

"Well, I must admit the plan didn't work out quite like I thought," she said bitterly. "Tom was over one day not long after the murder, begging me to come back to him, as usual, and when my back was turned he stole the earrings from my purse!"

Trish had to stall for time. "Wow, it seems like you're just surrounded by idiots." Out of the corner of her eye, she saw that Edna was moving again. Trish wanted Edna closer to her so that, when Clarissa made her move, she could get between Edna and Clarissa.

"You can say that again. Of course, he didn't know they were Susan's. He thought they were mine," she said, shaking her head at the irony and unaware of Edna's movements.

"Ouch, that must've rankled," Trish said, letting her grin show.

"Shut up!" Clarissa shouted as she dropped her arms to her side.

"Okay, okay," Trish said quickly, "settle down. Go on with your story."

Clarissa took a deep breath. "Well, then the stupid idiot gave them to that Mary girl! He owed her money for some bookkeeping work she had done when he was trying to get his own business going, and she wouldn't leave him alone about it. So, to shut her up, he gave her the earrings." Clarissa suddenly grinned. "Boy was she surprised when I turned up."

"I'll bet she wouldn't give them to you," Trish said, suddenly seeing the picture clearly. Mary would have refused to hand over the earrings, not realizing they were stolen from a murdered woman, and Clarissa killed her. *That poor woman,* Trish thought, as a feeling of nausea threatened to overtake her.

"You, my dear, would win that bet."

Trish took a deep breath, trying to settle her stomach and her nerves. They were out of time. So much of what they had suspected was true, and so much of it was shocking. There was no way Clarissa was going to get away with another two, possibly three, murders, but that fact didn't really make her feel any better right now. The goal was not to die tonight, but options to prevent it were becoming scarce.

She casually glanced along the counter to her right. Surely there was some kind of weapon she could use. A kitchen always held secret weapons, at least according to all the crime movies she had seen. But there was nothing except a crockpot and a toaster. She almost cried in frustration. If she survived this, she was going to plant small, heavy objects in all the drawers and on every available counter space.

Suddenly, Trish saw a slight movement behind Clarissa, and her heart slammed against her chest. It had to be Millie. *No,* she wanted to shout, *get out of here!* Instead, she looked at Clarissa and let her disgust shine through. "Mary was just an innocent bystander in all this," she said, hoping Clarissa would keep talking.

But Clarissa didn't get a chance to answer. All of a sudden, strong arms came around Clarissa, knocking the gun from her hand and throwing her to the ground. People were suddenly everywhere! Two uniformed men with rifles barreled through the small hallway into the kitchen, Joe was rushing toward Edna, his face as white as flour. Henry stood beside the doorway talking into a walkie-talkie. And, the man who had tackled Clarissa was none other than Larry. And then, finally, there was Millie, marching determinedly through all the commotion to give Trish a big hug.

"Did Joe get in touch with Sam last night?" Trish asked once Edna and Millie had sat down at the kitchen table.

Edna nodded. "Yes, and it was very emotional. Joe said Sam couldn't stop crying. He kept thanking all of us for believing in him and for finding Susan's killer. He'll be over later today."

"And how is Joe doing this morning?" Millie asked, stirring sugar in her coffee.

"He's fine, but I had a hard time convincing him to let me come over here alone this morning." Edna smiled, taking a sip of coffee.

"I imagine it's going to be a while before he's able to relax, you know." Trish set the plate of fresh cinnamon rolls in the middle of the table and sat down. "That man was scared to death."

"Oh, he wasn't nearly as scared as I was." Edna shuddered.

"You handled yourself very well," Millie said. "I was so petrified I couldn't move for hours, it seemed. But when I heard Clarissa call me an old bat, I knew she was crazy. I snuck into your office and called Henry. I didn't expect him to show up with a full platoon! I thought for sure he was going to blow it, but he told me they had parked down the street and he had left one man there to watch for Joe."

"Who would have thought Henry could have organized something that well?" Trish asked.

"Well, I did," Edna said. "But why did it take him so long to make his move against Clarissa? We were almost dead meat!"

"No, you weren't," Millie grinned. "He was getting her full confession on tape. No way is that crazy woman going to get out of this."

"It's a shame that Tom died before he could stand trial," Trish remarked with a sigh.

"I know. When Joe got to Tom's last night, he saw him sprawled at the front door. He had crawled there after Clarissa shot him, but he was still alive, if only barely." Edna shook her head sadly. "He was able to tell Joe about Clarissa, but he died right after that. Poor Joe—he was so worried. He was racing over here when the police stopped him at the corner."

"Larry is real proud of us, by the way," Trish said. "He's going to come by later today."

"He's such a sweet man," Edna said.

"And he's a good-looking one," Millie said with a twinkle in her eye. "We'll have to think of some way to keep him coming by, you know. It does an old heart good to see a handsome sight like that."

"Millie!" Edna exclaimed.

Just then the doorbell rang, and Trish grinned as she got up to answer it. "That's probably Joe. He figures you've been gone long enough."

But it wasn't Joe who followed Trish back into the kitchen a few moments later. "Have a seat, Henry, and I'll get you some coffee."

"Thanks," he said as he pulled out a chair and reached for a roll. "How are you all doing this morning?"

"We're doing fine, Henry." Edna smiled. "We are so

grateful for your quick actions last night. You literally saved our lives."

"Actually, Millie is the one who deserves the credit. She kept her head about her and did the right thing."

Millie sat up straighter and beamed. "Thank you. So, when is the female scumbag's trial going to be? I'd like to be a character witness."

Henry laughed as Trish placed a cup of coffee in front of him. "There won't be a trial. She's confessing to everything. It wouldn't matter, though. I have it all on tape."

"You know, Henry," Millie said, "all of this could have been prevented if you had only believed us from the beginning."

Trish winked at Edna as she sat down. Millie's good behavior couldn't have lasted much longer, anyway.

Henry cleared his throat and nodded. "I admit, at first I thought you ladies were blinded by your friendship with Sam. I was just following the evidence, and Tom made sure it looked like Sam had killed his wife. According to Clarissa, he even tampered with both Sam's and Claire's cars to stall them and make the situation appear even more suspicious. If it hadn't been for you, Sam may very well have been tried and convicted of the crime. You did a good thing, and I want to thank you. But—"

"No 'buts,' Henry," Millie stated, "because we were amazing, and you know it."

"*But,*" Henry continued with a stern glance, "what you did was extremely dangerous. You are very, very lucky I happened to still be in the office when Millie called."

Trish shuddered. "We know how lucky we are. I don't even want to think about what might have happened."

"Larry hinted that you were checking out some new information, Henry," Edna said. "Was he just trying to pacify us, or is what he said true?"

Henry reached for another roll. "No, he was telling you the truth. The main reason we suspected Sam from the beginning was that the fingerprint analysis on the radio showed Sam's print on the plug. We thought we had our man for sure. But, believe it or not, Larry and I were swayed by your conviction that Sam had been set up. There was an unusually long cord on the radio, a handmade splice job. And, there was another fingerprint on it, one we couldn't identify at the time."

Henry paused and sipped his coffee. "One of the officers at the crime scene remembered that Sam had touched the plug on the radio cord when he was asking him if he could identify it, so we stopped placing so much emphasis on that. Then, we finally got lucky. The fingerprint analysis finally hit a positive match: Tom Jones. He had just renewed his license a month before, and his fingerprints were on file."

"Wow," Trish breathed, "what a strange set of circumstances."

"We won't ever forget your help in this, Henry," Edna said softly.

"I don't care whether you forget it or not. What I want is your promise that you won't do anything so crazy again! Okay, look," he said, pushing himself up from the table, "I have tons of paperwork to do. I just wanted to come by and fill you in and to thank you for your part . . . and to threaten you within an inch of your lives if you ever do it again."

"You're welcome," Millie said sweetly.

After Henry left, Trish sank down in her chair and sighed. "Well, everything's back to normal, I guess."

"Hopefully so," Edna sighed. "It has been an exciting few weeks, though, hasn't it? We need to find something to do that will bring us the same stimulation, don't you think?"

"We could always take karate lessons," Trish suggested wryly.

"Actually," Millie said, "Michelle said there is something strange going on in her office. You know she works for that insurance company? Well, it seems that there has been an inordinate amount of stolen-car claims from their clients. Her boss is worried that it's going to put him out of business."

"No," Trish exclaimed, "don't even think about it."

"What? I was just telling you—"

"Come on, Millie," Edna said, grabbing Millie's arm, "I need to get home and you need to go cook something."

"Edna, you're being rude," Millie stuttered. Trish laughed as she followed them to the door. When she opened it, she looked out in surprise, and then let out a deep sigh. She had forgotten about her new yard man. Charlie waved as he pushed the lawnmower across her grass.

"I'll see you later, Trish," Millie said guiltily as she turned and hurried across the street.

"You ought to make Millie pay for your yard service, you know," Edna said wryly, shaking her head.

Trish grinned. "I should, shouldn't I? Well, I'll call you later." Trish leaned against the door frame for a moment and watched her friends leave. She was extremely lucky to have such warm, caring people in her life. They were truly God's gift to her, and she swore, then and there, that she would never take their friendship for granted.

Closing the door, she headed for the kitchen, a smile still on her face. It *had* been an exciting time, but now she had to get back to her normal life. Even the thought sounded boring.

After cleaning up the dishes, she walked over and looked at her exercise machine. She could always start her exercise program today, she thought to herself. Surely there was no chance of her being interrupted this time. But as she headed for the bedroom to change, she recalled Millie's words about Michelle's problem. Surely Millie had just been teasing—hadn't she?

Maybe she'd better just give Millie a call . . .